Paul Doherty was born in Middlesborough. He studied History at Liverpool and Oxford Universities and obtained a doctorate for his thesis on Edward II and Queen Isabella. He is now the Headmaster of a school in North-East London, and lives with his wife and family near Epping Forest.

Previous novels featuring Sir John Cranston and Brother Athelstan (written under the psuedonym of Paul Harding), *The Nightingale Gallery*, *The House of the Red Slayer*, *Murder Most Holy*, *The Anger of God*, *By Murder's Bright Light*, *The House of Crows*, *The Assassin's Riddle* and *The Devil's Domain*, are available from Headline and have been widely praised.

'Vitality in the cityscape . . . angst in the mystery; it's Peters minus the herbs but plus a few crates of sack'
Oxford Times

'The maestro of medieval mystery . . . packed with salty dialogue, the smells and superstitions of the 14th century, not to mention the political intrigues'   *Books* magazine

'As always the author invokes the medieval period in all its muck as well as glory, filling the pages with pungent smells and description. The author brings years of research to his writing; his mastery of the period as well as a disciplined writing schedule have led to a rapidly increasing body of work and a growing reputation'   *Mystery News*

'Medieval London comes vividly to life'
Publishers Weekly

The Field of Blood

Paul Doherty

HEADLINE

First published in 1999 by
HEADLINE BOOK PUBLISHING

First published in paperback in 2000 by
HEADLINE BOOK PUBLISHING

10 9 8 7 6 5 4 3 2 1

ISBN 0 7472 6073 7

Typeset by
Letterpart Limited, Reigate, Surrey

Printed and bound in Great Britain by
Clays Ltd, St Ives plc

HEADLINE BOOK PUBLISHING
A division of Hodder Headline
338 Euston Road
London NW1 3BH

www.headline.co.uk
www.hodderheadline.com

To a great fan
(Mrs) Veronica Hindmarsh
of
Stanley, Co Durham

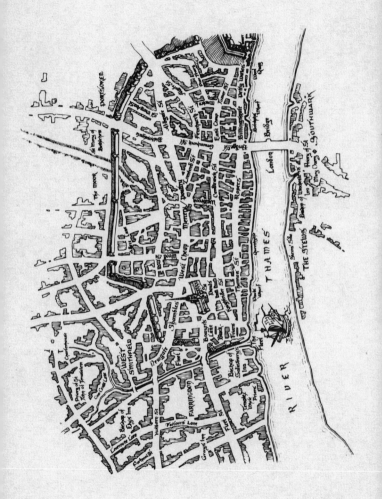

Prologue

'A place of ghosts! Soil soaked in blood! Houses and mansions built on the sweat of labourers! Graveyards full of corpses whose souls cry to God for vengeance! A pit of darkness with ground fertile enough to grow a thousand Judas trees!'

This is how the preacher who'd swept into London in the autumn of 1380 described the city.

'The whore of Babylon!' he had thundered from the steps of Cheapside. 'The place of the Great Dragon! Didn't its citizens see Satan, and all his fallen seraphs, rising like dark clouds, plumes of smoke from the spiritual battlefield, across the skies of London?'

The preacher's mouth was full of such choice phrases. Nevertheless, his words had little effect upon the citizens; they had even less upon the King's good fleet, fresh from patrolling the Narrow Seas and berthed at the different quays along the Thames. The sailors had swarmed ashore, filling the taverns and the streets with their raucous sounds and revelry.

The preacher, in disgust, took off his sandals, shaking the dust from them, a sign that his task was finished. He would have nothing more to do with the citizens of this new Babylon.

Now he sat in the Lion Heart tavern across the Thames on the outskirts of Southwark.

The preacher had gone down its narrow mean streets, the alleyways and runnels full of filth from the open sewers. He had seen the brothels and the whorehouses, the ale-shops and the taverns. Before dusk he had even stood in front of the pillory and watched a man, his ears pinned to the wood, have to pull those ears away leaving them torn and bloody: a sure sign that the King's justice had been done while the brand he'd carry all the days of his life.

Ah well, life was full of pain! The preacher had done his task. He'd leave London and go to the Cinque Ports. Some good ladies in Cheapside had given him silver pieces. The preacher had snatched them up only to spit in their faces.

'Women of London! Will ye not repent!'

He had pointed at their painted faces, plucked eyebrows, ornate headdresses covered in wisps of lawn. He mocked their damask-covered gowns with their narrow waists and brocaded stomachers, cut low to reveal swelling, creamy flesh and fluted swan-like necks, their beauty greatly enhanced by silver and gold collars.

The preacher leaned back against the taproom wall and licked his lips. He'd noticed one, youngish, big-bosomed and broad-hipped, with a naughty look in her eyes and a saucy pout to her lips. Would she be lively and enthusiastic in bed? He closed his eyes. He could just picture her, blonde hair falling down. Not like the common whore he had taken in that meadow near the mud flats.

The preacher felt a flush of excitement and opened his eyes. The young whore sitting across the taproom was ever so pert and comely. In fact, she reminded him of a woman he had glimpsed earlier in the day on Cheapside. The preacher, truly a wicked hypocrite, rubbed his stomach. He had eaten and drunk well. He'd done the Lord's business. Was this the Lord's way of rewarding him? Had not King David taken comely young maids to his bed to warm his blood and render him more fitted for the Lord's work? He clawed back his oily black hair and smiled across at the whore, then lifted his tankard. The whore turned away, glancing flirtatiously at him from the corner of her eye. The preacher studied her intently. He would not be brooked. He noticed her smooth face, the rich brown hair, its tresses piled high. She now took off her threadbare cloak, stretching forward. The preacher glimpsed milk-white breasts, the laces of her bodice half undone, and quietly groaned with pleasure. He took a silver coin out, twirling it between his fingers. Was not every saint tempted, he thought? And how could he know the depths of such sin if he did not plumb them himself? He would repent. He would reflect but, for now, his belly was full and the ale made his blood sing like a harp. The whore came over, her high raised pattens slopping on the floor. She moved rather languidly, submissively, head slightly down, hands hanging by her side.

'You want more ale, sir?' Her voice was like the

purr of a cat, green eyes studying the preacher from head to toe. 'You are thirsty, tired and in need of comfort?'

'I am in need of company,' the preacher replied.

The young whore perched herself demurely on a stool on the other side of the table. She leaned forward, head tilted, eyes half-closed, affording the preacher a generous view of her bosom and neck. He's a sailor, she thought, come across the Thames looking for fresh meat. And that silver piece in his hand? He'd be a generous customer, even though he looked rather wild and haggard.

'I'm thirsty,' she announced.

The preacher raised his hands as he had seen the young bucks do in the taverns. Mine host, standing near the barrels and tuns, smiled and called for a potboy.

'It looks as if Prudence is going to be busy tonight,' he whispered.

The potboy hurried across with two slopping blackjacks of ale.

'What's your name?' The preacher toasted her.

'Prudence.'

'Are you a whore, Prudence?'

'I bear no mark or brand on me,' she quipped. 'I have not been whipped in the pillory.'

'But would you like to be whipped, Prudence?'

'A little,' she simpered back, though her hand fell to the small knife in her girdle.

Prudence was from the countryside but she knew the darkness in men's hearts and souls. She intended to rise, make her fortune in this city of gold; become the mistress of some merchant. She had seen old whores and drabs with their pitted faces, toothless, drooling mouths, scars and cuts covering their bodies. Prudence knew all the tricks, this man had better not mark her! He certainly liked his ale and, when their bellies were full, men were easier to handle. She emptied her blackjack quickly. The preacher did likewise and ordered some more. He asked about her life. She told the usual mixture of lies about flawed innocence, flirting with her eyes, promising much. The preacher drank on until he could tolerate the tension no longer. He slammed the tankard down and lurched to his feet. Prudence looked up in alarm.

'Are you leaving now, sir?'

'If you wish.'

Prudence took his hand and led him out of the door, ignoring the salacious whispers and muted laughter of the other customers. Outside darkness had fallen. The cold night air revived the preacher.

'Where to now?' she asked. 'Do you have a chamber?'

The preacher shook his head. His lust cooled. He did not wish to be caught in some tavern stable and carted back into the city for punishment.

'Let's go somewhere,' he declared thickly.

Prudence pointed down the street to the mouth of the alleyway.

'In the fields beyond, stands an old, ruined house.'

'What house?' the preacher slurred.

'Simon the miser's. Burned down it was, killed the old miser. They say it's haunted but,' Prudence peered up at him, 'it's not. I've been there.'

The preacher grasped her hand more tightly. 'Come on girl!'

Such a place suited him. It was beyond the city in a place where no sheriff's men, bailiffs or constables would patrol. Slipping and slithering they went down the alleyway; the line of raggle-taggle houses gave way to a stretch of common land. The preacher slipped an arm round Prudence's waist.

'It's black as hell's pit,' he hissed. He stopped and fumbled at her breasts. 'I want to see what I buy.'

'Oh, you shall,' she whispered coyly and snuggled closer, a wild scheme already forming in her mind. She recalled how the downstairs parlour of the old miser's house was littered with thick pieces of wood. A sharp blow to the head and she'd empty this gull's purse and be away. And what could he do? Report her to the bailiffs?

They went down a gritty trackway across a wooden bridge. The preacher's eyes had now grown accustomed to the gloom. In the moonlight, the dark, stark outline of a ruined house rose over the brow of a hill. He began to regret his purchase but Prudence was climbing ahead of him.

At last they stood outside the ruined building. Once a magnificent, two-storied mansion, the roof had now fallen in, the windows were empty sockets. She led him through the doorway along a cracked stone passageway. The preacher paused.

'I heard something! A footfall?'

'Nonsense!' Prudence whispered back.

She led him into the parlour and across to a corner where she froze and cursed her fuddled wits. The room was warm, smelling of smoke as if a fire had been lit. She let go of the preacher's hand and turned. A shadowy outline now blocked the doorway. She heard a tinder scrape, as a candle was lit. Prudence and the preacher stood transfixed. In the pool of light they glimpsed a corpse, eyes open, throat cut, lying on the floor with this hideous figure above it. The preacher was the first to recover.

'What?' He stumbled across.

The crossbow bolt struck him full in the chest while Prudence could only stare in terror as the dark figure strode across the room towards her.

If London was regarded as a foulsome place, Newgate Prison, built into the old Roman wall, was the very antechamber of hell, a warren of passageways, pits, filthy chambers and damp dungeons.

Alice Brokestreet surveyed the murky, mildewed cell. Every time she moved, the gyves on her wrists and ankles chafed her skin. The tallow candle she had bought was now burning low on the stone ledge in front of her. Alice, who had definitely seen better days, wrinkled her nose at the fetid smells from the rotting straw and contemplated the bowl of gruel, which consisted of nothing more than slops with pieces of greasy meat and hard rye bread floating on the top. She tried to eat but couldn't, being so full of terrors. She closed her eyes. If she could blot out the shadows? Close her ears to the squealing and scampering of the rats? All would be well.

She was back in that tavern-cum-brothel, the Merry Pig, which stood on the corner of the Ropery near Pulteneys Inn. She was in the taproom and the customer, a fat-bellied clerk, was lurching towards her, screaming abuse. Alice had grasped a firkin-opener and, before she could think, had plunged it, two hands on the hilt, deep into the clerk's fat chest. He'd collapsed, choking on the blood bubbling in his throat.

Alice had expected help from other customers. They just stared hard-eyed back so she fled, out of the tavern along the needle-thin alleyway. Behind her the cries of 'Harrow! Harrow! Harrow!' were bellowed as the hue and cry was raised. Alice, not a young woman, had run demented, crazed with fear. In her panic, she'd turned, going down a runnel only to find there was no way out. She had slipped in the sewer and, before she could even rise, hands were grasping at her, tearing at her clothes and hair; her face was pummelled, her body kicked and punched. She had been caught red-handed, guilty of murder, and the bailiffs of the ward had committed her to Newgate.

In two days' time she would be taken out of this hell, thrown into a cart and hauled before the justices now sitting in judgement at the Guildhall. But what could she plead? Self-defence? The clerk had been unarmed. She was a woman, so benefit of clergy was denied her.

Alice jumped and screamed as the rats scurried across her bare ankles. She stared pitifully at the grille in the door. The gaoler had offered to stay with her for the night. Alice had refused. She shook her head despairingly. What did it all matter? The jury would find her guilty, the justices condemn her to hang. If only she'd not left the Paradise Tree. Mistress Kathryn Vestler had been kindly enough. The tavern had been clean with spacious gardens and a meadow stretching down to the Thames. From her garret

Alice could glimpse the turrets and soaring walls of the Tower.

Oh, she had been happy there! Alice had come from Maidstone in Kent. She had kept herself clean, her appearance good, and been hired as a chambermaid. Mistress Vestler had found her near the Si Quis door of St Paul's where men and women gathered to be hired. She had worked at the Paradise Tree for three months, cleaning rooms, sometimes helping Mistress Vestler, a widow, in her garden. At night, when the weather was good, she would stroll through Black Meadow, which stretched down to the river, a lonely haunted place. Alice had heard the rumours and gossip; how the tavern was supposedly built on the site of an ancient church, but Alice didn't know or care about such things. It was only scraps of gossip she had picked up. All had changed when a customer had told Alice how she could earn much more at the Merry Pig. She was comely enough. She could be a chambermaid and even save some coins. She could become a goodwoman. Perhaps a seamstress? In time buy her own alehouse or small tavern? Alice, guiled and tricked, had risen like a fish to the bait. The Merry Pig proved to be nothing more than a whore-shop. Perhaps that was why she had killed the clerk?

Alice closed her eyes as a spurt of anger coursed through her. She had tried to go back to the Paradise Tree but Mistress Vestler had been stony-faced and cold-eyed. Alice sighed. What secrets did she know about Mistress Vestler? Perhaps she could send a message? Ask for some help? The gaoler was uncouth but, in turn for a favour? She started as the key turned in the lock and the heavy door swung open. The gaoler lurched in. Alice's resolve weakened; he was such a shambling oaf of a man!

'Go away!' she hissed.

'Oh, it's not me, mistress,' the gaoler slurred.

He stepped aside. A shadowy, dark-cowled figure stood behind him.

'This good friar wishes to know if ye want to be shrived?'

Chapter 1

In the parish church of St Erconwald's in Southwark, Brother Athelstan, Dominican, parish priest and secretarius to the noble Sir John Cranston, coroner of the city, knelt on the steps before the high altar. He was praying that the new week would be uneventful. He tried to concentrate but his mind teemed with all the different goings on: the parish council was soon to meet. Athelstan privately regarded that as an occasion of sin, particularly if Pike the ditcher's wife decided to hold forth on everything and everyone. Huddle the painter wanted to start a new fresco in the sanctuary but Athelstan was cautious. The projected scene was Noah leading the animals into the ark, yet Huddle couldn't resist poking fun at his enemies in the parish. Athelstan knew it would be civil war if the two apes bore even the slightest resemblance to Pike and his wife. The Dominican gazed up at the brass crucifix standing on the white linen altar cloth.

'They are good people,' he prayed. 'Poor and dirty while the great ones consider them no more than worms in the earth. So, give me patience.' Athelstan paused. 'And good humour in dealing with them.'

Athelstan reflected on the good being done. Watkin the dung-collector and Pike had cleaned the cemetery up; a new death house had been built and the old one was now occupied by the beggarman Godbless and his little pet goat Thaddeus. Athelstan remembered to have a word with Godbless. The beggarman got his nickname because he attended the Mass and, at the kiss of peace, used the occasion to pick pockets. Nothing had happened in St Erconwald's but other parish priests were reporting how their parishioners were losing coins during the *osculum pacis*.

'I am too distracted.'

Athelstan gazed down at his ever-faithful companion, the great, one-eyed tomcat Bonaventure. The cat adored this little friar who provided him with delicious dishes of milk and salted fish. However, if the truth be known, Bonaventure was not sitting so quietly by his master out of any liturgical reverence; Bonaventure, the scourge and terror of the vermin in the alleyways of Southwark, had discovered that a party of church mice had taken up residence. He was now intently watching a far corner of the sanctuary for any sudden movement.

Athelstan rose and crossed himself. He genuflected towards the silver pyx hanging from a gold chain above the altar, put his stole about his neck and walked over to the small cubicle placed in one of the transepts. This was the shriving pew, fashioned out of oak by Crispin the new carpenter.

Everyone had admired it. It was a simple piece of wood, six foot high and fixed on a wooden platform. There was a lattice grille in the centre covered by a purple cloth. On one side was a small prie-dieu for the penitent, on the other a chair for the priest to hear confessions. Athelstan had announced that, every morning this week, in preparation for the Feast of All Saints, he would be here between the hours of nine and midday to hear confessions, shrive penitents and give absolution. The parishioners had all agreed. Athelstan said a quick prayer as he settled in the shriving chair that Sir John Cranston would not come gusting in from the city with news of a hideous murder, some bloody affray which would require their attention.

Bonaventure lay at his feet. Athelstan read his psalter, chanting to himself the divine office for the day. The door opened. He quickly peered round the screen. His parishioners were coming to confess, so Athelstan put the psalter down and rang a silver hand bell. The first penitent took his place.

'Brother, I've done nothing wrong!'

'Is that true, Crim?' Athelstan asked his altar boy. 'Then you are a most fortunate lad. You are good at home?'

'Oh yes, Brother.'

'And do you help your parents?'

'Of course, Brother.'

'And you've stopped making obscene gestures at Pike's wife?'

'Only when her back's turned, Brother.'

'And you never drink the altar wine?'

Crim coughed. 'Only when I have a sore throat, Brother.'

'Say a prayer for me,' Athelstan said as he smiled.

He gave Crim absolution and other penitents followed. Athelstan felt a deep compassion for the litany of sins they confessed. Men and women struggling against terrible poverty and oppressive laws still strove to be good, anxious when they failed.

'Brother, I think impure thoughts about Cecily the courtesan.'

'Brother, I drink too much.'

'Brother, I curse.'

'Brother, I stole some bread from a stall.'

Athelstan's responses were the same. 'God is merciful: His compassion will surprise us. Try to do good. Now I absolve you . . .'

The morning wore on. Athelstan was pleased. Quite a number of parishioners had turned up. Some were honest, others fey-witted. Pernell the Flemish woman, who dyed her hair a range of garish colours, confessed how she had slept with this man and that.

'Pernell! Pernell!' Athelstan broke in. 'You know that's not the truth. You dream.'

'I get worried, Brother, just in case I have!'

At last the church fell silent. Athelstan looked down at Bonaventure, glad that no hideous sin had been confessed: murder, sacrilege, dabbling in the black arts.

The church door opened. Athelstan could tell from the cough and the quick, light footsteps that a young woman had entered the church. She knelt on the prie-dieu.

'Bless me Brother for I have sinned.' The voice was low and sweet.

'I bless you.'

'I was last shriven before the Feast of Corpus Christi. I have been unkind, in thought, word and deed.'

'It is difficult to be charitable all the time,' Athelstan murmured. 'God knows I confess to the same sin.'

'Do you really, Brother?'

'I am a sinner like you. A child of God. He knows the heart and soul. Do continue.'

'Brother, I wish to commit murder!'

Athelstan nearly fell off his chair.

'I really do! I want to kill a woman, take a knife and drive it into her heart!'

'That is just anger.'

'No, I will do it! I swear by God I will do it!'

'Hush now!' Athelstan retorted. 'This is a sacrament in God's house. Can I pull back the curtains?'

'There's no need to, Brother.'

The young woman came round the screen and knelt before him.

'Why, it's Eleanor!'

Athelstan grasped her hands and gazed into the thin but very beautiful face of Basil the blacksmith's eldest daughter, a pale young woman with hair red as fire and the most magnificent green eyes Athelstan had ever seen. A shy girl but strong-willed, Eleanor always reminded Athelstan of what an angel must be: beautiful, modest with a dry sense of humour.

'Eleanor,' he pleaded. 'What is the matter?'

'Brother, I am in love.'

'You wouldn't think it.'

'No, Brother, I truly am. I deeply love . . .' She smiled.

'This is a secret?' Athelstan asked.

'Well, we've been very . . .'

'Discreet?'

'What does that mean, Brother?'

'Well, secretive, but not sly,' Athelstan added hastily.

A dreamy look came into the young woman's eyes. 'Its Oswald Fitz-Joscelyn.'

Athelstan recalled the eldest son of the owner of the Piebald tavern, his parishioners' favourite drinking-place.

'I truly love him, Brother.'

'How old are you, Eleanor?'

The young woman closed her eyes. 'This will be my eighteenth yuletide, or so Mother says.'

'And Oswald?'

'He loves me too, Brother, more than anything in the world! He bought me,' she touched the locket on a bronze chain round her neck, 'he bought me this on the Feast of the Assumption: Oswald said when he was with me, he felt as if he had been taken up into heaven.'

Athelstan hid his smile and nodded. Oswald was a personable young man. His father had already made him a partner in a very prosperous business. Joscelyn had plans to buy a tavern elsewhere, even apply for the membership of the Guild of Victuallers.

'If this is so,' Athelstan asked, 'why do you plot murder?'

'It's Imelda!'

'Oh no!'

Athelstan groaned and closed his eyes: Pike the ditcher's wife! The self-styled chronicler, herald and fount of all knowledge in the parish.

16

'What has she got to do with this?'

'She saw,' Eleanor blinked to hide her tears, 'Oswald and me in the fields beyond the ditch. She went and told Oswald's father.'

'And?'

'That harridan,' Eleanor spat the words out, 'maintains that my great-grandmother and Oswald's great-grandmother were sisters!' She glimpsed the look of anguish in the priest's face.

'And what proof does she have?'

'You know, Brother, what she is hinting at? She's never liked me and she blames Joscelyn for Pike's drinking, but the parish has no blood book.'

Athelstan glanced across the church at Huddle's paintings on the far wall depicting Lot's wife being turned into a pillar of salt. He recalled the furious arguments when Huddle had given the woman the same features as Pike the ditcher's wife.

'This is serious, isn't it, Brother?'

'It is, Eleanor.' Athelstan stretched a hand out and gently stroked her hair. 'We have no proper blood book. The last parish priest.' Athelstan shrugged. 'Well, you know what he was like?'

'He dabbled in the black arts, didn't he?'

'He not only did that,' Athelstan said. 'He either burned or stole every document the parish had. We have no records, Eleanor, but the Church strictly forbids marriage within the bounds of consanguinity.'

'I've heard of that, Brother. What does it mean?'

'That you and Oswald are related and that your children . . .'

'Now that I do know,' Eleanor interrupted heatedly. 'Imelda said the same. How, in isolated villages, such marriages give birth to monsters!'

'Now, now. Such tales of terror will not help the present situation. The problem, Eleanor, is that we do have a blood book. I instituted one, using what records and evidence I could collect, but it certainly doesn't go that far back.' He sighed. 'And Pike the ditcher's wife is sure about what she says?'

'Brother, you would think she had come straight from the Archbishop of Canterbury.'

Athelstan made a sign of the cross above her.

'Eleanor, I absolve you from your sins. I am sure God understands your anger but you must not do anything.'

'I'd love to silence her, Brother! I'd love to shut that clacking tongue! If it wasn't for her we'd be married at Easter!' Eleanor put her face in her hands. 'I do so love him.' She glanced up. 'Do you understand that, Brother?'

'No, Eleanor.' Athelstan smiled. 'I don't. Love can never be understood because it can never be measured, neither the length, the breadth, the height nor its depth.' Again he grasped her hands. 'In each of us God has breathed; that breath is our soul: without limit, without end. When we love, Eleanor, we are like God, and that includes Imelda.' He let go of her hands. 'Now you may do what you want, I cannot stop you. Or you can leave it to me. But, you must decide now.'

'Until the Feast of All Saints,' Eleanor replied tersely.

'Very well.' Athelstan sighed. 'Until the Feast of All Saints.'

Eleanor got to her feet. 'Thank you, Brother.'

'Smile!' Athelstan urged. 'I am sure, Eleanor, this can be resolved.' He pointed to the church door. 'And I'll meet you and Oswald there to witness your vows.'

He watched the young woman leave then put his face in his hands.

'Oh, Lord, what have I promised?'

He felt pressure on his leg and looked down. Bonaventure had lifted himself up, two forepaws on his knee; the cat's little pink tongue came out with a fine display of sharp white teeth.

'And how shall I forgive you, oh great killer of the alleyways?' Athelstan asked. 'Slaughterer on the midden-heap! Scourge of rats! Come on now!'

Bonaventure leapt into the friar's lap. Athelstan sat there stroking him, half-listening to the tomcat's deep purr as he reflected on Eleanor's problems. The new parish blood book didn't go back far so he would have to depend on verbal testimony. However, if Pike the ditcher's wife was bent on mischief, she might already have jogged memories in the direction she wanted. On the one hand Athelstan felt angry at such meddling but, on the other, if the ditcher's wife was correct, he would not sanctify Eleanor's and Oswald's marriage. So where could he start? What could he do?

The church door opened with a crash. Athelstan thought it was Sir John Cranston but Luke Bladder-sniff the beadle, his bulbous red nose glowing like a piece of fiery charcoal, stumbled into the church.

'Murder!' he screamed. 'Oh horrors! Murder most terrible!'

'In God's name Bladdersniff, what's the matter?'

'Murder!' the beadle shrieked. 'Come, Brother!'

Athelstan followed him out on to the porch. The day was fine, the sun shone strong. He could see nothing except Bladdersniff's large handcart in the mouth of the alleyway. Pike and Watkin were guarding it as if it held the royal treasure. Then Athelstan went cold as he glimpsed a bare foot, a hand sticking out from beneath the dirty sheet.

'In God's name!' he breathed. 'How many?'

'Three, Brother.'

Athelstan knew what Bladdersniff would say next.

'I brought them here because they were found in the parish. I do not recognise them, they are the corpses of strangers. According to the law, such relicts must be displayed outside the parish church for a day and a night.'

Athelstan inhaled deeply. 'Bring them forward, Bladdersniff!'

The beadle gestured. Watkin and Pike trundled the handcart across, Bladdersniff dramatically removed the canvas sheet and the friar flinched. He was used to death in all its forms, to gruesome murder, to stiff, ice-cold cadavers, hanged, hacked, stabbed, drowned, burned, crushed and mangled. These three corpses, however, had a pathos all of their own. The young girl looked as if she was asleep, except her face was blue-white and a terrible wound gaped in her throat. The dark-skinned, black-haired stranger looked like a sailor, his eyes still popping at the horror he must have experienced as the crossbow bolt took him deep in the heart. Athelstan inspected the feathers of the stout quarrel.

'This must have been loosed at close range,' he observed. 'No more than two yards.'

The third man was young, no older than his twenty-fourth or twenty-fifth summer, with close-cropped hair over a thin face rendered awful by death. Athelstan murmured a prayer and stepped back. The cart moved and the corpse of the young man rolled slightly so that his head fell back, showing the gaping wound in his throat, blue-black, ragged skin, half-closed red-rimmed eyes, his lips and nose laced with blood. Athelstan made a sign of the cross as he whispered the words of absolution. He felt his stomach pitch in disgust at such terrible deaths and the shock they caused. He had been in his church then murder, in all its hideous forms, had been thrust upon him. He sat down on the steps.

'God have mercy on them!' Athelstan prayed.

He tried to calm his racing mind. If only Sir Jack were here! He would know what to do. Athelstan prayed quietly for strength and glanced at his three companions. Only then did he notice that Bladdersniff must have vomited; his chin and jerkin were still stained. Watkin and Pike were burly fellows but their faces were pallid, and they were already distancing themselves from the cart's gruesome burdens.

'Where were they found?' Athelstan asked.

'In Simon the miser's house. I wager they had been there since at least last night.'

Athelstan studied the corpses.

'Where in the house? Who discovered them?'

'In the parlour downstairs,' Bladdersniff replied. 'Two children in the field nearby, chasing their dog. They went in and ran out screaming; their mother sent for me.'

'Do you recognise the corpses?'

Bladdersniff shook his head but Athelstan glimpsed the look of guilt which flitted across Pike's pallid face.

'Pike!' he shouted. 'Do you know anything?'

The ditcher shuffled his mud-caked boots, wiping the sweat from his hands on his shabby jerkin.

'I want to see you about a number of things, Pike, but, first, do you know anything about this young woman?'

'She may have been a whore, Brother. I am not too sure. I'll have to rack my memory.'

'Rack it!' Athelstan snapped.

He felt stronger and got to his feet. He studied the corpses more closely. The black-haired, sunburned man looked like a sailor with his shaggy, matted hair and beard but he was dressed in a gown and cloak rather than tunic and leggings. On his feet were stout walking boots though the brown leather was scuffed and scratched. The young woman was definitely comely. She wore a linen smock with petticoats beneath, pattens of good leather on her bare feet. A cheap bracelet still dangled round her left wrist. Athelstan went and pulled back the cloak of the dark-skinned man and tapped the wallet. It was empty, as was the purse on the cheap brocaded belt the young woman wore. He held out his hand.

'The money, Bladdersniff?'

The beadle coloured.

'Bladdersniff, you are my friend as well as my parishioner. I do not know the hearts and souls of murderers but I believe these people were killed, not for gain but for some other, more subtle, evil.' He paused. 'To rob the dead is a grievous sin.'

'I didn't rob them, Brother, I was just holding it.'

Bladdersniff dug deep into his own purse. He took out a handful of bronze and silver coins and thrust these into Athelstan's hand.

'Anything else?' the friar demanded.

The beadle was about to refuse but three more coins appeared from his purse.

'If I march you up the church, master beadle, and put your hands on the sanctuary stone, would you say, "That's all"?'

'I'll take the oath now, Brother.'

'Good!'

Athelstan sifted the coins of gold, silver and copper. He picked up a rather shabby medal on the side of which was a cross, on the reverse what looked like an angel with outstretched wings.

'Who had this?'

Bladdersniff pointed to the black-haired corpse.

The Dominican slipped the coins into his own wallet.

'If I remember the law, the goods and chattels of such murdered victims belong to the parish until they are claimed. These will go into the common fund.'

Athelstan studied the corpse of the younger man. He was dressed only in chemise and leggings.

'The shirt is of good linen,' Athelstan remarked. 'Leggings of blue kersey but where's his jerkin, his cloak, his boots and belt?'

'Brother, I assure you,' Bladdersniff protested, 'and Pike and Watkin are my witnesses, that's how we found him.'

Athelstan sat down on the steps and brought his hands together in prayer.

'Oh my Lord!'

He looked sharply to the left. Benedicta had come out of the cemetery and now stopped, mouth gaping, hands half-raised at this terrible sight. She walked forward like a dream wanderer, her dark hair peeping out from beneath the blue veil, her olive-skinned face pale. The beautiful dark eyes of the widow woman studied the three corpses.

'You shouldn't be here, Benedicta,' Athelstan said.

'No, no.'

Benedicta came over and sat beside him on the steps. She pulled her brown cloak more firmly about her as if the sight of these corpses chilled her blood, blotted out the light and warmth of the sun. Athelstan caught a faint whiff of the perfume she wore, distilled herbs, sweet and light, a welcome contrast to the horrors before him. He felt her close beside him and drew strength from her warmth, her quiet support. He smiled to himself. For a moment he felt like a man being joined by his loving wife.

'You shouldn't be here,' he repeated.

'Brother, I feel the way you look.' She half-smiled.

'Three corpses,' Athelstan explained. 'Found in the old miser's house in the fields at the end of the parish.' He pointed to the man with the crossbow bolt buried deep in his chest. 'He looks like a sailor or some wandering minstrel. The young woman? Pike thinks she may be a whore but this young man troubles me.'

'Why?' Benedicta asked.

'The other two appear to have been killed immediately: first the man by the crossbow bolt, then the young woman's throat was probably slit soon afterwards. She's light, rather thin. If the assassin was a man, she would pose no real problem. However, this other one.'

Athelstan got up and crouched beside the cart. He carefully examined the young man's head and noticed how the hair was matted with blood, masking a blow to the back of the head.

'Now, this victim was struck on the back of the head. He fell to the ground and his throat was cut: unlike the others, he's had his belt, jerkin, cloak and boots removed.'

'A thief?'

'But if it was a thief,' Athelstan continued, 'why didn't he steal the young woman's bracelet, or empty their purses?'

'So?'

'It's only a guess.'

Athelstan paused as Pike abruptly lurched back into the alleyway to be sick.

'He never did have much of a stomach,' Watkin growled. 'When Widow Trimple's cat was crushed under a cart and its belly split . . .'

'Yes, yes,' Athelstan interrupted, 'there's no need to continue, Watkin: Bonaventure might hear you.'

'You were saying about the young man?' Bladdersniff asked.

He looked longingly over his shoulder at the alleyway. The beadle wanted to head like an arrow direct to the Piebald and down as many blackjacks of ale as his belly could take.

'I believe,' Athelstan continued, 'the assassin attacked this young man in that deserted house. He knocked him on the head, cut his throat and was busy stripping him of any identification when he was surprised by these two. The young woman was a whore, the other man was one of her customers. God forgive them, they both died in their sins.' He got to his feet, fished in his purse and thrust a coin into Bladdersniff's hands. 'The labourer is worthy of his hire, master bailiff. The bodies will stay here for twenty-four hours, yes?'

Bladdersniff nodded.

'Watkin! Pike!'

The ditcher wandered back.

'You will take turns guarding the corpse. Hig the pigman, Mugwort the bell clerk, can all stand vigil!' He thrust another silver piece into Bladdersniff's hand. 'Each man of the parish who stands guard will be bought two quarts of ale by our venerable bailiff.'

Bladdersniff's red, chapped face glowed with pleasure. He blinked his bleary, water-filled eyes.

'Why, Brother, that's very generous of you.'

'On one condition,' Athelstan added sharply. 'When you stand guard you are sober. Now, Bladdersniff, show me where the corpses were found.'

'I'll come with you,' Benedicta offered. She rose unsteadily to her feet.

'I'd love your company.' Athelstan smiled, grasping her fingers and rubbing them between his. 'But, if you could clear the shriving pew, put my stole back, feed Bonaventure. Oh, and Philomel will need more oats,' he added, referring to his old war horse who spent most of his life eating or sleeping.

'Heaven forfend!'

Athelstan turned as Godbless the beggarman, with little Thaddeus the goat in tow, came out of the cemetery rubbing his eyes.

'Benedicta, you deal with him! Bladdersniff.' Athelstan grasped the beadle by the arm. 'If we stay here much longer we'll have the entire parish around us.'

He marched Bladdersniff across the open space and along the alleyway leading down to the main thoroughfare. Although he was of short stature, Athelstan moved briskly, keeping his eye on the water-filled sewer down the centre while trying to avoid the gaze of many of his parishioners.

'God bless you Brother!' a girlish voice shouted.

Cecily the courtesan was standing in the entrance to the Piebald tavern. Athelstan glared at her. She had her arm round Ronald, elder son of Ranulf the rat-catcher. On a bench beside her, Ursula the pig woman was sharing a tankard of ale with her big, fat sow. The pig snorted with pleasure. Athelstan bared his teeth at this great plunderer of his vegetable patch. Tab the tinker, Huddle the painter, Manger the hangman and Moleskin the boatman stood further down the thoroughfare grouped round Tab's stall.

'Is anything wrong?' Huddle called, flicking his long hair back.

Athelstan stopped. 'I need your help at the church,' he said sweetly. 'Go back there. Watkin will tell you everything. There's a quart of ale for each of you.' He held up a warning hand so Bladdersniff wouldn't add any gory details. 'For all who help.'

The whole group set off like greyhounds from the slips, eager to see what work would earn such a bountiful reward.

Athelstan pressed on. It was now early afternoon and the denizens of Southwark were out looking for mischief: pickpockets, foists, those shadowy inhabitants of the underworld eager for petty profit before darkness fell. Some avoided his eye; others raised their hands in salutation or shouted abuse about Bladdersniff and his fiery red nose.

At last they entered an alleyway which led down to the fields. They crossed the narrow wooden bridge which spanned the brook and went up the great meadow to the brow of the hill where the ruins of Simon the miser's house stood gaunt and open to the sky. Some children played at the far end of the meadow. A woman sat there keeping them busy plaiting garlands of grass. Athelstan raised his hand in benediction.

'Thank you!' he shouted across. 'Keep the children well away!'

Bladdersniff led him through the ruined front door, along a hollow passageway and into a dark, smelly parlour where the air reeked of animal urine and excrement. The walls were mildewed, the stone floor cracked and weeds now thrust themselves up through the gaps.

'A terrible place to die,' Athelstan noted. 'At night this place must be dark as . . .'

'Hell's window,' Bladdersniff offered hopefully.

'Aye, hell's window.'

At first Athelstan could see nothing untoward until he noticed the remains of a fire. He crouched down to examine it more carefully.

'A few twigs. But the nights aren't cold; this was lit to provide light rather than warmth.'

He crawled across the floor and noticed two pools of sticky blood.

'These belong to the young whore and her customer.' Athelstan pointed back to the doorway. 'Only God knows what happened but I believe this dreadful room witnessed hideous murder. The young man was either lured here and killed, or murdered elsewhere, and his corpse brought here to be stripped of any mark of recognition. The assassin lights a fire to provide some light as he carries out his grisly task.'

Athelstan went over and stood by the door.

'Suddenly,' he explained to the gaping Bladdersniff, 'the assassin hears voices: a young whore is bringing one of her customers in. He hurriedly stamps out the fire, takes an arbalest and allows his next victims into the room. He releases the catch, the man dies. The young woman stands terrified.' Athelstan strode across the room. 'She's like a rabbit before a stoat. Before she can recover, he's across, knife out, her throat is slashed and the assassin leaves.'

'By all that's holy!' Bladdersniff coughed. 'Brother, you must have the second sight.'

'No, I had Father Anselm.' Athelstan grinned. 'He owned a very hard ferrule.' He rubbed his fingers. 'Father Anselm believed in teaching logic through the knuckles. It's a marvellous way of concentrating the mind.'

'Athelstan! Athelstan!'

The friar lifted his head.

'All things conspire together,' he said to himself. He walked across to the doorway. 'Sir Jack, I'm in here!'

Bladdersniff cringed against the wall as Sir John Cranston, the most august coroner of the city of London, red face beaming, white moustache and beard bristling, strode like an angel come to judgement into this gloomy room of murder.

'Well! Well! Well!' Sir John stood, legs apart, thumb tucked into the belt from which hung the miraculous wineskin. 'Heaven bless my poppets! There's murder all around, Athelstan, and I need you in the city!'

Chapter 2

Athelstan dolefully followed Sir John down the steps and into the waiting barge to take them across the Thames. The coroner had almost dragged him out of the ruins and back to St Erconwald's to collect his cloak and chancery bag.

'You've got to come,' Sir John said heatedly.

He added how something evil was going to happen but, for the rest, he kept tight-lipped. Instead he rounded on the friar with a whole litany of questions.

'Three murder victims in St Erconwald's parish!' he exclaimed as they settled in the barge and Moleskin pulled away.

Athelstan winked at his burly friend and glanced quickly at Moleskin. Whenever the boatman pulled his hood up and bent over his oars as if absorbed in his task, that was the sign Moleskin was intently listening to what was happening.

'Old Moleskin won't tell anyone!' Sir John bawled for half the river to hear. 'I saw the three corpses and

31

that good-for-nothing Pike. He told me where you had gone. Three victims!' he repeated. 'And you know, Athelstan, I took a good look at that young man, the one without the boots. I think I've seen him somewhere.'

Athelstan looked out across the river; the tide had not yet turned, the day was sunny and warm. Everyone who owned a wherry, barge or bum-boat seemed to be out on the Thames. Victuallers were now gathering around the great warships berthed at Queenshithe, trying to sell the crews their produce. A wherryful of prostitutes were busy displaying their charms to entice officers of the watch. Royal barges, flying blue, red and gold pennants, made their way up and down to the Tower or Westminster. Three gong barges, full of ordure stinking to high heaven, were now midstream, the masked dung-collectors tipping the waste they had collected into the fast flowing river.

'You've seen all this before,' Sir John barked.

He took a quick sip from his wineskin and offered it to Moleskin. The boatman, resting on his oars, took a generous swig; he was about to take a second when the coroner snatched it back.

'Three victims,' Athelstan said. 'Killed, either last night, or the night before, I'm not too sure which. The girl and the dark-faced stranger were a whore and her customer. I think they surprised the assassin who killed that young man you seemed to recognise.'

'And the law says,' the coroner declared pompously, 'that they must lie on the steps of your church for a day and a night so they can be recognised. I hope it wasn't the work of any of your beloved parishioners. Someone will hang for such bloody deeds.'

'And where are you taking me, Sir John?'

Sir John hypocritically put a finger to his lips.

They berthed at Dowgate near the Steelyard, went up a busy alleyway along Walbrook and into Cheapside. The streets were busy, thronged with crowds. Shops and stalls were open, taverns and alehouses doing a roaring trade. A group of soldiers swung by, going down to the Tower. Debtors from the Marshalsea, manacled together, begged for alms on street corners for themselves and other inmates. A group of acrobats, three young women and a man, were tumbling and turning much to the merriment of a group of sailors who were throwing coins into a clack dish for the young women to turn on their heads and let their skirts fall down.

Athelstan thought Sir John might be taking him to his house, or his second home, the spacious Lamb of God tavern. However, the coroner, shouting good-natured abuse at the riff-raff who recognised him, forced his way through the crowds into the courtyard of the great Guildhall. Archers wearing the royal livery stood on guard. Men-at-arms in steel helmets patrolled entrances and doorways, shields slung over their backs, spear and sword in hand. Gaudily coloured banners hung from the great balcony above the main doors. Five shields displaying gorgeous arms, black martens, silver gules, golden fess, ornate crowns and helmets, were tied to the wooden slats.

'Of course,' Athelstan said, 'it's the Assizes . . .!'

'That's right, Athelstan, the royal justices of Oyer and Terminer are now in session.'

'Who are they?' Athelstan asked.

'The others don't concern me,' Sir John said briskly, 'but the principal justice is the Chief Baron of the Exchequer, Sir Henry Brabazon. A man who has little compassion and knows nothing of mercy.'

Sir John showed his seals of office and the guards let them through into the antechamber. The coroner plucked at Athelstan's sleeve and made him sit down on a bench just inside the doorway.

'Now listen, Athelstan, and I have this from a good authority: very shortly Mistress Alice Brokestreet, a tavern wench, possibly a prostitute, is to go on trial for killing a customer.'

'And is she guilty?'

'As Satan himself.'

'So, why are we here, Sir John?'

The coroner tapped his fleshy nose.

'Have you ever heard of approving?'

Athelstan nodded. 'It's a legal term?'

'Well, that's what the clever lawyers call it! Let me explain: Jack Cranston is put on trial for strangling Pike the ditcher.'

'That's possible,' Athelstan agreed. 'And, if you did, I'd probably help you.'

'No, listen. I'm found guilty. Now, I can throw myself on the King's mercy, be hanged by the purse, be exiled beyond the seas, imprisoned for life or, more usually, hanged by the neck. However, if I can successfully accuse, let us say, Watkin the dung-collector, of six other murders, I receive a pardon and old Watkin goes on trial. It's a rather clever and subtle method employed by the Crown's lawyers to resolve a whole series of crimes. Now, Watkin, being a man, could challenge me to a duel to prove his innocence. Or, I could challenge him.'

'Trial by combat?'

'That's right, my little monk.'

'Friar, Sir John, and what would happen if Watkin lost?'

'Oh, he'd hang.'

'And what would happen if you didn't accept the challenge?'

'Well, Watkin would go on trial. If found guilty, he'd hang and I'd go free.'

'And you think this will happen today with Alice Brokestreet? She will approve someone?'

'Just a rumour. As you know, Athelstan, I often speak to the bailiffs and gaolers of Newgate. Alice Brokestreet is as guilty as Herodias. You know, the one who killed St Peter?'

'No, Sir John, she killed John the Baptist.'

'Same thing! Anyway, Alice was once in the employ of Kathryn Vestler, a truly good woman, Brother. She has no children, she's a widow. Her husband, Stephen Vestler, was a squire at Poitiers. I've told you, haven't I, how we fought like swooping falcons?'

'Yes, yes, Sir John, you have.'

'Now Vestler is the owner of the Paradise Tree, a spacious hostelry in Petty Wales. You can see the Tower from its chambers. It has a lovely garden and a meadow at the back which stretches down to the river.'

'But surely, Sir John, you are not implying that this Brokestreet is going to accuse our good widow woman, an upright member of the parish, of being some secret, red-handed assassin?'

'I don't know, Brother. All I've been told, mere whispers and gossip, is that Alice Brokestreet exudes an arrogant confidence. She claims to have secrets to tell the justices: true, she may have done wrong, and this is where we come to the cutting edge; she says that she's not the only woman in London to have committed murder.'

'Oh come, Sir Jack.' Athelstan felt exasperated at being dragged away. 'Is that all?'

'No, it is not, Brother. Brokestreet is hinting that others she has worked for are guilty of more heinous crimes.'

'And where is Mistress Vestler now?'

Sir John sighed and got to his feet. 'In we go, Brother.'

They entered the Guildhall proper, down a spacious gallery. Its paving stones were covered in fresh straw, sprinkled with herbs. Soldiers stood on guard but Sir John, his seal wrapped round his hand, was allowed through. They went up a small flight of stairs and into a whitewashed vestibule. The doors at the far end were flung open and Athelstan glimpsed the court. At the far end of the hall, on a wooden dais draped in blood-red cloth, ranged the justices dressed in ermine-edged scarlet robes, black skullcaps on their heads. They sat on five throne-like chairs. Further down clerks sat grouped around a long table covered in a green baize cloth littered with rolls of parchment, inkpots and quills. To the judges' right was the jury: twelve men drawn from the different wards of London and, to their left, in wooden stands, sat onlookers, visitors and friends. At the bottom of the dais a great wooden bar stretched across the hall from one end to the other. Chained to this were different malefactors guarded by tipstaffs, bailiffs and archers. The room was hushed, the clerks apparently taking down something which had been said. Athelstan stood in the doorway fascinated by this process of justice.

'Brother, this is Kathryn Vestler.'

The friar turned. One glimpse of the widow woman's face and he felt a deep sense of unease. She was comely enough, her silver-grey hair hidden beneath a nun-like veil of dark green. A dress of the same colour was gathered by a white collar round her podgy neck. She possessed kindly grey eyes, a snub nose, a wide, generous mouth, but it was the almost tangible look of fear which caught his attention. He took her hand, soft, small and icy-cold.

'It was good of you to come, Brother and you, Sir Jack.' Kathryn Vestler dabbed at her eyes with a delicate kerchief sewn on to the cuff of her dress. 'I am so afeared! Alice Brokestreet had a nasty tongue and an evil mind.'

'She was in your employ?'

The woman closed her eyes. 'I do her an injustice, Brother. She was a good worker but she had her moods.'

Athelstan glanced behind her as a man came out of the shadows. He was tall, grey-haired, a white silken band around his throat. The shirt was of the whitest lawn while the dark-green leggings, tucked into soft polished boots, were of the purest wool. A fur-trimmed robe, slashed with red silk, hung round his shoulders. Athelstan recognised a lawyer from the Inns of Court. He was lean-faced, narrow-eyed, sallow-skinned with bloodless lips. A man who knows his rights, Athelstan reflected, a skilled adversary. He stood threading a silver chain through his fingers. Mistress Vestler caught Athelstan's gaze.

'Oh, this is Ralph Hengan, a lawyer and friend. He looks after my affairs.'

Apparently Sir John knew Hengan. He shook his hand and introduced Athelstan. The lawyer's severe face broke into a beaming smile. He firmly grasped Athelstan's hand.

'I apologise for being a lawyer, Brother. In the gospels we do not have the best reputation!'

'Well, it doesn't even mention monks and friars!' Sir John boomed then realised where he was and put his hand to his mouth. Hengan hitched the robe more firmly round his shoulders, a quick, delicate movement. He glanced into the courtroom.

'Mistress Vestler has fears,' he whispered. 'Perhaps we are wasting your time, Sir Jack, but I think we should go in. This case is drawing to a close. We can discuss matters afterwards. I am sure it's nothing but idle threats! We will soon be back in Mistress Vestler's tavern to broach its best cask of malmsey.'

Hengan had a word with the tipstaff at the door and, putting his finger to his lips as a warning to walk quietly, they went along the hallway, up some wooden steps and on to the hard, narrow benches. Athelstan quickly surveyed his surroundings. Above the justices a broad canopy displayed the arms of England; a great sheet at the back showed a mailed gauntlet clenching the sword of justice. At the tip of the sword rested a silver crown with the golden leopards of England on either side.

The five justices looked solemn: old men, they lounged in their chairs listening to the clerk read back some of the testimony given. The one in the centre was different. Athelstan guessed this was Sir Henry Brabazon, a large, florid-faced man, clean-shaven, his cheeks glistening with oil. Deep-set eyes were almost hidden by rolls of fat. He sat like a hunting dog, now and again lifting a sprig of rosemary to sniff noisily as if he found the odour from the prisoners offensive. The accused, chained to the bar, looked most unfortunate. They were dressed in rags, their hair and beards dirty and matted. The clerk finished his testimony.

'That is all, my lord.' He bowed low as if he were before a tabernacle.

Sir Henry consulted his colleagues on either side.

'Members of the jury.' Brabazon raised his head, his voice rich and sonorous. 'Do you need to retire to consider the evidence?'

The leader of the jury jumped up so quickly, in any other circumstances Athelstan would have found it amusing.

'Er, no, my lord.'

'Good heavens,' Athelstan whispered. 'Brabazon is not going to waste much time with these.'

'Good!' Sir Henry's face broke into a smile. 'And what is your verdict?'

The leader of the jury took this as a sign to consult his fellows. There was a great deal of muttering and whispering. The three prisoners chained to the bar looked despondent. Sir Henry sat tapping his foot.

'Well?' he barked.

Up stood the weasel-faced leader of the jury.

'My lord, we have a verdict.'

'On all three counts of murder?'

'On all three counts of murder, my lord.'

'My lord?'

A young attorney standing at the bar with the prisoners raised his hand.

'Yes, what is it, man?'

'My lord, one of the prisoners,' the lawyer tapped a young man, no more than sixteen summers, 'he was drunk as a judge when the crimes were executed.'

The lawyer realised what he had said and raised his hand to his mouth to hide his consternation as giggling broke out among both the jury and spectators.

Sir Henry leaned forward, gesturing with his hand for silence.

'Would you like to re-phrase that, sir?' he snarled.

'I, I . . . meant as drunk as a lord, er, my lord!'

Guffaws of laughter broke out in the court. Sir Henry banged the heel of his boot against the floor. Tipstaffs, waving white wands, moved threateningly towards both spectators and jury.

'We have heard the evidence,' Sir Henry bawled. 'Members of the jury, look upon the prisoners. Do you find them guilty or not guilty?'

'Guilty, my lord.'

'On all three counts?'

'All of them, my lord, on all three counts. But, my lord . . .'

'Yes!'

'We recommend mercy for the youngest.'

'I'll show him mercy. Tipstaffs, bailiffs, take the prisoner named,' he pointed to the youngest, 'away from the bar. He is to be exiled from this kingdom within a week. He is not to return for seven years on pain of forefeiture of life and limb!'

The fortunate prisoner was unmanacled and pushed to one side of the court. The young lawyer was profuse in his thanks; hands clasped, he kept bowing in Brabazon's direction. Everyone found the proceedings amusing but, when one of the clerks brought out a black silk cloth for the judge to place over his skullcap, a deathly hush fell on the court. Athelstan repressed a shiver.

'Thomas Shawditch, Richard Hadfield, you have been found guilty of the most heinous crime of the murder of three men at the Malkin tavern in the Poultry. Do you have anything to say before sentence of death is passed?'

One of the prisoners extended his hand and made an obscene gesture in the direction of the judges.

'Thomas Shawditch, Richard Hadfield,' Sir Henry continued undeterred. 'It is the sentence of this court that you be taken back to your cells and, on a day fixed by this court, no later than the feast of St Edward the Confessor, you are to be taken to the common scaffold at Smithfield and hanged by your neck until dead! May the Lord have mercy on your souls! Bailiffs, take them down!'

The prisoners shouted obscenities and curses but the bailiffs secured them, assisted by a few royal archers, and they were bundled out of the hall. Sir Henry now removed the black silk cloth and scowled at both jury and spectators.

'I hope my court,' he bellowed, 'will not be disturbed by further mockery and merriment. Bailiff, bring in the next prisoner!'

41

Alice Brokestreet's name was called. There was a slight delay before Athelstan glimpsed a shadowy figure come through the door escorted by two archers. She was brought to the bar of the court and manacled there by her wrists. She was dressed in a shabby grey gown, hair pulled back and tied by clasps in a tight knot. Athelstan's heart sank. He accepted the proverb 'Never judge a book by its cover' but Alice Brokestreet aptly summarised Sir John's whisper of 'trouble in petticoats'. She was sour-faced with high cheekbones, bold-eyed, her lower lip aggressively jutting out. She certainly seemed to nurse a secret and had no terror of the court or the charges levelled against her.

'Read out the indictment!' Sir Henry bellowed. 'And make it quick!'

The clerk jumped up as nimble as a grasshopper and fairly gabbled out the indictment, that Alice Brokestreet had killed Nicholas Tayilour in the Merry Pig tavern within the octave of the Feast of the Assumption.

'How do you plead?' the clerk asked Alice.

'I wish to go on oath,' came the tart reply.

A book of the gospels was brought, the oath hastily administered.

'Well?' Sir Henry leaned forward.

'My lord.' Brokestreet closed her eyes as if reciting lines. 'I wish to plead for mercy from God, the King and my peers.'

'On what count?'

Athelstan could see Sir Henry was deeply interested in the unusual turn of the proceedings.

'I plead guilty,' Alice said. 'But I killed in self-defence. I wish to approve.'

'Do you know what that means?'

'Yes, my lord. I have committed a terrible crime but I know of another who has done worse.'

'Continue. But be specific.'

'I accuse,' Brokestreet's voice rose, 'Kathryn Vestler, owner of the Paradise Tree, of the horrible murders of Margot Haden and Bartholomew Menster.'

Athelstan turned quickly. Mistress Vestler was sitting upright in shock.

'When did these murders occur?'

'Over two months ago, my lord.'

'And how do you know?'

'I helped bury their cadavers beneath an oak tree in Black Meadow which runs behind the tavern down to the Thames.'

'And how did these murders occur?'

'Margot was a chambermaid at the tavern. Bartholomew was a clerk of the records in the Tower. He was attracted to her and often visited the tavern. Mistress Vestler became jealous of their friendship. One night they stayed late, well after the chimes of midnight. I was roused from my sleep by Mistress Vestler.' She paused as her former employer began to weep noisily.

Sir Henry's head turned like a guard dog ready to attack.

'Silence in court!' he thundered.

Master Hengan put his hand on Mistress Vestler's shoulder.

'Hush,' he whispered. 'This is nothing but trickery!'

'Continue.'

'I was brought down to the taproom. Bartholomew . . .' Brokestreet's voice faded. 'And Margot were both slumped over the table. Mistress Vestler had administered a deadly potion.'

'No! No! No!' The accused woman jumped to her feet, eyes staring. She shook her hands. 'These are lies! This is not true!'

Sir Henry caught Sir John's eye and smiled thinly. His gaze shifted.

'Master Hengan, it is you, is it not?'

'Yes, my lord.'

'And this Mistress Vestler? Well, remove her from the court and compose her. But not too far: we may soon want words with her.'

Hengan, assisted by Sir John, helped the shaken, moaning woman to her feet, out of the makeshift gallery and down into the well of the court. Sir John returned to sit beside Athelstan.

'I am glad you are here. We may have need of your expertise,' Sir Henry cooed, as his pebble-black eyes moved to Athelstan. 'And your good secretarius. I saw you come, Sir Jack.'

Sir John leaned over to hide behind the man in front while he took a generous swig from the miraculous wineskin.

'If I wasn't so busy, Sir Jack,' Sir Henry called out without even glancing across, 'I'd ask for a drink from that myself!'

Before any eyebrows could be raised or questions asked, he gestured at Brokestreet to continue.

'The tavern was silent. The night was a black one, no moon, no stars.'

'Which month, Mistress Brokestreet?'

'I believe June, my lord: sudden storms had swept in.'

'You have a good memory?'

'My lord, Mistress Vestler said the rain would make the ground softer.'

'Proceed!'

'We brought a handcart into the taproom and placed the two corpses on. We took them out around the side of the tavern, through the herb gardens and into Black Meadow.'

'If it was so dark,' Sir Henry interrupted, 'how could you see?'

'Mistress Vestler lit lantern horns: two if I remember correctly. One she placed at the entrance to the meadow, the other at the foot of the great oak tree.'

'And the corpses?'

'We wheeled them out together. Mistress Vestler had a mattock and hoe. We dug a shallow pit and threw the corpses in. My lord, I was afeared. Mistress Vestler is a cunning woman and she threatened me. I later left her service and she gave me good silver to keep my mouth closed.'

'Heavens above!' Sir John whispered. 'I remember Bartholomew Menster. He was quite a senior clerk in the Tower. People wondered what had happened to him.'

Brabazon lifted the sprig of rosemary to his nose, sniffing at it carefully, eyes intent on Brokestreet. Sir John might be right, Athelstan reflected: the chief justice had a heart of flint but he was no man's fool. He had not taken a liking to the prisoner at the bar.

'You do realise what you are saying?' Sir Henry asked, lowering the sprig of rosemary.

'It is a very grave matter,' one of the other justices now asserted, 'to go on oath and accuse another citizen of hideous murder.'

'I will go even further,' Brokestreet answered defiantly. 'The Paradise Tree is a busy place. People coming and going as they pleased. For all I know, my lord, there may be other corpses in that field.'

'A true Haceldama,' Sir Henry said, quoting from the scriptures. 'A Potter's Field, a Field of Blood. Well, Mistress Brokestreet, you have thrown yourself upon the mercy of the court but, of course, you are not released. You will be taken back to Newgate, though lodged in more comfortable surroundings in the gatehouse. The court will pay good monies for your sustenance and upkeep while these matters are investigated. Do you have anything to add, mistress?'

The prisoner shook her head, a smile of triumph on her face.

'If you are wrong,' the chief justice continued, 'you shall certainly hang! Sir John Cranston, would you please come before the court?'

Sir John gave a great sigh, handed his wineskin to Athelstan then stopped abruptly. The friar followed his gaze, which was fixed on a royal messenger on the other side of the court. The man had just entered, his boots splattered with mud. He carried a small leather bag containing missives, documents for the court.

'Satan's tits!' Sir John breathed.

'What is it, Sir John? What's the matter?'

'I know your man, one of the victims.'

'Sir John Cranston!' the tipstaff called. 'The court awaits!'

Sir John pushed by and went down to stand, feet apart, before the bar.

'Sir Jack, it is good to see you. You are the King's coroner in the city of London? It is the wish of this court that you take Mistress Kathryn Vestler and place her under house arrest. If she attempts to flee, she is liable to forfeiture of life, limb and property. You are then to proceed to this field known as Black Meadow which lies behind Mistress Vestler's tavern. You are to take bailiffs and beadles from the city and discover the truth behind the prisoner's allegations.'

'And if they are lies, as I am sure they are, I will come back and assist in her hanging!'

'And if they are not,' Sir Henry bellowed, 'you are to arrest Kathryn Vestler and bring her before this court!'

Chapter 3

Sir John Cranston sipped from the blackjack of ale and stared up at the side of pork, wrapped in a linen bag, hanging from one of the rafters to be cured. He smacked his lips and gazed appreciatively round the taproom of the Paradise Tree. The sun was still strong, turning the late afternoon a mellow golden colour, with only a tinge of early autumn. The taproom was fairly empty. Athelstan walked towards a window seat from where he gazed across the lush herb garden at the red-painted wicket gate.

'That must lead to Black Meadow,' he observed.

'It certainly does.' Sir John joined him. 'And, if you go through the meadow, it will take you down to the Thames.'

He took the friar through the door and into the gardens. To the far right were some apple trees, heavy with ripening fruit. Above these soared the great turrets of the Tower.

'Old Vestler was a canny soldier,' Sir John said. 'He

fought in France and secured many ransoms. He came back after the Treaty of Bretigny, sold everything he had and bought this tavern. Even in lean times the Paradise Tree always prospered.'

Athelstan sniffed the air; he caught a tang of wood smoke and burning meat. That's not from the kitchens, he thought, I wonder where?

'Brother, look at this!'

Athelstan went over to where Sir John stood staring down at a gleaming sundial. The face, of burnished bronze with Roman lettering, was fixed into a thick stone cupola which rested on a squat column of ancient stone about a yard and a half high.

'A curiosity,' Athelstan said, noticing how the arm of the sundial rested between two numbers. 'I wonder how accurately it measures the passing of the sun?'

'I don't know,' Sir John growled. 'You're the student of the heavens!'

'Was Stephen Vestler?'

'No, he just loved collecting curiosities.'

'Ah yes, I noticed the old weapons fastened to the tavern walls.'

'Stephen bought them from the Tower garrison, a reminder of his warlike days.'

Athelstan walked back through the taproom, along a stone-paved corridor. The walls, clean and limewashed to repel flies, were decorated with old maces, halberds and shields. A snowy white cat crouched on the bottom step of the stairs leading to the rooms above. Athelstan grasped the newel post carved in the shape of the tree of forbidden fruit in the garden of Eden. He tried not to rouse the cat as he listened to the sounds of weeping. Hengan had taken Mistress

Vestler up to her chamber. The poor widow woman was distraught, beside herself with fear and anger.

'God save and protect them!' Athelstan said to himself. 'But the serpent has entered paradise and our golden day is about to turn to night!'

He heard sounds further up the path: the gate being opened, the crunch of boots on gravel. Henry Flaxwith, red-faced, lips pursed in self-importance, strode into the tavern. Chief bailiff to Sir John Cranston, Flaxwith carried a cudgel in one hand and the lead to his dog Samson in the other. Athelstan, out of charity, always smiled at the dog. Privately, he'd never seen such an ugly animal, which was a squat bull mastiff with a wicked face, gleaming eyes, slavering jaws and indescribable personal habits.

'Good morrow, Brother.'

Flaxwith moved his cudgel to the other hand and grasped Athelstan's. Samson immediately cocked his leg against the door post. The white cat rose, back arched, tail up, hissing and spitting. Samson growled and the cat promptly fled up the stairs.

'You'd best come with me,' Athelstan told him and led him into the taproom.

The door to the kitchen buttery now thronged with chambermaids and potboys. They all stood anxious-faced watching this drama unfold. Flaxwith greeted Sir John while his burly bailiffs squatted on stools, their mattocks, hoes and spades piled in a corner.

'Right lads!' Sir John rubbed his hands together. 'This is the Paradise Tree, property of a friend of mine, Kathryn Vestler. So, keep your sticky fingers to yourselves. I want you to dig a hole.'

He led them out into the herb garden and down through the wicket gate. Black Meadow was inappropriately named, for it consisted of a peaceful, broad swath of green fringed by hedges on either side. It swept down to where the Thames glinted in the distance. Even from where he stood, Athelstan could see boats and wherries, barges and heavy-bellied cogs making ready for sea.

'Why is it called Black Meadow?'

'God knows,' Sir John replied. 'Mistress Vestler leases it out for grazing.' He pointed to a small flock of sheep. 'And, of course, makes a pretty profit.'

Athelstan gazed at the thick grass, weeds twisted in wheels of fresh lushness, various coloured flowers dotted as far as the eye could see.

'That,' Athelstan pointed to the great oak tree, its branches stretching out to create a broad pool of pleasant shade, 'must be what Brokestreet meant.'

The oak was huge, five to six feet in girth. Its broad leaves were already tinged with gold as summer turned to autumn. In this lazy, pleasant spot lovers could meet or families take bread and wine out on Holy Days to eat and drink, lie in the cool grass and stare up at the sky.

'It's hardly a place for murder,' Athelstan commented.

Sir John marched his bailiff across towards the oak tree. The friar sat down and plucked at some daisies, twirling them in his fingers, admiring their golden centre, their soft white petals.

'Perfectly made. Not even Solomon in all his glory was as beautiful as you.' He smiled. 'Or so the good Lord said.'

He sat and watched as the harmony of this green pleasantness was shattered by shouts and oaths as the bailiffs began to dig.

'Brokestreet never said which side of the oak the corpses were buried. So dig a ditch lads, two foot wide and about a yard deep,' bawled Sir John.

They didn't get very far. Progress was hindered by the tough, far-reaching roots of the oak tree.

'They are not country people,' Athelstan noted.

The bailiffs had to pull back, a good two yards from the turn of the oak tree where they began again. Athelstan watched for a while but he was distracted by a plume of smoke at the far end of the field, rising above where the land dipped towards the river. He caught the smell of wood smoke and, once again, the fragrance of burning meat.

'There shouldn't be anyone there,' he muttered.

He got up, clutching his chancery bag more securely, and walked through the field past the sweating bailiffs. Sir John told Flaxwith to keep an eye on them.

'And that bloody dog away from the sheep!'

These had already glimpsed Samson's slavering stare and moved as close as they could to the far hedge.

'Where are you going, Brother?'

Athelstan pointed to the smoke.

'If this is Mistress Vestler's land, what's that? Travellers? Moon People?'

They breasted the hill and looked down. The meadow was cut off from the mud flats along the Thames by a thick prickly hedge. In the far corner stood a wattle-daubed cottage with a thatched roof.

From a hole in the centre of the thatch rose a plume of black smoke and, before the open door, a group of figures crouched before a fire ringed with bricks over which a turnspit had been fixed. Athelstan narrowed his eyes.

'Do you know these, Sir Jack?'

The coroner, however, was helping himself to a generous swig of wine; Athelstan shook his head when Sir John offered to share it.

'No thanks, Sir John, that blackjack of ale was enough for me. Who are they? At first glance I thought they were Franciscans.'

'They are wearing brown gowns, cords round their waists, there must be four all together. One man and three women. The fellow's head shaved as bald as a pigeon's egg. I wonder if they know anything?'

Sir John strode off, cloak swirling behind him. Athelstan hurried to keep up. The four figures were not alarmed by their approach but continued with their cooking, more concerned with turning the rabbit on their makeshift spit. The women were young but their faces were greasy, marked with dirt. The man, thin as an ash pole, was scrawny-faced, his bald head glistening with sweat. He came forward, hands extended.

'*Pax et bonum*, Brothers!'

Athelstan noticed the watery, constantly blinking eyes, the rather slack mouth. A man not in full possession of his wits, he reflected.

'*Pax et bonum*,' the stranger repeated as he grasped Sir John's podgy hand and kissed it.

'And a very good afternoon to you too,' Sir John replied. 'Who are you? What are you doing here?'

'I am the First Gospel.'

'I beg your pardon?' Athelstan intervened.

'Good afternoon.' The First Gospel stepped closer, raising his hand in benediction.

'I am Brother Athelstan, a Dominican from Southwark. This is Sir John Cranston, a coroner of the city. What are you doing here? What is your real name?'

The man stared at him, lips parted, to reveal two white teeth hanging from red sore gums.

'I am the First Gospel,' he replied. 'And these are my companions.'

He stepped aside to introduce the three women. They all looked the same, with black, straggly hair and fat greasy faces. They seemed friendly enough and waved shyly at him.

'This is the Second Gospel, the Third Gospel and the Fourth Gospel. We are the Book of the Gospels,' the stranger concluded triumphantly.

Athelstan chewed his lip. Sir John's face was a picture to behold, lips parted, blue eyes popping.

'Satan's futtocks!' he breathed. 'If I hadn't seen and heard myself, I wouldn't have believed it!'

First Gospel gestured to a log before the fire.

'Be our guests. Would you like something to drink? We have a small hogshead of ale, some good wine and, in a short while, rabbit meat stuffed with herbs. It is good for a man to eat. The body may be a donkey but it must be strong enough to carry the soul, yes, Brother?'

Athelstan took a seat beside the coroner and mentally beat his breast at his arrogance. This stranger seemed sharper-witted than he first thought. He watched as the Four Gospels bustled around. Such religious groups were now springing up all over the kingdom and beyond the Narrow Seas. The Illuminated, The Brides of Christ, The Flowers of Heaven, The Pillars of Jacob, The Tower of Angels. All filled with fanciful ideas that the end of time was nigh and that Christ would come again to mete out justice and establish a new Jerusalem.

One of the women kept turning the spit and Athelstan found his mouth watering at the savoury odour. The women looked happy, content, not as fey-witted or mad as members of other groups Athelstan had encountered.

'Who let you camp here?' Sir John demanded, finding it difficult to sit on the log. He unhitched his cloak and placed it on the ground beside his beaver hat.

'Oh, Widow Vestler,' First Gospel replied.

'She is a good woman,' Three Gospels chorused as one. 'We consider her to be one of the elect. In the new kingdom, when Michael comes, she will be given estates, palaces, full hordes for her tribute.'

'And who is this Michael?' Athelstan asked.

'Why, Brother, St Michael the Archangel.' The First Gospel pointed to a gap in the hedge. 'We watch the river for him.'

'I am sorry.' Athelstan kept his face straight.

'No, listen.' First Gospel wagged a warning finger as his voice fell to a whisper. He leaned forward, a fanatical gleam in his eyes. 'Brother, you will not believe this but, soon, St Michael will come up the Thames in a golden barge.'

'By himself?' Sir John interrupted. 'Or will he have Moleskin rowing him?'

First Gospel looked puzzled.

'We've never heard of him, sir. No, no, St Michael will come with the other archangels, Gabriel and Raphael. The barge will be rowed by massed ranks of seraphim.'

'I see,' Sir John murmured. 'I'm getting the full picture now. And so why should they come up the Thames?'

'Why, sir, to take over the Tower. Its roofs will turn to gold, its walls to gleaming white ivory. The angels will set up camp there and prepare a worthy tabernacle for the return of *Le Bon Seigneur* Jesu.'

At this surprising announcement all Four Gospels leaned forward, their brows touching the earth.

'And who told you all this?' Athelstan asked as they sat back on their heels.

'I had a vision,' First Gospel replied. 'I was once a shoemaker in the town of Dover. I went up on the cliffs and I heard the voices. "Go," they said, "go to the banks of the Thames, set up camp and await our return." '

'And these three ladies?' Athelstan asked.

'They are my wives. They, too, are included in the Great Secret.'

'I wish I had visions like that,' Sir John muttered out of the corner of his mouth. 'Good ale, fresh meat and all three in bed at the same time.'

'Hush, Jack!' Athelstan warned him.

'We came here four years ago,' First Gospel went on sonorously. 'At first Widow Vestler turned us away but then she thought otherwise. We set up camp. This cottage was already standing.'

'And when will St Michael come?'

'Why sir, the year of Our Lord, thirteen eighty-one.'

'Why not thirteen eighty-two?' Athelstan asked.

'One, three, eight and one make thirteen!' came the sharp reply. 'If you count the figures together, they come to thirteen. Now one and three is four, and we are the Four Gospels preparing the way!'

Athelstan gaped in astonishment. Of all the theories he'd heard, both sublime and ridiculous, this was the most bizarre. Yet the Four Gospels seemed harmless enough, probably swinging between sanctity and madness. He smiled to himself. Prior Anselm always believed the line between the two was very thin.

Sir John pointed to the gap in the hedge. 'And you go out there on to the mud flats to watch and wait?'

'Oh, yes, even at night.'

First Gospel got to his feet and led them through the gap in the hawthorn hedge. Athelstan was immediately caught by the contrast. It was like moving from one country to another. The lush green meadow, the sweet smell of cooking, the perfume of the flowers, gave way to the mud flats along the Thames, which even in the sunlight looked bleak and forbidding. The ground fell away like a sea shore, the steep incline cut by a barrier wall, probably built to resist flooding though the stones were crumbling and mildewed. He and Sir John made their way carefully down and stood on that. Beyond it the broad mud flats were dotted with pools, the hunting ground of gulls and cormorants which rose in clusters and with loud shrieks. The tide was still ebbing, the river itself quite peaceful now. Only the occasional barge or wherry, bearing the royal arms, made its way along to the Tower quayside.

'What is this?' Athelstan tapped his sandalled foot on the wall.

'Widow Vestler said it was Roman but that sharp lawyer of hers, Hengan, he came down here once to make sure all was well. He said all these lands once belonged to Gundulf, the man who built the Tower.'

'And why did Widow Vestler let you stay here?' Athelstan asked.

'Oh, she's kind-hearted, very generous. She gives us food and drink, says we are harmless enough.'

Athelstan glanced at the base of the wall and noticed the ground was charred and burned. The embers looked fresh.

'What is this?' He pointed.

'Widow Vestler allows us to build a fire at night and put an oil lamp here. We asked her permission,' First Gospel added warningly.

'Of course,' Sir John agreed. 'Just in case St Michael comes by night and can't see his way.'

'Oh, Sir John, you are a wise man,' one of the female Gospels simpered, standing behind them.

'Flattery! Flattery!' Athelstan nudged the coroner in the ribs. 'Another admirer, eh, Sir Jack!'

He glimpsed one of the standards flying from a passing barge and recalled Sir John's outburst in the Guildhall. He climbed down from the wall, tugging at the coroner's sleeve.

'Sir Jack, you mentioned that you know one of the victims?'

Cranston tapped his forehead with the heel of his hand.

'Lord save us, friar, I did.' He led Athelstan away from the Four Gospels. 'I am sorry, in the excitement

I forgot but, look you Brother, I glimpsed that messenger wearing the royal livery in the Guildhall, yes?'

Athelstan nodded.

Sir John swallowed hard. 'I believe that young man, the victim who had no boots, he, too, was a royal messenger. And, unless my memory fails me, a principal one.'

Athelstan's face paled. 'Oh no!' he groaned.

Sir John himself looked worried, clicking his tongue.

'I think he was called Miles Sholter.'

'Heaven forfend!'

'According to the law,' Sir John continued, 'if a royal messenger is killed, the parish or village in which his corpse is found is liable to a heavy fine unless it produces the murderer.' He looked over his shoulder to where the Four Gospels were chattering excitedly among themselves. 'Southwark is known as a nest of sedition and rebellion. The peasants under their secret council, the Great Community of the Realm, have strong support in St Erconwald's parish and elsewhere.'

'I follow your reasoning, my lord coroner,' Athelstan intervened. 'They'll maintain this royal messenger was ambushed by rebels and murdered while these same traitors killed the whore and her customer.'

'The fine would be great. In Shoreditch, two years ago, the parish of St Giles was fined four hundred pounds sterling and, because they couldn't pay, the leaders of the parish council went to prison.'

'But . . .?'

'Sir John Cranston, my lord coroner!'

Henry Flaxwith stood at the top of the hill, gesturing at them to come.

'Truly, we are launched upon a sea of trouble,' Sir John remarked. 'Brother, they must have found something.'

They hurriedly climbed back up the hill. Flaxwith, red face perspiring, leaned on his shovel.

'Oh, Sir John, Brother Athelstan, you have to see this! Eh, come back!'

The bailiff shouted as Samson, a bone in his slavering jaws, raced by them down towards the Four Gospels. As they turned away, Athelstan heard the chaos breaking out behind them. Samson had a nose for food; he would probably have dropped the bone and headed straight for that cooking rabbit.

Athelstan followed Sir John's quick stride to the great ditch dug around the oak tree. His heart sank at the sight of the two pathetic bundles lying on the grass. He glanced into the ditch and groaned. At least four other skeletons lay sprawled as if they had been killed, their cadavers bundled into a hastily prepared grave.

'You found them like this?' Sir John barked.

'Four here, Sir John, and two more on the other side. Between each skeleton there's at least half a yard. There may even be more.'

The skeletons lay in different positions: on their sides, backs or faces down in the dirt. Scraps of clothing, pieces of leather boots, rusting buckles were strewn around. One was apparently a female whose bony fingers still clutched a leather bag while the brooch which had pinned her hair lay in the mud beside her.

'Can you say how they died?' Sir John asked as he eased himself into the pit.

'There's no mark of violence on them, Sir John,' Flaxwith replied.

Athelstan murmured a quick requiem and also climbed into the pit. He and Sir John moved the skeletons over but they could find no blow, no crack where sword or dagger had sliced bone or skull. Athelstan hastily sketched a blessing, clambered out and crossed to the two soiled bundles. Flaxwith pulled back the dirty canvas sheets. The corpses beneath were in the last stages of decay: the flesh had dried, shrivelled and peeled off. This made the skulls even more grisly with their sagging jaws and empty eye-sockets. One corpse had the remains of a cloak about it. The other, certainly a woman, shreds of her kirtle, yellow and blue in colour. A pair of pattens were still lashed to her feet while the boots the man wore, though cracked and grey with dirt, were of good Spanish leather. Sir John knelt down beside the cadavers. He slipped the ring off the dead man's finger.

'It bears the royal insignia,' he declared, getting to his feet. 'There is little doubt these are the cadavers of Bartholomew Menster and Margot Haden.'

Helped by Athelstan, he scrutinised the corpses further, turning them over. Now and again they had to rise and walk away gulping in the fresh air.

'A pit of putrefaction,' Sir John breathed. 'They bear no mark of violence, no blow to the head or body!' He faced the friar. 'Satan's bollocks! Alice Brokestreet is apparently telling the truth!'

They walked back to the pit, Sir John issuing orders and distributing largesse.

'Henry, I want you and one of your burly lads to come with me. The rest are to sheet these corpses and take them to the Guildhall.'

'There may be more,' Flaxwith pointed pout.

'Aye, there may well be.' Sir John wiped the sweat from his brow. He strode off, not even waiting for Athelstan who had to hurry to catch up.

'What's the matter, Sir John?'

The other man stopped, tears welling in his eyes.

'Ten years ago, Brother, on the great north road leading to York, stood a hostelry, the Black Raven, a spacious, well-endowed tavern. It was managed by a taverner and his two sons. A lonely place out on the moors, though welcoming enough. Rumours sprang up, about travellers, pilgrims, chapmen disappearing. At first people shrugged these off. Travellers often became lost on the moors. The mists come swirling in, hiding paths and trackways and the unwary can blunder into a marsh or mire. However, the local sheriff investigated. He is a friend of mine, keen of wit and sharp of eye. To cut a long story short, Brother, the taverner was murdering solitary travellers and burying their bodies out on the moors.'

'And you think Mistress Vestler did the same?'

'Athelstan, corpses don't appear under oak trees unless they are put there!'

'But you said Mistress Vestler was a good woman?'

'Oh, she and her husband were kind and friendly but they did have a partiality for gold and silver.' He stamped his boot on the ground. 'God knows what lies beneath here but I don't think Kathryn will placate Sir Henry Brabazon with coy smiles and fluttering eyelids.' He turned round.

Flaxwith and another bailiff were following. Behind them, triumphant as a knight returning from a tourney, waddled Samson, a half-roasted rabbit between his jaws.

'Brother, I thought life had become too quiet and peaceful. Now we have Mistress Vestler, a murderess, perhaps many times over, while your parishioners are going to receive the shock of their lives.'

He marched back through the garden into the taproom.

Master Hengan appeared in the taproom but Sir John shook his head, gesturing at him to leave. He beckoned at the ale-master who was standing in the kitchen doorway, scullions and maids thronging behind him.

'Come in here!' Sir John ordered. 'Go on, all of you, take a seat!'

The maids and scullions did. The potboys sat on the floor, the spit-turners took their place on either side of the fireplace.

'Now, I have questions for you. Do any of you recall a clerk known as Bartholomew Menster who came here, sweet on a chambermaid, Margot Haden?'

'Oh yes.' The ale-master spoke up. 'A tall man, Bartholomew, quiet and studious.' He moved his body in imitation. 'Shoulders rather hunched. He really liked our Margot. He often came here after he had finished work in the Tower.' He pointed to the far corner near the garden door. 'He'd always sit there and eat, wait for Margot to finish.'

'And did Mistress Vestler encourage this?' Athelstan asked.

'She was welcoming enough,' the ale-master

replied. 'But she often scolded Margot for wasting time. She was kind enough to Bartholomew because he paid well and brought other clerks here.'

Sir John sat down on a bench, Athelstan beside him. The friar touched his chancery bag but he was too tense, too anxious to write; he would remember all this later on when he returned to St Erconwald's.

'And what happened to Bartholomew and Margot?'

'You know, my lord,' one of the potboys piped up.

'No lad, I don't, remind me,' Sir John asked sweetly.

'About three months ago we'd all been out to the midsummer fair. Margot and Bartholomew disappeared soon afterwards. Officers came from the Tower to enquire about the whereabouts of Bartholomew but we couldn't help them.'

'And Margot disappeared at the same time?'

'Of course.' The boy rubbed his nose on the back of his hand. 'Gone like a river mist they were.'

'And what did Mistress Vestler say?'

'She thought they had eloped.'

'Aye that's right,' a maid intervened. 'But the officer from the Tower, a tall beanpole of a man, he said that couldn't be true, Master Bartholomew had not taken any of his property with him.'

'You are sure of that?' Athelstan asked.

'Yes and we thought it strange because, just after they disappeared, Mistress Vestler said she had kept Margot's belongings long enough. Nothing much, just a gown, a cloak, some trifles. She was in a fair temper. She burned them on the midden-heap in the yard.'

'Why did she do that?' Athelstan asked.

'Mistress Vestler said her tavern had enough clutter. Margot was not coming back and she wouldn't get a price for any of the goods.' The maid shrugged.

'Did you notice anything else untoward?' Athelstan asked. 'About their disappearance?'

A chorus of no's greeted his question. Sir John got to his feet and pointed to the ale-master.

'I'm appointing you as steward. You will answer to the Crown on what happens here.'

The ale-master's face paled. 'And Mistress Vestler?'

'I have no choice,' Sir John replied. 'I must arrest her for murder and commit her for trial before the King's justices!'

Chapter 4

This declaration was met by horrified silence.

'It's impossible!' the ale-master whispered.

'I must tell you,' Sir John replied, 'that we have been out to Black Meadow. Aye, and it's well named. We have discovered the corpses of both Margot and Bartholomew.'

One of the maids started to sob.

'And worse yet,' the coroner continued, 'the skeletons of six others.'

One of the potboys began to shake; he crept like a little child to sit with one of the maids who put her arms around him. Athelstan studied them carefully. These were not hard men and women but good people, simple in their loves and hates, their work and lives. The evil Sir John was describing was well beyond their experience. If Kathryn Vestler was guilty of such hideous crimes, her servants were certainly innocent. Athelstan rose and walked into the centre of the taproom.

'In Christ's name,' he declared, 'and I ask you now, as you will answer for the truth before Christ and His court of angels, do any of you know anything about these deaths?'

The assembled company just looked at him.

'Then I have my answer. So, I ask you this, solemnly, on the Eucharist, the body and blood of Christ.' He paused. 'Over the last two years, has anyone ever come here, making enquiries about people who stayed at the Paradise Tree?'

The ale-master stepped forward and two of the chambermaids raised their hands.

'Brother, in the last few months to my recollection, strangers have come asking, "Did so and so reside here? Did they hire a chamber? Did they eat and drink?" '

'I have heard the same.' One of the maids spoke up.

'Who were these people?' Sir John asked.

'Oh strangers, chapmen, pedlars, tinkers, people coming in and out of the city.'

'Aye and enquiries were made about Bartholomew and Margot,' another offered.

'There's more.' The potboy came forward, his little thin arms hanging by his side like sticks. 'I have seen Mistress Vestler burn possessions.'

Athelstan glanced at the coroner, who usually maintained his bonhomie, his fiery good humour, but his rubicund face had paled. He looked haggard, rather old.

'Oh, Sir John,' Athelstan sighed. 'What do we have here?'

'You'd best go about your duties,' Sir John told the tavern workers. 'Brother Athelstan, come with me.'

They went out up the wooden staircase. The Paradise Tree was well named. The floorboards were polished and cleaned. The windows on the stairwells were full of glass, some even painted with emblems. Bronze brackets for candles were fastened into the wooden panelling. Flowers and pots of herbs were tastefully arranged along shelves and sills. The first gallery even had woollen rugs to deaden the sound; small pictures in gilt frames decorated its walls. At the far end a door stood half-open. Inside Kathryn Vestler was sitting on a chair, Hengan beside her on a stool. The tavern-mistress's face had aged, pale, her eyes red-rimmed, her podgy cheeks soaked with tears. She had a piece of linen in her hands which she kept twisting round and round, staring at a point above their heads, lips moving wordlessly. Beside her on the floor was a half-filled goblet of wine. Hengan looked pitifully at them.

'Sir John, we have heard the rumours.'

'I am innocent!' Mistress Vestler protested. 'Before God and His angels, Sir John, I am innocent of any crime!'

Athelstan moved over to a small desk and stool while Sir John took a chair just inside the door and sat in front of the widow woman. He leaned forward and clutched her hand.

'Kathryn, I must tell you we have discovered a horrid sight.'

He then informed her in pithy phrases everything they had seen and learned since their arrival. Mistress Vestler grew more composed; Athelstan wondered if Hengan had slipped an opiate in the drink.

'I know nothing of the corpses. Margot Haden

disappeared about midsummer, Bartholomew with her. True, officers came from the Tower but I could not tell them anything.'

'Why did you burn Margot's possessions?' Sir John asked.

'They were paltry,' she stammered. 'Nothing much. I, I . . . didn't think it was right to sell or give them to someone else, so I burned them. Bartholomew was a clerk, a fairly wealthy man. I thought Margot had left them here as tawdry rubbish. Her swain, her lover would buy her more.'

'Did you like Bartholomew?' Athelstan asked.

'He was a good, kindly man. But, Brother, I have suitors enough. Bartholomew was of little interest to me.'

'And the others?' Sir John asked.

'What others?' the woman snapped.

'Your own servants. Enquiries have been made here of people who visited the Paradise Tree.'

'That is nonsense!' Hengan spoke up heatedly.

'In what way, sir?'

'The Paradise Tree is a busy tavern. It stands near the Tower and the river. People often visit here. It is logical that enquiries were made. Did so and so come? Where have they gone?'

'But they also said you burned the possessions of people who stayed here?'

'Sir Jack,' Mistress Vestler replied. 'There are at least twenty chambers in this tavern. Guests come, they leave scraps of clothing, items of saddlery which are broken or disused. I keep a clean and tidy house. What crime is there in burning such paltry things?'

Sir John got to his feet and, in the time-honoured fashion, touched her shoulder.

'Mistress Kathryn Vestler, by the power granted to me by the King and his city council, I arrest you for the murder of Bartholomew Menster, Margot Haden and other unnamed victims!'

Mistress Vestler bowed her head and sobbed.

'You will be taken to Newgate and lodged there to answer these charges before the King's justices at the Guildhall.'

Hengan got to his feet.

'Sir John, may I have a word?'

The two left the chamber. Athelstan looked across at the weeping woman. He did not know what to think. In his time he'd discovered that murder could have the sweetest face and the kindliest smile.

'I shall pray for you, Mistress Vestler,' he murmured.

The woman's face came up, her eyes hard.

'Pray, Brother? What use is prayer now? Alice Brokestreet has had her way. Will you pray for me when they turn me off the ladder at Smithfield?'

'That has not yet happened. Put your trust in God and Sir John.'

Gathering up his chancery bag, Athelstan joined Sir John and Hengan out in the gallery. The lawyer was deeply agitated.

'Sir Jack! Sir Jack! What can we do?'

'Master Hengan, I've told you the evidence. What other explanation could there be?'

'Is it possible that Alice Brokestreet and another murdered Bartholomew and Margot then buried their corpses in Black Meadow?'

'What proof is there of that?' Athelstan asked.

Hengan, anxious-eyed, stared back.

'Master Hengan, you are a lawyer,' Athelstan continued. 'I merely ask what Chief Justice Brabazon will demand. Why should Alice Brokestreet and this mysterious accomplice kill these two people? Why should they take them out and bury them in Black Meadow where they could have been seen by anyone in the tavern or that motley crew, the Four Gospels, whom I've just met?'

Hengan's face creased into a smile.

'Mistress Vestler let them stay here out of the kindness of her heart,' he countered. 'Perhaps they can be of assistance? They must have seen something, surely? Corpses cannot be trundled out and buried in such a place without someone noticing!'

'Precisely,' Sir John confirmed, taking a swig from his wineskin. 'And the justices will ask the same question.' He looked up at the white plaster ceiling. 'Master Ralph, you will defend Mistress Vestler?'

'Of course!'

'Then let me speak to you privately.'

Sir John strode to the top of the stairs and bawled for Flaxwith, who came lumbering up. Sir John told him to guard Mistress Vestler then gestured at Hengan and Athelstan to follow him. They went down through the taproom and out into the garden. A small, flowery arbour built out of trellis wood stood at the far side, a cool, secretive place with a quilted bench round its curving sides. They took their seats, Sir John bawling for tankards of ale. While they waited till these were served, Athelstan studied the different plants and herbs: matted sea lavender, bog bean, pea flower, fairy flax; bees buzzed above them, butterflies, white and deep coloured, flitted from plant to plant. A mallard from the small stew pond at the other end of the garden strutted around. Swallows swooped across the grass and out over Black Meadow, somewhere a woodpecker rattled noisily against the bark of a tree. Athelstan could scarcely believe that this peaceful, pleasant place masked bloody murder and hasty burial.

'You'll represent Mistress Vestler?' Sir John asked again.

The lawyer stroked the tip of his sharp nose, lower lip coming up.

'I am not skilled in such legal matters, Sir John. I only advise Mistress Vestler on her business affairs. However, I will prove her innocence in this matter.'

'She has no children?' Athelstan asked.

'None whatsoever, nor kith or kin.'

'But she must have a will?'

Hengan sipped from the tankard and wiped the white foam from his lips.

'She brews the best ale on this side of the Thames,' he said. 'She's no murderess. Yes, she has drawn up a will and I am her executor. Mistress Vestler has laid down clear provision. On her death the tavern is to be sold for the best possible price and all proceeds are to be sent to the Knights Hospitallers at their Priory of St John's in Clerkenwell.'

'Of course,' Sir John trumpeted, his good humour returning. 'Stephen, her late husband, was a bit of a noddle-pate. He maintained that, if Kathryn died before him, he'd journey east and join the Hospitallers in their struggle against the Turks.'

'The will is very short and terse,' Hengan confirmed. 'And cannot be denied. I even tease Mistress

Vestler that she hasn't left one penny to me.'

Athelstan looked at him sharply.

'A jest, Brother. I have sufficient riches.'

'She is a widow woman,' Athelstan pointed out. 'Comely and wealthy. Surely she had suitors? After all, Master Ralph, you are a lusty bachelor yourself.'

Hengan put his tankard down. 'Oh, suitors came and went: adventurers, profiteers, Kathryn would have none of them. There's a chamber in the tavern, Brother, used by her late husband, Stephen. She has turned it into a shrine to her husband's memory with his writing-desk, his sword, his shield and armour, the pennant he carried at Poitiers. Mistress Vestler is a comfortable woman, happy in what she does. She has vowed never to remarry.' He held the tankard up in a mock toast. 'And, as for me, Brother.' He sighed. 'I speak in confidence?'

'Of course, Master Ralph.'

'I am a man, Brother, how can I put it? The company of women is pleasing enough.' His kindly grey eyes held Athelstan's. 'But I have no desire to bed one.'

'And what will happen now?' Athelstan persisted. 'If Mistress Vestler is found guilty and sentenced? Because, in this secret place, Master Ralph, I speak the truth, unpalatable though it be. If the jury find her guilty there'll be no pardon for what she has done.'

'Brother, I take your warning. Mistress Vestler stands in great danger of being hanged. If that happens . . .'

'The tavern and all its moveables,' Sir John interrupted, 'are forfeit to the Crown.'

Athelstan cradled his tankard; his deep friendship with Sir John, whatever his troubles in Southwark, committed him to this matter. In conscience he must do all he could to prove Mistress Vestler's innocence.

'Has anything untoward occurred?' he asked. 'Is there anyone with a grievance against Mistress Vestler?'

The lawyer shook his head.

'Does anyone desire the tavern? Or its properties?'

'Mistress Vestler was very fortunate,' Hengan replied. 'She and Stephen bought this when prices throughout the city had fallen after the great pestilence. The tavern was not what it is now. These gardens, the carp pond, the chambers are all their doing. Mistress Vestler is a skilled cook. Her venison pies, baked in spices, are famous through the city. Now, to answer your question bluntly: about eighteen months ago a member of the Guild of Licensed Victuallers, Edmund Coddington, did offer a price for the tavern. Mistress Vestler refused.'

'And where is this Coddington now?' Sir John asked.

'Oh, Sir Jack, he died of some ailment or other. Apart from him, no one else.'

Athelstan recalled the Four Gospels and repressed a shiver. They looked and acted fey-witted but what if their smiles concealed some secret purpose? They would not be the first so-called witnesses to truth who masked their nefarious practices under the guise of religion. He finished his ale and got to his feet.

'Sir Jack!'

He gave the surprised coroner his empty tankard.

'I shall be with you shortly.'

Athelstan strode into Black Meadow. He paused at the pit where the bailiffs were now sheeting the skeletons and two corpses.

'Can I help you, Brother?' One of the bailiffs leaned on his mattock. 'Dark deeds, eh?'

'Dark deeds certainly. Tell me, sir, where did you find the two corpses? The man and the woman?'

The bailiff scratched a cut on his unshaven chin.

'Ah, that's right.' The fellow pointed. 'Over there, Brother.'

Athelstan went to the spot indicated and looked back towards the lych gate. The bailiff came over, his mattock resting against his shoulder like a spear.

'What's the problem, Brother?'

'Let's pretend I'm a murderer.' Athelstan smiled. 'Or we are both murderers. We have corpses to dispose of. So, when do we bury them?'

'Why, Brother,' the surprised bailiff replied, 'at the dead of night.'

'Now we can't be seen,' Athelstan said, 'from the bottom of the meadow.'

'Ah, you mean where that strange group live? Yes, you're right, Brother, the swell of the hill hides all view.'

'And if we dig this side of the oak tree?' Athelstan asked. 'We are hidden from any view of people in the tavern. Correct?'

'Agreed.' The fellow, now enjoying himself, was preening at being patronised by this friend of the powerful lord coroner.

'So, how would you bring the corpses here?' Athelstan continued. 'If they're taken from the tavern, chambermaids, servants might see us.'

'Ah yes, Brother, but, at the dead of night, everyone's asleep. And look.' He walked away, gesturing with his hand. 'We can see the tavern, its roofs and gables but, have you noticed, the trees hide the view from most of the windows?'

'Sharp-eyed.' Athelstan smiled, dug into his purse and gave the man a coin. The bailiff almost danced with embarrassed pride.

'So, it's possible the corpses were brought from the tavern at night, loaded on to a handcart, or barrow, its axles newly oiled, the wheels covered in straw?'

'Yes, that's what we do in the city, when we take a cart out at the dead of night. Otherwise, it's a complaint to the mayor.'

'But let's suppose that they didn't come from the tavern. It's too dangerous to bring them from the river because, as you say, those strange people are there, waiting for St Michael.' The bailiff looked mystified. 'Come on, Sharp Eyes,' Athelstan joked. 'Where else could the murderers have come from?'

'From the east.' The bailiff pointed to the hedge at the far end of the field. 'That leads to common land and the great city ditch. While to the west, what is there now?' He scratched his head. 'Yes, there's another field which stretches down to a hedgerow and, beyond that, Brother, lie the alleyways of Petty Wales.'

Athelstan dug with his sandalled foot at the earth beneath the oak tree.

'Wouldn't this be hard to dig?' he asked.

'Not really, Brother. My father was a peasant owning land in Woodford. As long as you avoid the roots, the ground under the branches of a tree like this is always softer. The leaves shade it from being baked by the sun while, when it rains, the branches collect the water and drench the ground beneath.'

'Of course.' Athelstan recalled his father's small farm. How he and his brother Francis would dig around the small pear trees in the orchard to strengthen the roots. 'But wouldn't someone notice?' Athelstan asked. 'Let's say we brought two corpses here at the dead of night, sometime in midsummer, so it must be well after midnight.'

'Don't forget, Brother, it was a very wet summer. The ground was truly soaked and the sod easy to break.'

'How deep was the pit in which they were found?'

'The two corpses?' The bailiff lowered his mattock and dug it into the ground. 'No more than half a yard.'

'And the two were thrown together?'

'Yes, lovers in life, lovers in death, if the gossips are to be believed.'

'So, we put the corpses in,' Athelstan continued. 'But, surely, next morning someone is going to notice.'

'Not really, Brother. First, if we were burying . . .' The bailiff grinned. 'My lord coroner, God forbid!'

'God forbid!' Athelstan echoed.

'I'd remove the top layer followed by the rest of the soil, put his magnificent corpse in, cover it up, place the sods on top and stamp down. Then I'd go into the field.' He pointed to the long grass. 'I'd cut some of that and sprinkle it over the grave.'

'True, true,' Athelstan murmured. 'And this is a lonely place. Unless you made careful scrutiny.'

'While in full summer, Brother, the grass soon grows again . . .'

'And the secret's kept,' Athelstan finished the sentence for him.

He thanked the bailiff and walked across the field. The sheep scattered at his approach, bleating at this further disturbance to their grazing. Athelstan examined the thick privet hedge which divided the field from the common land which stretched down to the city ditch. In most places it was thick and prickly, in others there were gaps, probably forced over the years by travellers, lovers or people seeking a short cut between Petty Wales and the fortress. The same was true of the hedge on the other side. Athelstan heard shouts and turned; the bailiffs were finishing, the corpses sheeted. They were now taking them up to the tavern and the waiting cart. Athelstan waved farewell and walked down towards the Four Gospels. This time they were not so friendly; they were sitting by the fire eating cheese and sliced vegetables piled on makeshift platters.

'We lost our rabbit,' First Gospel moaned. 'That bloody dog has the mark of Cain upon it!'

Athelstan apologised, dug into his purse and handed over a coin. Their mood changed at the sight of the twinkling piece of silver.

'Thank you very much, Brother. Remember that!' First Gospel lifted a hand, fingers extended. 'When St Michael comes along the Thames, let Brother Athelstan's name be inscribed in the Book of Life. May he be taken by the angels into their camp.'

'Quite, quite,' the friar broke in. 'But I've come to ask you some more questions.'

'About the corpses found beneath the great oak tree?' First Gospel asked, his long face solemn. 'Oh yes, we've heard of bloody murder and hideous crime.'

He was about to launch into another paean of praise about what would happen when St Michael came but Athelstan cut him short.

'Have you seen anything untoward?'

'In Black Meadow?' First Gospel asked; he shook his head. 'We keep to ourselves, Brother. The doings of the world and the flesh are not our concern. Sometimes we hear lovers, poachers, men of the night.' He pointed to the open cottage door. 'But, until the angels come, we are well armed. I have a bill hook, a sword, a bow and six arrows.'

'Did you see anything?' Athelstan insisted. 'Someone brought two corpses into this field, dug a grave and buried them.'

'We saw nothing, Brother.' One of the women spoke up. 'Eye does not see.' She broke into a chant. 'Nor does the ear hear while the heart is silent to the tribulations of this world.'

Athelstan decided it was time to take another coin out of his purse.

'But the river is another matter,' First Gospel declared in a red-gummed smile.

'In what way?'

'Oh yes,' the women chorused, eager now to earn another coin.

Athelstan quietly prayed that the Lord would understand his distribution of coins taken from the corpses earlier that day.

'What happens on the river?' he asked.

'Well, we light our fire and maintain our vigil,' First Gospel declared. He leaned closer, eyes staring. 'But we've seen shapes at night, Brother: boats coming in from the river, men cowled and hooded.'

'You are not just saying that for the silver coin?'

'Brother, would we lie? Here, I'll show you.'

He sprang to his feet and led Athelstan out through the gap in the hedge, down over the old crumbling wall which overlooked the mud flats. He pointed to his right towards the Tower.

'There, you see the gallows?'

Athelstan glimpsed the high-branched gibbet. He could just make out the bound and tarred figure of a river pirate hanging from the post jutting out over the river.

'Just there, near the gibbet! Barges come in. We've glimpsed lanterns, figures, shapes moving in the night.'

'You are sure they are not soldiers, men going to the Tower?'

'No, Brother, why should they stop there? It's only mud and what are they doing?'

'How often do they come?' Athelstan asked.

First Gospel blew his cheeks out. 'About once a month. They don't mean well, Brother. If it wasn't for the glint of a lantern, we'd hardly know they were here.'

'And where do they go?'

'I watch them. But this is all I know. They go into the common lands beyond Black Meadow.' He turned, gripping Athelstan by the elbow, his eyes gleaming with expectation. 'At first we thought it might be the angels,' he whispered. 'But, surely,

Brother, they'll come with fiery lights, banners unfurled and trumpets braying?'

'I suspect they will. I thank you, sir.' Athelstan followed the First Gospel back to the rest grouped around the fire. 'I want to ask you another question.' He handed the coin over.

First Gospel took it and smiled triumphantly at his women.

'A good day's work, sisters! Proceed, Brother: your visit proves that the Lord giveth as well as taketh away.'

'Or rather that Samson the dog does,' Athelstan replied. 'You are correct! Two corpses have been dug up beneath the great oak tree. We know who they are.'

First Gospel's face flinched. He blinked and licked nervously at a sore on his lip.

'You probably know,' Athelstan continued, 'the man is Bartholomew Menster, a senior clerk from the muniment rooms in the Tower. The other was a young chambermaid, Margot Haden. They were sweet on each other, that's what the gossips say. Bartholomew often visited the Paradise Tree. Around midsummer they both disappeared. You did know them, didn't you?'

Athelstan sensed a shift of mood in the group: no more fawning smiles or air of innocence. He studied their close-set faces: you may not be what I think you are, he thought. The friar now understood why the group had not been troubled as they quickly hid behind an air of surly aggressiveness.

'Brother, we travel here and there.'

'That wasn't my question.' Athelstan shifted on

the log, picked up his chancery bag and placed it in his lap. 'I only seek information. It's good to do it on a sunny autumn afternoon. However, I can petition Sir John Cranston and continue my questioning at another time and in a place much less congenial.'

'There's no need to threaten.'

'I'm not threatening. I'm giving you my solemn promise. Horrendous murders have taken place. Justice must be done for Margot and Bartholomew.'

'We knew them.' One of the women spoke up, ignoring First Gospel's angry glance. 'They often came into Black Meadow and walked down towards the river, hand in hand, cheek to cheek.'

'They were pleasant people?' Athelstan asked. 'They must have stopped and talked to you?'

'Oh, they did.' First Gospel spoke up. 'Usually about the river but the clerk, Bartholomew, he was full of tales about the Tower: about its history and the gruesome deeds it had witnessed.'

'And?'

'He talked of Gundulf the Wizard.' First Gospel closed his eyes. 'That's right, the sorcerer who built the Tower for the Great Conqueror. He said that in or around the Tower . . .'

'Go on!' Athelstan insisted.

'Gundulf had buried a great treasure.'

Athelstan's heart quickened. 'And where was this treasure buried?'

First Gospel smiled slyly and tapped the side of his head.

'Many people think our wits wander, Brother, so they talk to us as if we were children.'

'What did he say?'

'Go on!' the woman urged. 'Tell him. It was an interesting tale.'

'Bartholomew was a scholar,' First Gospel added slowly. 'I am not sure, Brother, but sometimes I got the impression that he knew where that treasure was.'

'Did he say as much?'

'I asked him once. He and his sweetheart, I am not too sure whether she understood. Bartholomew said: "It shines like the sun, lies under the sun, so we have to find the sun." I laughed at the riddle for the sun we see but Bartholomew shook his head and would say no more.'

'And did he give any other clue?' Athelstan asked.

'That's all he said, Brother.'

'And did they talk of Widow Vestler?'

'The clerk never did but the young woman often complained, said she was a hard task mistress though she could be kind.'

'Brother.' One of the Four Gospels had taken a crude, silver-grey medallion from her purse. 'Take this, it will provide you comfort and protection. It depicts St Michael . . .'

'No thank you!'

Athelstan glanced across the field. The shadows were lengthening as the sun dipped in the west. He felt weary, slightly frightened, but he didn't know why. The meadow didn't look so pleasant now. He made his farewells and walked back towards the tavern.

Chapter 5

At the end of the alleyway leading up to his parish church, Athelstan paused, closed his eyes and muttered a quick prayer. Sometimes he was a simple parish priest, more concerned with ensuring Huddle painted the gargoyle's face correctly or Bonaventure didn't drink from the holy water stoup. Or the children came on a Saturday so he could teach them divine truths and take them through the life of Christ, using the paintings on the church wall. He'd meet the parish council; now and again tempers were lost but there was also the bonhomie, the sheer comedy of parish life, truly a gift from God. Sometimes, however, in his dreams, Athelstan glimpsed murder come shuffling along this alleyway, a yellowing cadaver dressed in a red cloak and hood while behind him clustered dark shapes, carrying corpses, the bloody work of sudden death.

'You are hungry, Athelstan,' he reminded himself. 'And you are tired. Don't let the mind play tricks on the soul.'

He drew a deep breath and marched up the alleyway. Athelstan expected to see the enclosure in front of the church crowded with those three grisly cadavers laid out on a sled. He stopped in surprise. It was empty! No sled, no corpses! No one, except Benedicta sitting on the steps, Bonaventure beside her. The widow woman had taken off her veil and her hair, black as a raven's wing, fell uncombed down to her shoulders. She was talking to Bonaventure, sharing a piece of cheese with him.

'A true mercenary,' Athelstan said to himself. He stood in the shadows and watched this beautiful woman with her perfect face and those kindly eyes, always full of merriment. Athelstan never knew whether he loved Benedicta or not. He'd admitted to this attraction in confession.

'You do love her,' Prior Anselm had replied. 'Being a friar, Athelstan, does not build a defence round the heart but you must remember your vows. You are a priest dedicated to God. You do not have time for those relationships which are so important to others: there can be no distraction to your work as a priest.'

Bonaventure suddenly espied him. Athelstan, embarrassed, stepped out of the shadows and walked across. Benedicta clapped her hands and got to her feet.

'I thought you were never returning.' She caught the friar's hand, eyes dancing with laughter. 'I am so pleased to see you. The house is swept. Philomel has eaten and Merry Legs was kind enough to send two pies. He solemnly swore he'd baked them today.'

'But the corpses?'

Benedicta's face became grave. 'Thank God they've

been recognised, Brother. The young woman was a whore, Prudence. She plied her trade at the Lion Heart tavern. The swarthy man was one of her customers.' She gave a half-smile. 'Apparently a preacher who warned against the lusts of the flesh. I suppose,' she added tartly. 'he wanted to find out whether they are as delicious as they sound. Bladdersniff took the cadavers away.'

'Where will they be buried?'

'The common grave at St Oswald's. Bladdersniff declared that God's acre in St Erconwald's had its fair share of strange corpses, which nearly led to a fight between him and Watkin.'

'And the young man?'

Benedicta's lips tightened. 'He's been recognised too: Miles Sholter.' Benedicta indicated with her head. 'His widow and friend are in the church.' She moved closer. 'Brother, is the rumour correct? Was Miles Sholter a royal messenger? They say he and his companion, Philip Eccleshall, were taking messages from the Regent John of Gaunt to the Earl of Arundel, who is on pilgrimage to Canterbury. Is it true, Brother,' she insisted, 'that if a royal messenger is murdered, the parish where his corpse is found is held responsible until the killer is found?'

'All things are possible,' Athelstan told her. 'But let me see them.'

Now he was back in his parish, Athelstan did not feel so tired or weary. Inside the church the young widow, Eccleshall beside her, was sitting in the far corner near the steps to the tower. They rose as Athelstan entered and came out of the shadows. Eccleshall was tall, blond-haired, podgy-faced. He was dressed in a dark-brown jerkin with slashed, coloured sleeves; a war belt strapped round his waist carried sword, dagger and leather gauntlets. His leggings were bottle-green, tucked into high-heeled riding-boots in which spurs still clinked. He carried a cloak over his arm; on his chest were emblazoned the royal arms and he carried a small wrist shield which bore the same insignia. A soldier, Athelstan thought, a man used to camp and warfare. Mistress Sholter was tall, dark-haired, with an imperious face, high cheekbones and slanted eyes. Her painted cheeks were now stained with tears. Like Benedicta, she was dressed in a gown of dark-brown wool with a cloak fastened over her shoulder by a silver brooch. Around her neck hung a silver harp on a gold chain.

'This is Brother Athelstan, our parish priest,' Benedicta said.

'I'm Philip Eccleshall, Brother, royal messenger and this,' Eccleshall flicked his fingers as if his companion were beneath him, 'is Bridget Sholter.'

The young woman started to cry, shoulders shaking, and went towards Athelstan, hands out. The friar caught her cold fingers and gripped them.

'I've heard the news, Brother,' Eccleshall informed him.

Athelstan waved them to the bench.

'Sit down! Sit down!'

His guests did so. Athelstan and Benedicta lifted across another bench to sit opposite them.

'Can I offer you something to eat or drink?' the friar enquired.

The woman shook her head. Eccleshall, too, refused.

'We must be gone soon, Brother. Miles's corpse has been taken to Greyfriars near St Paul's. I have paid the good brothers to dress it for burial.'

'Tell me what happened,' Athelstan began.

'Miles and Mistress Bridget live in Mincham Lane.'

'That's off Eastchepe?' Benedicta asked.

'We have a house there.' The young woman lifted her head. 'I am a seamstress, an embroiderer. I buy in cloth and sell it from a small shop below.' Her lower lip quivered. 'Miles and I had been married four years. He was well thought of. Why should anyone . . .?'

'Tell me what happened,' Athelstan repeated. He leaned across and patted the young woman on her hands.

'The day before yesterday,' Eccleshall replied, 'I went down to Westminster and received the Regent's letters for the Earl of Arundel. I then journeyed back to the royal stables in Candlewick Street where, by the Chancellor's writ, two horses and a pack pony were ready.'

'What time was this?' Athelstan asked.

'After three o'clock in the afternoon. I then journeyed on to Mincham Lane. Miles was already waiting. He made his farewells and we travelled down Bridge Street across the Thames and through Southwark. A pleasant journey, Brother, no trouble. We decided to lodge for the night at the Silken Thomas.'

'Wouldn't you travel further?'

'No, once you get beyond Southwark the highway becomes lonely, rather deserted. Miles and I had decided to rest overnight and leave before dawn. By riding fast and changing horses, we could be in Canterbury by nightfall.'

'And nothing happened?'

'We arrived at the Silken Thomas. I hired a chamber while Miles took our saddlebags up. A simple, narrow room, two cot beds, the promise of a meal with bread and ale before we left in the morning. We must have stayed there about two hours. The sun was setting. I was dozing on the bed when Miles shook me awake. "Philip," he hissed. "I've forgotten my silver Christopher." Show him, Bridget.'

The young woman undid her purse and took out a silver chain with a medal of St Christopher hanging on it. The medal was large, about two inches across. Athelstan took it and studied it carefully. It weighed heavily, probably copper-gilt with silver.

'Miles had always been a royal messenger,' she explained. 'And, whatever the journey, he always took this with him. But, before he set off, he changed and left this on a stool in our bedchamber.'

'And he went back for it?' Athelstan asked.

'He wouldn't listen to me.' Eccleshall shook his head. "I'm going back," Miles said. "It won't take long." He put on his cloak and hood and went downstairs. I followed and said that I would wait for his return, he replied he wouldn't be long and galloped away.'

'And what happened then?'

'He never came home.' Mistress Sholter spoke up. 'But there again, Brother, I did not expect him. After Miles had left, I closed up the shop and went up to Petty Wales to buy some goods and provisions. I returned.' She fought back the tears. 'I thought Miles and Philip were safely on the road to Canterbury.'

'When he didn't return,' Eccleshall said, 'the next

morning I travelled back into the city. I thought something had happened but, when I visited Mistress Bridget, she said she had not seen her husband. I then began my search. I heard rumours of corpses being found and came here.' He shrugged. 'I recognised Miles immediately but the other two I've never seen before.'

'And what was Miles wearing?' Athelstan asked.

'The same as me, Brother: a tabard, war belt, boots and cloak.'

'A strong man?'

'Oh yes, vigorous, a good swordsman.'

'So, if he was attacked, he would defend himself resolutely.'

'Brother, both Miles and I were soldiers.'

Athelstan paused and looked at the wall painting behind his visitors, depicting David killing Goliath.

'Let us say,' Athelstan began slowly, 'that Miles was attacked as he travelled back into Southwark. The first question is why?'

'He was a royal messenger, Brother. He wore the tabard and shield.'

'But why should someone attack him?'

Eccleshall shrugged. 'For any money he carried, his horse and weapons, not to mention the despatches.'

'But he wasn't carrying them that night, was he?'

'Oh no, Brother, I had them with me at the Silken Thomas.'

'Very well.' Athelstan played with the tassel on the cord round his waist. 'Had anyone a grudge against Miles? Was it possible that you were followed to the Silken Thomas and, when Miles left . . .?'

'No, Brother,' Bridget Sholter intervened. 'Miles

was a merry soul. No one had a grudge or grievance against him.'

'So, it has to be put down to either robbery or treason?'

'It's possible. The Great Community of the Realm often attacks royal messengers.'

'And what happens then?'

Eccleshall looked surprised.

'I mean,' Athelstan explained, 'are their bodies left in a hedgerow or a ditch?'

'No, Brother, they generally tend to disappear. So no one can take the blame.'

'I agree.' Athelstan moved on the bench. 'Now, Master Eccleshall, you are a soldier. I, too, have fought in the King's wars. Here we have a strong, well-armed young man riding his horse along the country lanes back into Southwark. You and I, Master Philip, are rebels. What do we do? We must get this man to stop and dismount.'

'One of us could lie down,' Eccleshall replied. 'Pretending to be injured.'

'But would you do that?' Athelstan asked.

'No, Brother, I wouldn't.'

'Of course not,' Athelstan retorted. 'It's a well-known trick and royal messengers, I understand, are under strict instructions to be wary of such guile and knavery. Miles Sholter was an experienced messenger, a soldier. Even if he was dismounted he would still be a powerful adversary. What I am saying, Master Eccleshall, is that Miles Sholter, if attacked by rebels or robbers, would first have been struck by an arrow.'

'It's possible, Brother, that his horse was brought down beneath him.'

'Yes, yes, I hadn't thought of that.'

'I understand your unease, Brother,' Eccleshall continued. 'But bailiff Bladdersniff said that Miles's corpse was found in a derelict house, an old miser's home in the middle of a field.'

'Yes, and that's the mystery. How did Miles get there? Where is his horse, his tabard, his war belt? And you see, Master Philip, we know that the two others, the whore and her customer, were killed because they surprised the slayer.'

'In what way, Brother?'

Athelstan rubbed the side of his head.

'I don't know. Sholter was apparently killed the day before yesterday, his corpse taken to that derelict house. The following evening the killer returns to strip it completely but he's surprised, so he slays his unexpected visitors.'

Athelstan tapped his foot on the floor. Bonaventure took this as a sign to jump in his lap and sat there purring.

'I'm intrigued,' Athelstan continued. 'Would robbers or rebels go to such lengths? Surely they'd drag poor Sholter off his horse, kill him and flee?'

'I disagree, Brother. Rebels would certainly hide the corpse and show little mercy to anyone who disturbed them.'

'Them?' Athelstan asked.

'It must have been more than one to attack a man like Miles Sholter.'

Athelstan caught the note of pride in Eccleshall's voice.

'And then to kill two more people. I've seen the corpses: both the whore and the other man were young, vigorous. They would have resisted, wouldn't they?'

Athelstan stared at the royal messenger: what Eccleshall said made sense.

'But you know what will happen?' the friar said quietly. 'The corpse of a royal messenger has been discovered in my parish, at a time when the shires round London seethe with unrest.'

'I'm sorry, Brother: what the Regent does is not my concern. I know a fine will be levied but you could argue the murder didn't take place here.'

'That's not the law!' Athelstan snapped. 'Master Eccleshall, Mistress Sholter, I grieve for your loss, I truly do. I shall remember Miles and the other victims at Mass. However, hideous murders have taken place! Blood cries to God for vengeance and, if I know the Lord Regent, justice will be speedily done. It has not been unheard of for Gaunt to hang people out of hand as a warning to others. Whoever killed those three unfortunates could have more blood on their hands.' He rose to his feet. 'If you learn anything at all?'

Eccleshall promised that he would return immediately. Athelstan gave them his blessing and they both left the church. Benedicta locked the door behind them.

'Is that safe?' Athelstan smiled. 'What if Pike the ditcher's wife comes? Benedicta the widow woman and the parish priest locked in the church?'

'Bonaventure's my escort,' Benedicta teased back.

Athelstan looked down at the cat; Bonaventure stretched, then padded over into the corner to search out the cause of certain sounds, only to return and stare up at his master.

'You are worse than a monk,' Athelstan teased. 'You know the hours and times for food.'

'What do you think?' Benedicta sat down on a bench.

'Benedicta, God forgive me, I am in God's house but what I say is the truth between the two of us. Miles Sholter, the preacher, and that pathetic young woman were murdered. I don't think Sholter was attacked by rebels or robbers. An arrow wound to the back or one loosed deep into the heart: that's the mark of the night people.'

'So what?' Benedicta asked.

'I don't know.' Athelstan shook his head. 'I sit in confession and listen to people's sins.' He paced up and down. 'I was taught by Prior Anselm to use logic and reason yet, at other times, it's good to forget these and listen to the heart.'

'Are you saying that Eccleshall and Mistress Sholter are assassins?'

Athelstan sat next to her on the bench.

'Listen Benedicta,' he said quietly. 'Here we have a young man, a royal messenger, happy and content. He leaves London and reaches a tavern. He finds he has forgotten his St Christopher medal and comes rushing back. On his way home he is brutally attacked and murdered, that would be Saturday evening. On Sunday his corpse is discovered in a derelict house by two people who are killed for their intrusion. All three corpses lie there until Luke Bladdersniff, our most industrious bailiff, finds them. Now, what's wrong with the theory that all three were killed by night-walkers?'

'Well. We know robbers or rebels do not act like that!'

'Good, Benedicta! Now we enter the realm of logic and evidence. Why should their corpses be kept? This is where the assassin, or assassins, made a mistake. I am sure Sholter's corpse would either have been destroyed by fire or hidden so it was never discovered. Matters, however, were complicated by the two intruders, so the assassin had to be careful. Hiding one corpse is relatively simple but three? The assassin, or assassins, returned on Sunday evening to finish their work with Sholter but the killing of the other two foiled that plan. Fire was the best solution but to burn a house requires oil and kindling. It's out in the countryside and such grisly preparations might be observed.'

'So, he was planning to return?'

'Possibly. When people were looking elsewhere for Sholter, the assassin, or assassins, would return, probably Monday evening, burning the house to the ground and consuming the corpses hidden inside. However, there's something more interesting. Tell me, Benedicta, when you leave your house what do you do?' He grasped her hand. 'Close your eyes. Tell me precisely what you do!'

'I put my cloak on. I make sure I am carrying my wallet, purse and belt. I check that there are no candles or fires left burning.'

'Good, honest woman.'

'I close the windows, lock the door and put the key in my wallet.'

'Go on!' Athelstan encouraged her.

'I am walking down the street. I am thinking about what I am going to buy. I am also worried about a certain meddlesome priest . . .' Benedicta rubbed her eyes. 'Who doesn't eat properly.'

'Terrible man,' Athelstan answered. 'But what else, Benedicta? What do you check?'

'That my key and any monies I carry are safe.' She laughed deep in her throat. 'The St Christopher medal!'

'Oh *mulier fortis et audax*, brave and bold woman,' Athelstan replied, quoting from the scriptures. 'You have said it, Benedicta! Here is a messenger leaving his young wife. He will stop at a tavern on Saturday evening and continue his journey on Sunday. He's riding through open countryside. He's well armed and protected: however, he's a young man who has a deep devotion to St Christopher and knows such journeys can be dangerous. Isn't it strange, Benedicta, that he never feels his neck for the chain, never realises it's missing until he reaches the Silken Thomas?' Athelstan held a finger to his lips. 'What he does next is both reasonable and logical. He hurries back but, surely, he wouldn't have forgotten it in the first place? And, even if he had, he must have noticed it was missing long before he reached the tavern?'

'There's only one flaw in your logic.'

'I am sure there is. And it would take a woman to find it.'

'What if Eccleshall is telling the truth? What happens if Sholter deliberately left the medal behind to provide a pretext for returning home?'

Athelstan raised his eyebrows. 'Prior Anselm would like you. It's possible! Sholter, for some reason unknown to us, distrusts his pretty young wife so he goes to the tavern and decides to return. He rides through the night, reaches Mincham Lane where his wife is entertaining someone else. A quarrel breaks out. Sholter is killed.' He glanced at Benedicta. 'And what next, mistress of logic?'

'The corpse is put into a cart, covered or hidden, and taken out to that derelict house.'

'Now, that is possible. But a cart would be seen, it would leave marks. It has to be trundled through busy streets and why go there? Why not take it out through Aldgate, hide it in the wild countryside north of the Tower?' He tapped Benedicta on the nose. 'But I accept your reasoning. Yet I am certain either one, or both, of that precious pair are implicated in Sholter's murder.' He fought back his anger. 'For which this parish is going to pay.'

'There are other difficulties,' Benedicta pointed out. 'What if we can prove that Mistress Sholter stayed in her house on Saturday evening and Master Eccleshall never left that tavern?'

Athelstan got to his feet and clapped his hands at Bonaventure.

'That, my dear Heloise, would pose a problem!'

'Who's she?'

'A beautiful woman who fell in love with a priest called Abelard.'

'I've never heard of him,' she replied tartly.

'Come.' Athelstan walked to the door, Bonaventure trotting behind him. 'Let's feed the inner man.'

They left the church. Outside the day was dying. Athelstan expected to see some of his parishioners but, apart from Ursula the pig woman disappearing down the alleyway, her great sow trotting after her, ears flapping, the church forecourt was empty. Philomel was leaning against his stall busily munching.

Athelstan found his small house swept and cleaned, a fire ready to be lit. On the scrubbed table stood two pies covered with linen cloths and an earthenware jug of ale. Bonaventure went and lay down in front of the empty grate. Athelstan brought traunchers and goblets from the kitchen, horn spoons from his small coffer. He was about to say grace when there was a knock on the door and Godbless, followed by his little goat, bustled into the house. The beggarman was small, his hair dishevelled, eyes gleaming in his whiskered weatherbeaten face. Athelstan noticed the horn spoon clutched in his hand. Thaddeus went across to sniff at Bonaventure but that great lord of the alleyways didn't even deign to life his head.

'I am hungry, Brother.'

'Godbless, you always are. When you die we'll say you were a saint.'

Godbless looked puzzled.

'You can read minds,' Athelstan explained.

'I've been in the death house.' Godbless rubbed his stomach and looked at the pies. 'I've had some cheese and bread but I knew about these pies, Brother.'

'It's not the death house,' Athelstan reminded him. 'Pike and Watkin have built a new one and, from now on, you are to call your little house the "porter's lodge". You are the guardian of God's acre. I don't want Pike and Watkin getting drunk there or Cecily the courtesan meeting her sweethearts in the long grass. If I've told that girl once, I've told her a thousand times: only the dead are supposed to lie there.'

Godbless solemnly nodded.

'And I'm going to offer you a reward.' Athelstan gestured at him to sit. 'I have this dream,' the friar continued, pushing a trauncher towards the little beggarman. 'To actually plant vegetables which I, not Ursula's sow, will eat.'

'I've driven that beast off before, Brother.'

'Beast is well named,' Athelstan quipped. 'That pig fears neither God nor man.'

'I'm glad I'm here.'

Godbless watched as Benedicta cut the pie and held his trauncher out. Athelstan filled the earthenware cups with ale.

'That young woman in the cemetery, she is such doleful company!'

The friar nearly dropped the jug. 'What young woman?'

'You know, Eleanor, Basil the blacksmith's daughter. She's just sitting under a yew tree muttering to herself.'

Athelstan was already striding towards the door. Godbless happily helped himself to another piece of pie and began to eat as fast as he could. The friar, followed by Benedicta, hurried through the enclosure along the side of the church and into the cemetery where Athelstan climbed on to an old stone plinth tomb. It supposedly contained the bones of a robber baron who had been hanged and gibbetted outside St Erconwald's many years ago.

'What's the matter?' Benedicta asked.

'Eleanor!' Athelstan shouted. 'Eleanor! You are to come here!'

He glimpsed a flash of colour. Eleanor rose from where she was hiding behind a tomb, head down, hands hanging by her sides. She came along the trackway. Athelstan climbed down.

'Eleanor, what are you doing here?'

'I feel as if I want to die, Brother. I just miss Oswald but our parents will not allow us to see each other and it's all due to that wicked vixen's tongue.'

'You'll die soon enough. And then you'll go to heaven. In the meantime you've got to live your life. God has put you here for a purpose and that purpose must be fulfilled.'

'I feel like hanging myself.'

Benedicta put her arm round the young girl's shoulder and stared in puzzlement at the friar.

'She loves Oswald deeply,' Athelstan explained. 'But, according to the blood book, a copy of which we haven't got, they are related.'

'Ah!' Benedicta hugged the young woman close.

'Come back with me,' Athelstan suggested. 'Have some pie and ale. A trouble shared is a trouble halved.'

They returned to the kitchen. Godbless sat, his chin smeared with the meat and gravy, a beatific smile on his face.

'You are worse than the locusts of Egypt,' Athelstan complained. 'But, come, sit down.' He sketched a hasty blessing. 'Lord, thank You for the lovely meal and let's eat it before Godbless does!' Athelstan raised his cup and toasted Eleanor. 'Now, let me tell you what happened today because it will be common knowledge soon enough in the city.'

Athelstan half closed his eyes, his mind going back to Black Meadow: the Four Gospels, those shadowy shapes slipping in from the river at night and, above all, that dreadful pit and the skeletons and corpses it housed.

'Brother?'

Athelstan glanced at Benedicta.

'It's a tale of murder,' he replied. 'And, I'm afraid, before God's will is known, more blood will be shed!'

Chapter 6

Athelstan was up early the next morning. He celebrated a dawn Mass with Bonaventure as his only congregation. He tidied the kitchen, checked on Philomel, Godbless and Thaddeus while trying to make sense of what had happened the day before.

The business of Kathryn Vestler he put to one side. It was too shadowy, too insubstantial, but he still held to the conclusion he had drawn about the murder of Sholter and the other two. However, his real concern was Eleanor, Basil's daughter, and, when Crim appeared to serve as altar boy for his second Mass, he sent him round to members of the parish council. Afterwards Athelstan hastily broke his fast, went back to his bed loft and knelt by a chair to recite the Divine Office. He kept the window open and eventually heard the sounds of his parishioners arriving. He flinched at Pike's wife screeching at the top of her voice. He closed his eyes.

'Oh Lord, please look after me today as I would

103

look after You, if Athelstan was God and God was Athelstan.'

He crossed himself. He often recited that prayer, particularly when he was troubled or anxious. Then he put away his psalter, climbed down from the bed loft and went out across to the church.

Athelstan always marvelled how his parishioners sensed some impending crisis. The whole council had turned up, eager to learn any tidbits of scandal and gossip. They all now sat in a semi-circle at the back of the church where he and Benedicta had met their two visitors the previous evening. The benches were neatly arranged, the sanctuary chair had been brought down for himself.

Of course there had been the usual struggle for positions of authority. Athelstan groaned at the way Pike's wife was glaring at Watkin's bulbous-faced spouse, for her expression suggested civil war must be imminent. Watkin, as leader of the council, sat holding the box which contained the blood book and seals of the parish. These were the symbols of his authority; the way Watkin gripped them and looked warningly at the rest from under lowered bushy brows reminded Athelstan of a bull about to charge. Pike sat next to him. Hig the pigman, his stubby face glowering, looked ready to pick a quarrel with the world and not give an inch. Pernell the Fleming woman had tried to change the dye in her hair from orange to yellow. Athelstan tried not to laugh. The result was truly frightening. Pernell's hair now stuck up in the most lurid colours. Benedicta sat next to her, whispering to assuage the insult one of the rest must have levelled at the poor woman. Mugwort the bell clerk, Manger the hangman, Huddle the painter, eyes half-closed, and Ranulf the rat-catcher: from the huge pockets on his leather jacket Ranulf's two favourite ferrets, Ferox and Audax, poked out their heads. Cecily the courtesan wore a new bracelet and looked like a cat which had stolen the cream. Basil the blacksmith and Joscelyn from the Piebald tavern were also present. The door was flung open and Ursula the pig woman hurried in, her great sow trotting behind her. The ferrets sniffed the air and disappeared. The pig would have headed like an arrow straight into the sacristy but Ursula smacked its bottom and it sat down immediately. Athelstan looked daggers at the offended sow. If I had my way, he thought, I'd bring bell, book and candle and excommunicate that animal!

'We are ready, Brother,' Watkin announced sonorously. 'The council is in session.'

'Do you know what that means, Watkin?' Pike jibed.

'Shut your mouth!' Watkin's wife retorted. 'My man knows his horn book, he can make his mark. Unlike some of the ignorant . . .!'

'Thank you. Thank you,' Athelstan intervened. 'Remember we are in God's house. The Lord is a witness to what is going to happen. I do thank you all for coming.'

Before anyone could object, Athelstan made the sign of the cross and intoned the 'Veni Creator Spiritus'. He sat down.

'We are in session!'

'We need more sinners for the choir!' Mugwort spoke up: his remark immediately provoked roars of merriment. 'I mean singers,' he corrected himself.

'In St Erconwald's,' Athelstan said, 'it's the same thing. We are not here for singers.' He continued, 'You know the reason why. Eleanor, Basil's daughter, is deeply in love with Oswald, Joscelyn's son. They are both good young people. I hope to witness their vows here at the church door. We will have dancing, singing, church ales . . .'

'Aye and a lot of fun in the long grass in the cemetery!' Pike's wife snapped, glaring at Cecily.

'Why, is that what you do?' the courtesan answered in mocking innocence.

'However,' Athelstan continued remorselessly, 'we have a problem. The Church's law is very clear on this matter. You cannot marry within certain blood lines. It would appear that Basil and Joscelyn's great-grandmothers were sisters. Now, you know that, although we have a blood book, it does not go back to those years.'

'What years?' someone asked.

Everyone looked at the blacksmith.

Basil flapped his leather apron and folded his great muscular arms. 'I don't know.'

'It must have been in the time of the young King's great-grandfather, Edward II,' Athelstan put in.

'Wasn't he the bum-boy?' Mugwort asked, eager to show his knowledge. 'Didn't they kill him by sticking a hot poker up his fundament?'

'That's disgusting!' Watkin's wife exclaimed. 'Anyway, how could they put a poker . . .?'

'Listen,' Athelstan continued. 'We have a blood book but it doesn't go back that far. What we are missing . . .' He waved his hand. 'Well, you know the previous incumbent?'

'He was a bad bastard, Brother,' Pike said darkly. 'Dabbled in the black arts, out at the crossroads in the dead of night.'

'He was sinful and he was wicked,' Huddle added. 'He didn't like painting. He kept the church locked.'

'He also stole things,' Athelstan continued. 'And probably sold them for whatever he could, including our blood book.'

'Yet, what's the harm in all this?' Joscelyn asked. He sat awkwardly, the empty sleeve, where he had lost an arm at sea, thrown over his shoulder, his other hand stretched out to balance himself. 'I mean, Brother, if they marry? Our great-grandmothers lived years ago, the blood line must be pure.'

'Not necessarily,' Pike's wife retorted. 'Things can still go wrong. We don't want monsters in the parish.'

'True, true,' Ranulf murmured. 'We have enough of those already.'

'How do we know they were sisters?' Athelstan asked. 'That's the reason for this meeting. Who will speak against me proclaiming the banns? You know what they are. I ask you formally. Who, here, can object to such a marriage taking place? It is a very grave matter. You must answer, as you will to Christ Himself.'

All eyes turned to Pike's wife.

'There is a blood tie,' she declared, adopting the role of the wise woman of the parish. Her voice became deeper, relishing the importance this proclamation gave her. Pike looked down and shuffled his feet.

'And what proof do you have of this?'

Athelstan's heart sank at the spiteful smile on the woman's face.

'Proof, Brother? No less a person than Veronica the Venerable.'

'Oh no!' Basil groaned.

'And you are sure of this?' Athelstan asked.

'Go and see her yourself, Brother. She may well be four score years and ten but her mind is still sharp and her memory good. I know the rules. If two witnesses speak out against a marriage, it cannot take place.'

Athelstan lowered his head. Veronica the Venerable was an ancient crone who lived in a tenement on Dog Tail Alley just behind the Piebald tavern. She claimed to be too old to come to church so Athelstan sometimes visited her. She was old, frail, but her mind was sharp. A cantankerous woman who had a nose for gossip and a memory for scandal, she had lived in Southwark for years and claimed she even watched Queen Isabella's lover Roger Mortimer being hanged, drawn and quartered at Tyburn some fifty years earlier.

'Why are you so hostile against the marriage?' Benedicta asked.

'Widow woman, I am not, I simply tell the truth!'

Aye, Athelstan thought, and you love the pain it causes. He saw the pleading look in Basil's eyes while Joscelyn just sat shaking his head.

'I will visit Veronica.' Athelstan tried to sound hopeful. 'I will make careful scrutiny of all this and perhaps seek advice from the Bishop's office. Now, there's another matter.'

Bladdersniff raised his head. His cheeks were pale but his nose glowed like a firebrand.

'The corpses?' he asked.

'I'll be swift and to the point,' Athelstan said. 'Three

people were murdered in the old miser's house beyond the brook. God's justice will be done but, unfortunately for us, so will the King's. One of the victims was a royal messenger.' He paused at the outcry. 'You know the law,' Athelstan continued. 'Unless this parish can produce the murderer, everyone here will pay a fine on half their moveables. The King's justices,' he stilled the growing clamour with his hand, 'are sitting at the Guildhall. I have no doubt a proclamation will be issued. The fine would be very heavy.'

Athelstan felt sorry for the stricken look on their faces.

'It could be hundreds of pounds!'

All dissension, all rivalry disappeared at this common threat.

'You know what I am talking about. The justices will rule that the royal messenger was killed by the Great Community of the Realm. By those who secretly plot rebellion and treason against our King.'

'It's not against the King!' Pike protested. 'But against his councillors!'

'Now is not the time for politicking,' Athelstan warned him, 'but for cool heads. We will not take the blame for these terrible deaths so keep your eyes and ears open. Sir John Cranston is our friend, he will help and we'll put our trust in God.'

Athelstan rose as a sign that the meeting was ended. He was angry at Pike's outburst but determined to use it.

'The day has begun,' he added softly, 'and I have kept you long enough. Thank you. Pike, I want a word with you.'

Athelstan walked up the nave and under the rood

screen, Pike came behind shuffling his feet. He knew his outburst had angered his parish priest and he was fearful of the short and pithy sermon he might receive. Athelstan knelt on the altar steps.

'Kneel beside me, Pike.'

The ditcher did and stared fearfully up at the silver pyx hanging above the altar.

'Pike,' Athelstan began. 'We are in the presence of Christ and His angels.'

'Yes, Brother.'

'I know you are a member of the Great Community of the Realm but, if you ever make an outburst like that again, I'll box your ears, small as I am!' Athelstan glanced wearily at the ditcher. 'Don't you realise,' he whispered, 'if one of John of Gaunt's spies heard that, they could have you arrested.'

'I, I didn't mean . . .'

'You implied you knew the rebels, that's good enough.'

'I'm sorry, Brother.'

'Don't be sorry. Just keep your mouth shut and the same goes for Imelda. Young Eleanor is very angry. She spent last night crying.'

'Father, she . . .'

'Never mind,' Athelstan cut him off. 'I want you to do something for me, Pike, and I don't want any objections. You are a member of the Great Community of the Realm.' He held up his finger just beneath Pike's nose. 'Don't lie to me. For all I know you may even be a member of its secret council. I want you to do one favour. Ask your fellow councillors: do they know anything, and I mean anything, about the death of that royal messenger?'

'Brother, I really can't.' Pike's voice faltered at the look in Athelstan's eyes. 'I'll do what I can, but I'm not the only one.'

'I'll wager you are not. I wouldn't be surprised if Ursula's sow also attends the meetings though she's too busy in my cabbage patch to do me that favour. Now, cross yourself and go!'

Pike did so and Athelstan closed his eyes.

'I'm sorry, Lord,' he prayed. 'I really am but, one of these days, Pike is going to get his neck stretched.'

He heard the door crash open behind him.

'Good morning, Sir John.'

'How did you know it was me, Brother?'

'Only one person opens that door as if he were the Angel Gabriel.'

'Oh, don't talk about angels. It brings back memories of those madcaps in Black Meadow.' Sir John knelt beside Athelstan and made a quick sign of the cross.

'And what brings you here?' Athelstan got to his feet and genuflected.

Sir John followed him into the small sacristy.

'Mistress Vestler is committed at Newgate. What is today, Tuesday? On Thursday she is to appear before Justice Brabazon in the Guildhall.'

Athelstan studied his friend. Sir John's bonhomie was forced, the coroner looked deeply worried.

'What is it, Jack?'

Sir John drew out a small scroll of parchment. He tapped Athelstan on the shoulder with it. The friar felt a shiver of cold run up his back.

'You know what it is, Athelstan. Don't ask stupid questions!'

Athelstan undid the scroll: the seals at the bottom

were of the chief justices, the mayor and justices sitting in session at the Guildhall. They proclaimed, in the name of the King, that Miles Sholter, 'piteously slain by person or persons unknown in the parish of St Erconwald's Southwark, was a royal messenger carrying the King's insignia and coat-of-arms. An attack upon him was an attack upon the Crown. Accordingly, the parish of St Erconwald's and all its inhabitants must, within forty days, surrender the person, or persons unknown, into the hands of the King's officers or suffer a fine of two hundred pounds sterling.'

'I am sorry,' Sir John said. 'It's the best I could do. I personally went to see John of Gaunt. If Brabazon had his way it would have been six hundred pounds.'

Athelstan found he couldn't stop trembling.

'It's still onerous, Jack. We are a poor parish!'

'There are ways and means. There are ways and means.'

Sir John took a sip from his wineskin. 'We'll catch the killer, Brother, while I know merchants in the city. We'll raise the monies. Meanwhile, that must be nailed to the door of the church, and I mean securely, Brother.'

'It will be.'

Athelstan regained his composure and wrapped the roll up. He stared at the crude wooden crucifix fastened to the wall above the vestry table.

Please, he prayed silently. Please do not let this happen.

The coroner was still looking woebegone.

'And there's something else, isn't there, Sir John?'

Cranston shook his head and sat down on a stool.

'I stride around, Brother, bellowing good mornings, quaffing ale, laughing and joking but, as God knows, I am deeply worried.'

'Kathryn Vestler?'

'It goes from bad to worse. Kathryn is now in Newgate gatehouse. She's stopped weeping, I find her stronger than I thought and she's become hard-eyed, evasive. Last night I questioned her again regarding the enquiries about Margot Haden, and others who visited the Paradise Tree, but she shrugged them off. She can find no explanation. Brabazon is now threatening to dig the whole meadow up.' Sir John clutched his beaver hat in his hands. 'I loved her husband Stephen like a brother. I owed him my life. I know, I know, I talk about Poitiers but there were other occasions. What happens if Stephen and Kathryn were killers? Murdering poor travellers, looting their possessions and burying them in that field of blood?'

'Alice Brokestreet is the key,' Athelstan countered.

'She is a murderess, desperate to save her neck. I've been to see her as well. She's obdurate in her story, hinting at other things, other crimes.'

'Such as?' Athelstan asked.

'What I thought.' Sir John scratched his chin. 'Let us say Kathryn Vestler is a murderess and she does plunder her victims. Now I can accept that she destroyed the goods of a poor chambermaid . . .'

'I follow your reasoning, Sir John. If Vestler was a robber, as well as a murderess, she killed for gain. What would happen to the goods she stole?'

'Precisely. Now Vestler couldn't very well go into the markets with baskets full of plunder. People would become suspicious. It's my feeling that she would sell them to someone else who would take them to a different part of the city, even to another market beyond the walls, and sell them there.' Sir John's light-blue eyes caught Athelstan's change of expression. 'What is it, Brother?'

The friar told him how the Four Gospels had described dark shapes coming off a barge and slipping, either through Black Meadow or beyond.

'There's only one place they could be going,' Athelstan concluded. 'The Paradise Tree.'

'Oh, Lord save us!' Sir John put a hand to his mouth. 'I can see how this will go. Vestler was hand-in-glove with a band of robbers. She'd kill a traveller and sell the goods to others.' He sighed. 'In which case she's lying. I asked Kathryn if there was anything she knew. Had she been involved in anything against the law? Even when she replied, I suspected she was lying.'

'And there's more!' Athelstan told Sir John about the Wizard Gundulf and the treasure 'which lay under the sun'. 'It's a riddle,' he concluded. 'But what can it mean?'

'Bartholomew was a clerk in the Tower,' Sir John replied. 'Let us say, for sake of argument, and remember Brother, I am writing a treatise on the governance of the city, that Bartholomew was a historian. Now, there are supposed to be treasures buried all over London. Every year the Crown lays claim to treasure trove, either from the river or dug up in some field or cemetery. Bartholomew may have stumbled on such a story. Is it possible he was murdered for that?'

Athelstan closed the small cupboard fixed to the

wall which contained the sacred species. He absent-mindedly took the key out and put it into his purse.

'And what if,' he continued Sir John's theory, 'Bartholomew believed the treasure was buried somewhere under the Paradise Tree? He goes to Mistress Vestler and shares the secret with her?'

'So she decides to kill him? I have a friend,' Sir John continued. 'Richard Philibert. He's an old clerk who once worked in the royal treasury. He sat at the Exchequer and audited the sheriff's accounts when they were presented at Westminster.'

'What has he got to do with this?' Athelstan asked.

'Well, Brother, yesterday as I sat sunning myself in the garden, I had a close look at the Paradise Tree. The garden is beautiful: the eaves, the roof, the furnishings within, everything is in a pristine state.'

'But Mistress Vestler does a good trade?'

'Aye, but Hengan said something interesting: how Kathryn had gold and silver salted away with the bankers.' Cranston got to his feet and patted his stomach. 'My friend Philibert will look at the accounts of the Paradise Tree. I'd wager a wineskin against a firkin of ale that Kathryn's income is excessive and Brabazon will swoop on that like a hawk. I've seen him before in court. A man for minutiae is Chief Justice Brabazon. He can pick at a prisoner like a raven does a corpse; he'll wonder whether she and Bartholomew found this treasure.'

'Will Hengan defend her?'

'Oh yes, but he's troubled. I called at his house this morning on my way here. He looked as if he hadn't slept. So, what shall we do, Brother?'

'First things first.' The friar rubbed his hands. 'Sir

John, we face an army of troubles, but it's not for the first time. If Mistress Vestler is a killer then there is little we can do to save her from the scaffold. What we must ask is, if she didn't kill Bartholomew or Margot, then who did?'

Sir John stared bleakly back.

'Think of it as a tapestry, Sir John,' Athelstan insisted, 'which tells a story. We have Mistress Vestler. We have the victims. Who else could have killed those people? Be responsible for the grisly remains in Black Meadow? Come on, Sir John, think! Because if you don't answer that question, Chief Justice Brabazon will make sure he hangs your friend on it!'

'We have Alice Brokestreet,' the coroner replied slowly. 'It's possible she could have killed them.'

'Perhaps.'

'I asked the gaoler at Newgate,' Sir John continued, 'if Alice Brokestreet had any visitors. He claimed a friar had visited to give her solace and shrive her. Now the priests come from many of the houses in London. There are more friars in London than there are flies upon . . .!'

'Thank you, Sir John! Your opinion of friars is well known!'

'Well, Newgate is near Greyfriars House so I went in to see Father Prior. They're Franciscans aren't they, not one of your coven?'

'Thank you, Sir John.'

'According to his records, the friars are responsible for the prisoners in Newgate. They provide comfort and consolation. However, not one of his brothers seemed to have any knowledge of Alice Brokestreet.'

Athelstan smiled. 'So, Brokestreet has an accomplice?'

'It's possible.'

Athelstan was going to reply but paused as the bell began to toll for mid-morning prayer. He sighed and hid his exasperation. Sometimes Mugwort remembered his duty, other times he was too drunk to forget. Now, the way the bell was tolling it seemed as if Mugwort were summoning everyone in the city to prayer. He waited until the clanging had stopped.

'Who could this accomplice be?'

'I don't know, Brother but I've got old Flaxwith and that damnable dog sniffing away. Remember Brokestreet worked in a brothel.'

'Who are you looking for, Sir Jack?'

'An old acquaintance of ours, the vicar of hell.'

'Oh no!' Athelstan groaned. 'I remember that rapscallion!'

'He may be able to help. Flaxwith will track him down. So, where to now, Brother? Hengan will meet us at the Tower . . .'

'Sir Jack.' Athelstan clapped him on the arm. 'You have problems, so have I. Let me tell you a story about our murderers here in Southwark. But first . . .'

Athelstan led him back into the church and out through the main door. Members of the council were still standing around. Athelstan walked over and thrust the scroll into Bladdersniff's hands.

'You are the parish bailiff aren't you, Luke? Nail that up and make sure it stays there.'

And, before anyone could ask questions, Athelstan walked round to the priest's house. Benedicta was in the kitchen washing the goblets and traunchers from the night before. Bonaventure was helping her. He'd jumped on to a barrel and was busy trying to lick one of the platters. Athelstan handed her the keys of the church and the widow woman, once she had freed herself from Sir John's bear-like embrace, agreed to look after the parish until he returned.

'You are welcome to them all,' Athelstan told her. 'At this moment in time, I feel like running into the countryside and hiding beneath a tree.'

'Strange,' Sir John mused, winking at Benedicta. 'I used to do the same when I was a little boy. And, if the truth be known,' he added in a mock whisper, 'I still do it when the Lady Maude is in one of her rages.'

Athelstan collected his cloak and chancery bag, absentmindedly made his farewells and, followed by a mystified Sir John, strode out of his house, taking the trackway down into Southwark. His parishioners shouted farewell but Athelstan walked on, lost in his own thoughts.

'What's the matter, monk?'

'Friar, Sir John, I'm a friar and a very angry one. We have the Vestler business in London, God knows what the truth behind that is; I have a young maid, daughter of Basil the blacksmith, who wants to marry a young man but there are rumours that they are related by blood. Now I have the mysterious death of Miles Sholter, not to mention a heavy fine!'

'You are not thinking of leaving, are you?' Sir John caught him by the shoulder. 'Oh, don't say that, Brother!'

Athelstan stared up at his sad-eyed friend and felt his temper cool.

'No, Jack, I'm not leaving you. I am just angry. Do you know what I think about evil, about the devil? He's not some great beast, some fallen angel shrouded in hideous majesty. Ah no! To me, Sir Jack, evil is like a malicious child who plays a trick and then hides in the shadows and giggles with glee at the damage done. You are the coroner, responsible for law and order. I am a friar, a priest, answerable to God for the care of souls. Now we're lost in a maze because people want to thwart God's will. So, I'll tell you: we're off to the Silken Thomas tavern and, as we go, my dear coroner, I'll tell you what happened last night and the reason for our visit.'

Sir John linked his arm through that of the friar.

'Then, Brother, let's proceed. I'll hear your confession.'

And the lord coroner and his secretarius walked on through the mean trackways and runnels of Southwark, totally unaware of the shadowy figure, trailing far behind, watching their every step.

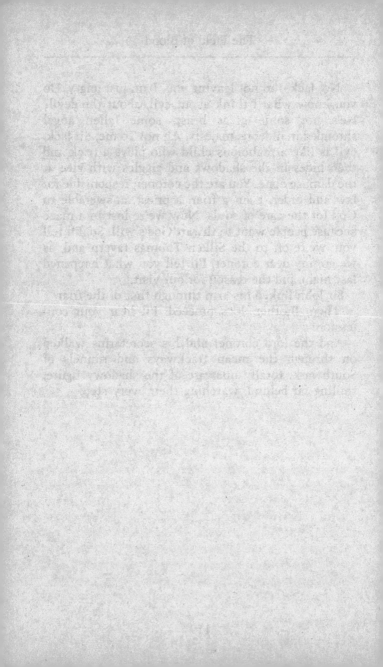

Chapter 7

They crossed the brook and went up the hill to the derelict house.

'What was his name?' Sir John asked. 'The old meanthrift who lived here?'

'Simon the miser, but that wasn't his real name. They say he was a priest, a Benedictine who escaped from his monastery and took some of its treasure with him. He died just after I arrived here. The house and this field were seized by the Crown. If I remember rightly, there's some legal battle over whether it was common land or can be sold. Naturally the house has been stripped of lead, tiles, anything valuable.'

Sir John stopped, huffing and puffing, and mopped his brow. He looked up at the house; the walls were dingy, only battered gaps where there had once been windows. Of the roof only a few beams remained, sticking up like blackened fingers towards the sky.

'It's also haunted,' Athelstan said. 'They say by

Simon's ghost. A good place to hide a corpse. The assassin must have known few people came here.'

The two went through the ruined doorway and into the parlour where the corpses had been found. Athelstan described how he thought the murders had taken place. Sir John agreed.

'But let's look around.'

'What for, Brother?'

'You'll know when you find it. Oh, be careful, the upper stories are not safe.'

Sir John looked up at the ceiling and noticed the rents.

'Aye, it would be a fool who went up there.'

'The stairs have long disappeared,' Athelstan said. 'Taken, no doubt, by some inhabitant of my parish for firewood.'

The lower rooms were the same. Anything of value had long disappeared. The floor was of stone but lintels, doors, window frames had all been plucked out. Athelstan came out of the scullery and noticed the steps leading down to what must have been a cellar. He went carefully down. The air was mildewed and smelt of coal and firewood.

'Simon must have used this as a storeroom,' he shouted, his voice sounding hollow. 'It's dark as . . .'

'Satan's armpit!' Sir John bellowed.

Athelstan undid his wallet and took out a thick candle and a tinder. He struck but no flame came. He tried again and, at last, the wick was lit creating a small circle of light. Athelstan gazed around. Nothing but cobwebbed walls and ceilings. The cellar was no more than a stone box, a pile of black coal dust gleaming in the corner. Athelstan waited until his companion came gingerly down the steps.

'Hush now!' the friar warned.

'What is it?'

Athelstan closed his eyes. He'd always been warned by Prior Anselm never to look for any spiritual experiences. 'Resist such occurrences,' the prior had urged. 'God rarely moves through visions but the ordinary things of life. There are more miracles on a tree in spring than in many of our so-called visionaries' dreams.'

Nevertheless, Athelstan felt tempted. He thought of the assassin cowled and hooded, face masked. Poor Miles had probably been killed on Saturday evening, just after he left the Silken Thomas. His corpse hidden here till Sunday when the other two had stumbled on the assassin.

'Brother! Brother!' Sir John urged him back to business.

'Hush!' Athelstan lifted a hand, eyes still closed. 'The assassins, Sir John, killed someone on Saturday but came back on Sunday to dispose of the corpse. So, where would they keep it? This cellar has been used to store coal: yet I can't remember any coal dust on the victim's clothing. Ergo, either the corpse was never placed here or the coal dust was on the upper garment and his boots which, as we know, were later removed. The leggings were dark green. They would hide such stains and moving the corpse would also loosen the dust.'

'Agreed!'

'So, what we are looking for, Sir John, is any stain or mark which shouldn't be here: that will be the deciding factor.'

Athelstan crouched down, holding the candle out, and moved slowly across the floor. He stopped at a clean patch against the wall and stared at the dark mark in the centre.

'A piece of sacking has been laid here. Look, Sir John. This stain.' He rubbed it with his fingers.

'It could be anything,' Sir John said. 'Spilt wine . . .'

'Or blood,' Athelstan added. 'Sholter's corpse was probably hidden here before being taken to the room above where the assassin was disturbed. Right, Sir John, now for the Silken Thomas.'

The tavern lay at a crossroads just outside Southwark where the common scaffold and stocks stood. These were empty but in the tavern yard swarmed chapmen with their pack ponies, pedlars and tinkers. Some Moon People in their motley-coloured rags had wandered in, two men and a woman; they were offering to tell fortunes and read palms but all they received were dark looks and muttered curses. The woman came across and tried to grasp Athelstan's hand.

'Will ye not let me see?' she asked in a harsh, strange accent. 'All of us have a future, pretty ladies perhaps.'

'I doubt it! But here, mistress.' He pressed a penny into her callused hand. 'That's not to read fortunes but to leave us alone!'

The Moon woman scurried off. Athelstan looked about him. The Silken Thomas was a three-storied building, its plaster and black beams hidden by creeping ivy which climbed up around the windows, giving it a pleasant serene appearance. A prosperous enough place but nothing like the Paradise Tree: the wooden sills were chipped, only some of the windows had glass. Others were covered by oiled paper or were simply boarded up with wooden shutters. Inside, the taproom was a large, ill-lit, sprawling place with benches and stools in different corners; a huge trestle table down the centre served as the common board. At the far end, just near the door leading to the kitchens, ranged the great tuns and vats above which ranged shelf after shelf of blackjacks and tankards, pewter mugs and cups. A tinker sat at a table, displaying a white rat in a cage which would go round and round on a makeshift wheel like that of a water-mill. Others were laying bets as to how many times the rat would turn it before it wearied and climbed off. A pickpocket, recently released from the stocks outside, was loudly complaining about his stiff neck. A little boy stood on a table and tried to massage it for him. The tavern-keeper swept out of the kitchen wiping his hands on a bloody rag which he stuffed beneath his stained apron. He took one look at the coroner and bustled across.

'Good day, sir. Can I help you? Our ales are the best you'll find on the Canterbury Road. Indeed, anywhere in Southwark, if that's your direction.'

'Miles Sholter!' Sir John barked, showing his wax seal of office. 'And Philip Eccleshall. Two royal messengers, they arrived here last Saturday evening.'

'What was it sir, two quarts of ale? A piece of chicken pie? Or we have eel pastries? I am a busy man, sir.'

'And I am a King's officer!'

'Two quarts of ale and a chicken pie would do nicely.' Athelstan pulled out a silver piece. 'And we'll sit over in the corner.'

The taverner's oily face broke into a smile. Athelstan tried not to flinch at the blackened stumps and his yellowing teeth, jagged and broken. He looked at the man's dirty fingernails.

'On second thoughts,' he added, 'just two quarts of ale.' He pressed his sandalled foot on the toe of Sir John's boot. 'I do urge you, sir, to help us or Sir John Cranston here, who is coroner of the city, might come back with his merry boys.'

The taverner held his hands up as if in prayer.

'Sir Jack Cranston. I've heard of you, sir.' He hurried across and wiped two stools with his rag. 'Make yourselves comfortable. The ale is free, my gift.'

'No, it isn't.' Athelstan put the silver piece on the table. 'We pay for what we drink and for what we learn.'

Despite his ponderous girth the taverner moved quickly. He roared out the order and a slattern hurried across. The blackjacks were large and looked clean, the ale frothing at the top and running down the sides.

'Now, sir, how can I help you?' The taverner pulled a stool across.

'Miles Sholter and Philip Eccleshall,' Sir John repeated. He sipped from the tankard and smacked his lips in appreciation. 'Tell the truth and, bearing in mind the ale is fragrant, I'll forget your earlier rudeness.'

'They arrived here on Saturday evening. You know the way they are. They came bustling in, cloaks on, hoods up, spurs clinking, sword belts on. One, of medium height, had long dark hair, the other was taller.'

'And what happened?' Athelstan asked.

'They gave their names, Sholter and Eccleshall, and their office. Sholter was rather quiet but Eccleshall was full of his own importance.'

'Did they order food or drink?'

'No, they immediately hired a chamber. I took them up to one on the first floor, the best we have: two beds, a chest, coffer, table and a . . .'

'Thank you. Just tell us what happened.'

'They stayed there. One of the maids took some food up, about an hour after they arrived. One was lying on the bed, the other was mending a spur. Their saddle-bags were unpacked and they were talking about their journey. About seven or eight in the evening, one of them came clattering downstairs all in a hurry, the other behind him. The taller one, Eccleshall, was arguing with his companion. "Why not leave it?" he cried. But the other said no and demanded his horse be saddled. They had already paid for their chamber so I didn't object and off the other one went.'

'Did you know he was murdered?' Sir John asked.

The taverner shook his head and wiped his face with a rag.

'Who was murdered?'

'The one who left.'

'So, that's what happened.'

'What do you mean?' Sir John demanded, glaring across at the group of chapmen whose shouts and curses shattered the peace of the taproom. The ped-lars, who'd overheard that Cranston was a King's officer, immediately fell silent.

'Well, the taller one, Eccleshall, after his companion left, he came down here.' He pointed to the inglenook. 'He just sat there looking into the flames.'

'And he never left?' Athelstan asked.

'Never.'

'You are sure of that?'

Athelstan felt a surge of disappointment.

'Well, you see, Brother . . .?'

'Athelstan. I am Sir John's secretarius. I am also parish priest of St Erconwald's.'

'Ah.' The taverner tapped the side of his fat nose. 'I've also heard of you. Look, I tell the truth. Eccleshall drank deeply that night. I could see he was worried. He had great difficulty climbing the stairs and that was long after closing. Now, like all taverners, I'm frightened of fire. I always go round and check that some drunken bugger has not left a candle alight. We deliberately do not put locks in our rooms because of that.' He grinned. 'If a man and his lady friend wish a little privacy, they can always put a stool against the door. Anyway, it must have been well after midnight. I opened the door to Eccleshall's chamber, the candle was out and he was snoring like a pig on the bed. We also have a groom guarding the stables. No one disturbed him.'

'And the next morning?' Athelstan asked.

'Eccleshall, rather heavy-eyed, came down to break his fast. He was very agitated, asking everyone had they seen his companion? Of course, we hadn't. He ordered his horse to be saddled and left. Oh, it must have been about nine in the morning.'

'And you are sure,' Athelstan insisted, 'that two came here?'

'Of course! Eccleshall and the other, Sholter, slightly shorter, dark-haired, fresh-faced.'

Athelstan thanked him and the taverner went back to the kitchen, chuckling at the easy silver he had earned.

'It seems you are wrong, Brother.' Sir John patted him gently on the shoulder. 'Sholter and Eccleshall came here. Sholter left but, if Eccleshall had anything to do with his murder, I can't see how he could be in two places at once!' He looked round the taproom. 'Brother,' he said quietly, leaning across the table. 'What happens if the Great Community of the Realm were here? One of their so-called officers? You heard the taverner. Eccleshall and Sholter swagger in, loudly proclaiming who they are, then one abruptly leaves just before darkness falls.'

'You mean he was followed out and killed?'

'It's possible.' Sir John licked his lips. 'That ale was nice.'

'No, Sir John, you've drunk enough.' Athelstan pushed his tankard across. 'Or, at least I have, you can finish mine then it's back to Southwark and across to the city!'

They left the Silken Thomas and made their way into Southwark. The streets were now busy, the small markets which stood on each street corner doing a busy trade in second-hand goods.

'Or what they've stolen from the other side of the river,' Sir John commented.

Many people recognised Athelstan and his burly companion. In the main, good-natured abuse was called but, on one occasion, the coroner had to draw his sword as some dried dog-turds struck the house wall beside him. The group of roaring boys gathered in an alehouse doorway quietly slunk back.

'Let's move on,' Athelstan urged. He went down an alleyway.

'Brother, I thought we were going to the bridge?'

'No, Sir John, just bear with me. I have a little parish business to do. The Venerable Veronica.'

They found Dog Tail Lane. The Venerable Veronica lived in a mean, shabby tenement thrust between an old warehouse on one side and a dingy cook shop on the other. Her chamber was at the top of rickety stairs which stank of urine. The walls were cracked and split, the flaking plaster covering the shabby, wooden steps like a coating of snow. The Venerable Veronica, however, was welcoming enough and her chamber was neat and tidy. She was sitting on a stool, hand over a small dish of glowing charcoal fixed on a tripod. In a far corner stood a cot bed screened off by a tawdry cloak which hung from hooks fixed into the ceiling.

Despite her great age, Sir John was surprised how striking the old woman was. She was small, narrow-faced; her skin looked lined and seamed but her eyes were sharp and bright as a sparrow's. She responded quickly enough, asking her visitors to bring across a bench so they could sit near her while she 'warmed her poor hands' over the charcoal.

'I should go to church more often, Brother,' she began. 'But my old knees and back hurt.'

'I could bring you the sacrament when I come,' Athelstan offered. 'It's easy enough done.'

'Would you really, Brother, and shrive me?'

'Of course, whenever I visit, just ask.'

The old woman peered up at him, moving her hands as if washing them above the charcoal.

'You are different from the other, Brother, the one who came before you. He was born in sin, he lived in sin and he died in sin. He took everything, he did: chalices, cups, breviary. William Fitzwolfe sold them all.'

'Including the blood book?' Athelstan asked.

The Venerable Veronica sighed and nodded.

'That's why I am here, Mother,' Athelstan continued. 'We truly have a problem in the parish. Eleanor, daughter of Basil the blacksmith, wishes to marry Oswald, Joscelyn's son.'

'Ah yes, yes.' The old woman blinked her eyes, head up, mouth open. She rocked herself backwards and forwards. 'The harridan, that fishwife Imelda, the one who's married to the ditcher, the troublemaker. I met her in the lane below. She was all hot with the gossip, like a sparrow on a spring morning.' Veronica glanced at Athelstan. 'Perhaps I should have kept my words to myself, Brother, but I was so lonely and I wanted someone to talk to. I told them Eleanor's and Oswald's great-grandmothers were sisters. They shared the same womb and the same blood line.'

'And is that the truth?'

Sir John took his wineskin off its hook on his belt, and the old woman immediately got up and fetched three cups.

'Oh, you are kindly, sir.'

Athelstan winked at Sir John who had no choice but to fill three cups to the brim. The old woman drank hers in one gulp and held it out for the coroner to refill.

'I am afraid it is the truth, Brother.'

'You can remember such detail?'

'It's not so much that! They always called each other "sister", that's how I remember: it was "sister this" and "sister that".'

'You'd go on oath?' Sir John asked, quietly marvelling at how this old woman could quickly down two cups of claret and appear none the worse.

'If I had to, I'd swear it's the truth.' She extended her cup.

Athelstan took it and gave her his.

'In which case, Mother, I think we should leave.'

They were at the door when the old woman called out, 'Brother, I've got something for you!'

The Venerable Veronica got up, moaning and grumbling under her breath, and went across to a coffer from which she brought out a small calfskin tome with a glass jewel embedded in the centre. She hobbled across and thrust this into Athelstan's hands. He opened the covers and saw the strange symbols depicted there.

'It's a book of spells,' she explained. 'Left by that wicked priest, Fitzwolfe.'

'And how did you get hold of it?'

'When he left the church, Brother, he just fled: the King's officers were pursuing him. I used to tidy his house until I got tired of his games. Anyway, the morning he left, I went in and found this lying beneath his bed. He had apparently hidden it there and forgotten it.'

Athelstan leafed through the pages. It contained crude drawings of gargoyles, a dog depicted as a human, spells and incantations.

'It's a grimoire,' he explained. 'A sorcerer's book.'

'I thought I should throw it away, Brother, but I was frightened.'

Athelstan slipped it into his chancery bag and tapped her on the shoulder.

'Don't worry. I'll burn it for you.'

They went down the stairs and out into the street, Athelstan briskly informing Sir John of the latest crisis in the parish council.

'It's serious,' Sir John agreed, glaring across at two ragged boys who were standing beside a wall seeing who could pee the highest. 'I've heard of many a marriage that's been forbidden because of that.'

They left the lane and went down the main thoroughfare to London Bridge. A cart trundled by. Inside, their hands lashed to the rail, were a group of whores, heads bald as eggs, their wigs piled into a basket pulled at the tail of the cart. Behind this a beadle blew on a set of bagpipes, inviting all and sundry to come and mock these ladies of the night being taken down to the stocks and pillories near London Bridge. Most, however, ignored the invitation. The women were local girls and most of the abuse, both verbal and clods of mud, was directed at the hapless beadle.

Cranston and Athelstan waited a while to let the cart move on. They passed the Priory of St Mary Overy, pausing now and again to greet parishioners. They reached the bridge but, instead of making their way down the narrow thoroughfare between the houses, Athelstan knocked on the metal-studded door of the gatehouse. It was flung open and Robert Burdon, the mannikin keeper of London Bridge, poked his head out. His black hair was greased in spikes, his face half-shaved. In his hand he grasped a horse comb and brush.

'What is it you want, friar? You'd best come through!' The little mannikin jumped from foot to foot. 'The lady wife is out. She has taken all nine children down to the fair at Smithfield so I am doing my heads.'

Sir John snorted in surprise.

'Don't look at me like that, Sir John Cranston! You may be a King's officer but so am I. I am responsible for the gatehouse, and am constable and keeper of the bridge. I also have my heads!'

He led them down a narrow passageway and out into the garden beyond, a small plot of grass with flower beds stretching down to the high rail fence which overlooked the river. Just before this ranged six poles driven deep into the soil.

'Oh, Lord save us!' Athelstan whispered.

On three of the poles were severed heads, freshly cut, the blood flowing down the wooden posts. Thankfully they were turned the other way facing out towards the Tower.

'Must we stand here?' Sir John murmured, feeling slightly sick.

'The court says,' the mannikin replied, 'that these heads are to be displayed before sunset. River pirates, Sir John, caught in the estuary they were. Sentence was carried out on Tower Hill just after dawn this morning. I comb their hair, wash their faces.' He pointed further down where the long execution poles jutted out over the river. 'And then I'll place them there.'

Sir John took a swig from his wineskin then cursed

as he realised the Venerable Veronica had already emptied it for him.

'Come on, Athelstan, get to the point!' he growled.

Burdon was gazing longingly at his heads.

'Do you know what, Robert?' Athelstan asked. 'You are one of the few adults smaller than me. Anyway, I have one question for you. On Saturday evening, about five o'clock, did two royal messengers ride across the bridge?'

'Of course they did. Cloaked and cowled, carrying their warrants and, according to custom, they showed me their commissions before they left the city.'

Athelstan clasped the little man round the shoulder.

'In which case, Robert, we won't keep you from your heads any longer.'

And, not waiting for the mannikin to lead them, they went back through the house and on to the bridge.

'I'd forgotten about that.' Cranston nudged Athelstan playfully. 'Of course, every royal messenger leaving the city by the bridge must, by regulation, show his commission to the gatekeeper. Why, what did you suspect?'

'Oh, that something had happened to Miles Sholter and perhaps only one of them left. I don't know.' Athelstan shook his head. 'Now, Sir John, before we go to the Tower, I must have words with Mistress Sholter in Mincham Lane.'

Sir John gazed dolefully up at the sky.

'Here we are, Brother, on London Bridge, between heaven and earth! My feet are sore, my wineskin's empty and everywhere we turn there's no door, just brick walls without even a crack to slip through.'

'We'll find one, Jack,' Athelstan replied. 'And the sooner the better.'

They crossed the bridge as quickly as they could. Athelstan tried not to look left or right between the gaps in the houses. He always found the drop to the river rather dizzying and disconcerting.

They left the bridge, went down Billingsgate and up Love Lane into Eastchepe. Sir John wanted to stop at an alehouse but Athelstan urged him on. At the entrance to Mincham Lane they found the way barred by a group of wandering troubadours who were playing a scene using mime. Athelstan stood fascinated. The troubadour leader was challenging the crowd to say which scene from the gospels they were copying. Athelstan watched.

'It's the sower sowing his seed!' he called out.

The troubadour's face became stern. Athelstan realised he had solved the riddle and should collect the reward. The rest of the troupe stopped. The troubadour picked up the little silver cup which was the prize. He looked down at it then at Athelstan.

'Run for it, lads!' he bawled.

And the whole group took off down an alleyway pursued by the jeers and cat-calls of their small audience.

'Very good, Brother.' Sir John grinned. 'I've never seen that trick before. They collect money from the audience and, if anyone solves the problem, they are off like the wind.'

They went further along into Mincham Lane, a broad thoroughfare with pink plaster houses on either side. Most of the lower stories served as shops with stalls in front displaying clothing, felts, shoes and caps. The sewer, unlike those in Southwark, was clean and smelt of the saltpetre placed over the night soil and other refuse.

Mistress Sholter's house was at the far end, a two-storied building with a pointed roof and jutting gables. A well-furnished stall stood outside the front door, the lintel of which was draped in mourning clothes.

'Is your mistress within?' Sir John asked the two apprentices manning it.

'Yes, sir, she's still grieving,' one of them replied lugubriously. 'She's there with her maid and Master Eccleshall.'

Sir John and Athelstan entered the house and waited in the hallway. It was clean and well furnished. Pieces of black lawn now covered the gleaming white plaster on either side. A young woman, her hair gathered up in a mob cap, came out of a room to their right.

'I beg your pardon, sirs?'

'Sir John Cranston, coroner, and his secretarius Brother Athelstan.'

'Oh, do come in,' a voice called.

The maid stepped aside. Cranston and Athelstan entered a well-furnished parlour where Mistress Sholter and Eccleshall were seated on either side of the hearth. A sewing-basket in the window seat showed where the maid had been sitting. The widow and her companion rose. Athelstan made the introductions and the coroner quickly accepted Mistress Sholter's offer of refreshment.

Sweet wine was served and a small tray of crusty, sweet marchpane. Athelstan refused this but Sir John took a number of pieces, murmured his condolences and slurped at the wine cup.

'I'm sorry to intrude on your mourning.'

Athelstan noted that most of the hangings on the walls were hidden by funeral cloths.

'However, I need to ask further questions.'

Bridget Sholter's face looked even paler, framed by her dark hair under a mourning veil which fell down beneath her shoulders.

'What questions, Brother? I've been sitting here with Philip wondering what had happened.'

'Tell me again?'

'I've told you,' Eccleshall said. 'Miles and I left here about four o'clock.'

'And you reached the Silken Thomas?'

'Oh, about six.'

'You travelled slowly?'

'What was the hurry? We'd decided to stay at the Silken Thomas and leave before dawn. We would be refreshed and so would our horses.' He shrugged. 'Measure out the distance yourself. It takes an age to get across the bridge; we stopped to pray at the chapel of St Thomas à Becket. Then, of course, we had to wait for that officious little gatekeeper.'

'True, true,' Sir John agreed. 'A leisurely ride from here to the Silken Thomas would take that long.'

'And you, Mistress Bridget?' Athelstan asked.

She made a face and gestured at her maid.

'Hilda here will attest to this: shortly after Miles went, I closed the stall, after all it was Saturday afternoon. I left the house and went down to the markets in Petty Wales.'

'Then you came back here?'

'Well, of course, Brother.' She laughed softly. 'Where else could I go?'

'It's true what my mistress says,' the maid said. 'The master left. As he did so, the apprentices were bringing the goods in. The mistress then dismissed me and she took her basket out.'

'You don't sleep here?'

'Oh no, Brother, I live with my own family in Shoe Lane.'

'Our house is very small,' Bridget Sholter explained. 'We have a parlour, kitchen and scullery while the upper rooms are used as bedchamber, a small chancery office and storerooms.'

'But I came back here later,' Hilda said.

'At what time?'

'Oh, it must have been just before curfew, between ten and eleven o'clock.'

'What is your name?'

'Hilda Smallwode: when the Master's away, I always come and see that all is well.'

'Why these questions?' Bridget Sholter asked, getting to her feet. 'What are you implying?'

'I am implying nothing, madam.' Athelstan also rose. 'We are investigating the dreadful murder, not only of your husband, but of two other souls. My parish faces a heavy fine and the people I serve are poor. I need to know every detail if I am to lodge an appeal.'

Eccleshall spread his legs out, stretching them until the muscles cracked.

'Well, Brother, now you have it: Miles and I left shortly after four o'clock. We crossed London Bridge. We stopped to say a prayer at the chapel of St

Thomas à Becket. The gatekeeper, after some delay, let us through. We must have arrived at the Silken Thomas just before six o'clock. At some time before eight Miles decided to return for his St Christopher medal.'

'Yes, can I see that?' Athelstan asked.

Bridget Sholter, looking narrow-eyed, made to refuse but Sir John coughed and shuffled his feet.

'I'll get it for you.'

She left and came back. The medal was really a large locket, gold gilt on a silver chain. Athelstan prised the clasp open to reveal on one side a picture of Christ, on the other a St Christopher bearing the Infant Jesus. Athelstan snapped it shut and handed it back.

'I thank you mistress, Master Eccleshall.'

They made their farewells and went out into Eastchepe.

'What was all that about?' Sir John asked.

Athelstan led him through a porchway.

'Sir John, Miles Sholter was murdered. I am sure, as God made little apples, those two are responsible!'

Chapter 8

Athelstan stared up at the great keep of the Tower. On the green around him the women of the garrison were washing their clothes in great iron-hooped vats. Children also played in these, splashing water, jumping out and chasing each other. Soldiers lounged in the shadows drinking ale and playing dice. A lazy, pleasant place. The autumn sun was now warm and the grounds of the Tower seemed more like the setting for a midsummer fair than a formidable fortress. The mangonels, catapults and battering rams were all covered with tarred sheets. A horseman rode in, the hooves of his mount clattering on the cobbles. Grooms shouted and ran out to help take off the harness and lead the horse away. Cooking smells drifted from the kitchens and, from the royal menagerie, came the powerful roar of the lion sent as a gift by the Prince of Barbary to John of Gaunt.

The great hall, which lay next to the Chapel of St Peter ad Vincula, had its door flung open. Servants

141

and retainers were bringing out the greasy laden trestle tables to be scraped and washed once the women had finished with the vats of water. Two great hunting dogs snarled and fought over blood-spattered bones. Athelstan's gaze travelled to the parapets where archers, supposedly on guard, sought shade against the autumn sun.

Athelstan eased his writing bag off his shoulders and sat down on the grass. One of the great hunting dogs came over, chased by a child; it would have licked his face but the little boy grabbed the dog and pulled it away. Athelstan turned back to study the keep which soared up into the sky six or seven storeys high, built of dressed stone. Athelstan wondered at the ingenuity of the builder, Gundulf.

'He was a Bishop of Rochester,' he said to himself. 'He may not have been much of a churchman but, as a mason, he had a real gift.'

Athelstan glanced across at the Chapel of St Peter ad Vincula which lay to his left. The old church was being refurbished and Athelstan noted how the derelict cemetery had been turned into a pleasant green yard; the old tombstones and other monuments had been removed then the ground grassed over.

Athelstan loosened the cord round his waist and made himself comfortable. Sir John had met Flaxwith at the Tower gates and despatched him on certain errands. He had then gone to report to the constable, Sir Marmaduke Mountjoy. However, this newly appointed official was out hunting on the marshes so Sir John had to do business with the surly-faced lieutenant, Colebrooke. The coroner now sauntered back out of the hall whistling under his breath. One of the great dogs ran up. Athelstan was always amused how animals loved Sir John. The coroner skipped away.

'Nice dog! Nice dog!' he said. 'Now go and eat someone else!'

'What are we waiting for, Sir John?'

Athelstan saw Colebrooke, dressed in a brown leather jerkin, green leggings and battered boots, come out on to the steps of the half-timbered great hall, thumbs stuck into his war belt. Sir John crouched down on the grass and indicated with his head.

'Old Merry Eyes over there,' he declared sardonically, 'will take us up into the chamber where Bartholomew Menster worked and kept his possessions. Thank God the place has not been cleared. They are still looking for a replacement. When I called this morning, I told Master Hengan to meet us here around noon. Look, Brother.' The coroner made himself comfortable. 'You really believe that precious pair we've just visited are guilty of murder? But how could it be done? Sholter was definitely seen leaving the city, crossing the bridge and arriving at the Silken Thomas.'

'I don't know, Sir John, but, as you often say, I feel it in my water.' Athelstan plucked at a piece of grass and chewed on it.

'Are you hungry, priest?' Sir John unstoppered the wineskin. 'Old Merry Eyes over there filled it.' He took a swig, pulled a face and spat it out. 'Satan's futtocks! It's vinegar!'

'It will clean the wineskin,' Athelstan replied, his mind going back to Mistress Sholter and Master

Eccleshall. Two killers, posturing in mock innocence. She, the grieving widow, he the understanding friend. You played the two-backed beast together, he thought. You've committed adultery and, in some subtle way, you killed that poor man. My parishioners will now pay for your wickedness. Time will pass and, by Easter, you will be married, adding blasphemy and sacrilege to your sins.

'Be of good cheer, Brother. Here comes Master Hengan.'

They got to their feet as the lawyer strode across the grass towards them. He clasped their hands; despite the smile, Hengan looked worried.

'I've been to see Mistress Kathryn at Newgate.' He scratched his thinning hair. 'She's in good spirits, but she just sits and keeps her own counsel.'

'Master Colebrooke!' Sir John bawled.

The lieutenant came down the steps and walked as slowly as possible across the grass.

'Look at that sour face,' Sir John whispered. 'It would turn piss sour.'

'Sir John.' The lieutenant forced a smile, his eyes watchful.

Athelstan had done business before with Colebrooke. A red-haired, testy-tempered young man full of his own importance, constantly bemoaning the fact that he was always lieutenant and never constable.

'Ah, Master Colebrooke, if you could show us to Bartholomew Menster's chamber?'

Colebrooke sighed, jingled the keys on a ring on his belt, and led them across the green into the Wakefield Tower. They tramped up the spiral stone staircase passing different chambers, their doors open. Some were empty, others housed clerks poring over rolls of vellum. Near the top Colebrooke stopped outside a nail-studded door, unlocked it and threw it open. The chamber was large and circular. It smelt musty and stale. Colebrooke hastened to open the shutters, allowing in bursts of sunlight and fresh air. The bed had been stripped; only a straw-filled mattress remained and two dark-stained bolsters. A cloak hung from a peg on the wall, other garments from hooks on the inside of the door. There were tables and stools, a tray of pewter cups and a cracked flagon. A wooden lavarium, bearing a bowl and jug, stood in the corner. Some saddlebags lay piled next to coffers and chests beneath a crucifix.

'He never took anything with him,' Athelstan remarked. 'I mean, at first it was thought Bartholomew had eloped with the young tavern wench.'

Colebrooke rubbed his nose on the back of his hand.

'I never believed that: Bartholomew was a quiet, studious man. He loved working in the Tower, constantly chattering about its history, searching among the records and old manuscripts.'

Athelstan walked over to the table and touched the rolls of vellum, the well-thumbed ledgers sewn together with black twine.

'God have mercy on him,' Colebrooke continued. 'Fancy a man like Bartholomew being killed by a woman, eh?'

'When was his last day of work?' Athelstan asked.

'We had the midsummer fair on the Feast of St John, the twenty-fourth of June, that was a Thursday. I remember seeing him the following day.'

'That would be the twenty-fifth?'

'Yes, then he disappeared.'

'Did he say or do anything untoward?' Sir John asked.

He had taken off his wineskin and ostentatiously poured the wine into a chamber pot he had pulled from underneath the bed. Colebrooke smirked.

'You don't like our wine, Sir John?'

'No, I don't. But answer my question!'

'When he went missing, I made careful search.' Colebrooke shook his head. 'I could discover nothing. A close, secretive man, Bartholomew. All we knew was that he was sweet on a tavern wench.'

'Did he have friends?' Athelstan asked.

'No family to talk of. Bartholomew lived and slept here, until he took up with the wench.' Colebrooke walked to the door. 'If you want, I shall have refreshments sent up.' With another smirk he left.

Sir John went and kicked the door shut with his boot.

'Right, gentlemen.' The coroner rubbed his hands. 'I'm hungry, but nothing that a pot of ale and a meat pie wouldn't cure. So, let's begin.'

They soon listed Miles's paltry possessions: some robes, clothing, belts, a sword and rusty dagger; two skullcaps, a felt hat, wallets and empty purses.

'I wager any money he had soon disappeared,' Sir John said. 'Colebrooke's got the eyes of a jackdaw.'

Athelstan, seated at the desk, was piling all the manuscripts together. These he divided out and asked his companions to go through them.

The day wore on; now and again broken by the sound of a bell or the blowing of a horn as the hunters returned to the Tower from the moorlands to the north. Most of the manuscripts were old accounts and ledger books which provoked nothing of interest. Two or three were letters written by Bartholomew to different people in the city. Athelstan was determined to find something and, after a while, he pushed these aside, going quickly through the pile until he brought out a yellowing piece of parchment sewn together with twine. As he thumbed through this, the pages crackling, the ink slightly faded, he noticed a fresh piece of parchment had been inserted. He studied the entry most carefully.

'This is an extract from a chronicle,' he exclaimed. 'An account of the building of the Tower.' Athelstan sifted quickly among the manuscripts. 'And here's a map, crudely drawn.'

The parchment was stiff, blackened at the edges. Athelstan studied the map, aware of the other two standing behind him. He pulled the small candle closer.

'It's a mason's drawing, done in black ink, though this is faded. Look, there's the keep. Here are the Tower walls.' Athelstan moved his finger to the left. 'And there's Petty Wales, beneath it the river. And look at this.' He pointed to the faded words *ecclesia Romana*, 'the Roman Church.' 'This chronicle was written two hundred years ago by a very old man who was one of Bishop Gundulf's scribes. He describes how the Tower was constructed. He also comments on the Roman ruins. Apparently, the Paradise Tree is built on the ruins of an old Roman church.' He turned over the pages and noticed the fresh marks in the margin. 'That's Bartholomew's writing. The chronicler is telling of Gundulf's treasure. Apparently the old bishop had it melted down and fashioned into a great ingot. A foot in diameter and, listen to this, nine inches thick!'

'Satan's futtocks!' Sir John breathed.

'The chronicle then goes on to say that before he died, "*Gundulfus celavit hunc thesaurum, quod fulgebat sicut sol, in ecclesia prope turrem.*" Gundulf hid this gold,' Athelstan translated, 'which glowed like the sun, in the church next to the Tower.' He paused. 'In my view the church next to the Tower is a reference to the old Roman ruins.'

'The site of the Paradise Tree?' Sir John exclaimed.

'Bartholomew must have believed that Gundulf hid his treasure somewhere in the vicinity of the tavern.' Athelstan turned his stool round. 'Did Bartholomew ever discuss this matter with you or Mistress Vestler?'

Hengan shook his head. 'Never to my knowledge, Brother.' He tapped the map. 'If any treasure were buried beneath that tavern, I doubt if it's there now.'

'Why is that?'

'Brother, I deal in property: bills of sales, searches and scrutiny. If the old Roman church was destroyed and a tavern built, the treasure must be under it.'

'Of course,' Athelstan replied. 'It's near the river and the ground becomes water-logged.'

'This was written over two hundred years ago,' Hengan pointed out. 'The Thames often breaks its banks. It's a common occurrence every autumn: the soil crumbles, the river swells and floods the mudbanks.'

'So it could have been swept away?'

'Perhaps but, there again, if the treasure were hidden and protected by the old foundations . . .'

Athelstan recalled the Four Gospels.

'I wonder,' he mused, 'if our little religious group chose that spot to await St Michael or to continue their own searches? Master Hengan, they told me a story about barges which come up the Thames late at night carrying dark figures which, if the Four Gospels are to be believed, disembark and steal towards the Paradise Tree.'

'Oh, Lord save us!' The lawyer rubbed his eyes. 'I hope Whittock doesn't get hold of that.'

Athelstan looked across the chamber to where Sir John stood half-listening while going through other pieces of manuscript. At the mention of Whittock, the coroner strode across.

'Odo Whittock, the serjeant-at-law?'

'The same,' Hengan replied.

Sir John glimpsed the puzzlement in Athelstan's eyes.

'Odo Whittock,' he explained, 'is a young, ambitious serjeant-at-law: a veritable limner, a sniffer-out of crime. He works for the Barons of the Exchequer but, now and again, he does pleas for the Crown.'

'In other words a prosecutor?'

'Yes, Brother, a prosecutor,' Hengan said. 'I have heard good rumour that Sir Henry Brabazon has appointed Whittock to investigate this matter. Let me put it this way. Brabazon will loose the arrows.'

'But Whittock will be by his side,' Athelstan finished, 'holding the quiver?'

'Precisely, Brother. If Whittock gets hold of that sort of story, of which I know nothing, it will go badly for Mistress Kathryn.'

'I remember Odo,' Sir John intervened. 'Tall, thin-faced, nose like a falcon's beak. Eyes which never miss a trick. Prisoners at the bar are more frightened of him than they are of torturers in the Tower. A good friend but a bad enemy.'

'Did Bartholomew ever try and buy the Paradise Tree?' Athelstan asked, returning to the matter in hand.

'Not to my knowledge. But, as I have said, Mistress Vestler might sing a different tune.'

'Oh, look at this.'

Sir John, who had gone back to his searches, came and threw a scrap of parchment into Athelstan's lap. Athelstan picked it up and quickly translated the Latin.

'Who is Geoffrey Bapaume? Oh yes, I see, a gold-smith! Good heavens!' Athelstan exclaimed. 'It's a list of monies, five hundred pounds sterling, lodged by the said Bartholomew Menster in Bapaume's coffers. Bartholomew must have been careful with his monies: this was dated the sixth of June of this year. It would seem our dead clerk was collecting all his monies together.'

'I'll visit Bapaume before the scrutineers from the Exchequer do,' Sir John said. 'Now Bartholomew is declared officially dead, they'll search out every penny he owned. If there were no heirs, the royal treasury will sweep in the lot.'

'So, what do we have here?' Athelstan got up and paced the floor. 'Firstly, we know that Bartholomew was a careful clerk, sweet on the tavern wench, Margot Haden. He held a post here in the Tower which he used to search out the lost treasure of Gundulf, Bishop of Rochester. Secondly, we know Bartholomew found an old chronicle, written some years after Gundulf died. The writer was probably repeating a legend, or one that he may have learned from his old master, that Gundulf melted his gold down and hid it in a church near the Tower. Thirdly, we know that Bartholomew was deeply interested in this secret. This probably accounts for his visits to the Paradise Tree and his relationship with the young chambermaid. He made a cryptic reference to the Four Gospels about the treasure glowing like the sun and being hidden beneath the sun; that was an allusion to the line from the chronicle. Fourthly, we know that Bartholomew's last day on this earth was probably the twenty-fifth of June, but that's as far as we go. What else, Sir Jack?'

'Bartholomew would work here until just before sunset. In summer time that would be seven or eight o'clock in the evening, so he and Margot must have been murdered after that on the evening in question. That's some time ago. Memories dim. We know there was no mark of violence on the corpses, no blows to the skull or the ribcage of either. Therefore, we can safely deduce that death was by poison which must have been concealed in something they ate or drank.'

'Excellent, my lord coroner.' Athelstan smiled. 'Sharp as a cutting sword; ruthless as a swooping hawk.'

Sir John beamed with pleasure. 'Master Hengan, would you agree with this?'

The lawyer scratched his chin and nodded.

'Bartholomew was a clerk.' The lawyer picked up the story. 'But he had seen military service. Margot was a young woman, vigorous and strong; their deaths must have been by stealth . . .'

'Which leads us to two conclusions,' Athelstan interrupted. 'They were either killed at the Paradise Tree and their bodies taken out in the dead of night . . . He stopped as he recalled that great oak tree with its overhanging branches, the shade it would provide on a hot summer's evening. A good place to sit and take the cool breezes from the river.

'Or what?' Sir John asked crossly.

'Maybe their bodies didn't have to be taken out? Maybe they were sitting under the oak tree and the assassin, like a serpent, entered their Eden. Was there a third, or even fourth, person there? Or did the Four Gospels invite them down to their cottage? After all, Bartholomew had referred to treasure in their presence. Just because that precious group are waiting for the return of Michael and all his angels doesn't mean they are averse to taking a little gold.'

'I have another theory.' Sir John spoke up. 'What about those dark shapes? The shadow men who come up the Thames at the dead of night? They could have stumbled on our clerk and his sweetheart, or even been involved in this hunt for Gundulf's treasure.'

'I know what Whittock will say of all this,' Hengan broke in mournfully. 'Kathryn Vestler had the best opportunity for murdering Bartholomew and Margot.' He pulled a face. 'As well as the means. Kathryn does keep poison in the Paradise Tree, as all taverners do, to destroy rats and vermin.'

'But what about the motive?' Athelstan asked.

'Master Hengan, was there any hint of a relationship between Mistress Vestler and Bartholomew?'

'None that I knew of. Bartholomew was an amiable man. Kathryn was nice enough to him but nothing singular.'

'I have another theory,' Sir John proudly declared. 'Let us say our clerk truly believed Gundulf's treasure was buried somewhere in or around the Paradise Tree and shared this knowledge with Mistress Vestler. What happens if they've already discovered it?'

'You mean thieves falling out?' Athelstan asked.

'Possibly. Whatever the case, as Master Hengan's said, if all these matters come to light, Sir Henry Brabazon and Master Whittock will make great play of them. Indeed . . .' He paused and spread out his fat fingers.

'Indeed what?' Hengan asked.

'I don't know how to say this, Master Hengan, but, as an officer of the Crown, I have the right to conduct a search.'

'Into what?' Hengan coloured.

'I think you know already,' Sir John said quietly. 'The accounts for the Paradise Tree. It's a very prosperous tavern. Perhaps too prosperous.'

Hengan put his face in his hands.

'I've asked my bailiff Master Flaxwith to seize the accounts books and take them to an old acquaintance of mine.'

Hengan lowered his hands.

'Kathryn is a shrewd businesswoman,' he replied. 'The Paradise Tree is very popular: clean, fragrant, well-swept while the food its kitchen serves is delicious. But, yes, Sir John, on a number of occasions I have questioned Kathryn about the large profits she makes.'

'And what did she say?'

'At the time she laughed.'

'She won't laugh now,' Sir John observed. 'All of London will be agog with this. Did Mistress Vestler make a profit out of the customers she killed? Or has she already found Gundulf's treasure? The tavern owns a forge; gold can be smelted down. By the time Sir Henry Brabazon has finished with her, she'll not only be accused of murder and robbery but stealing treasure trove from the Crown and that's petty treason. A fine mess, master lawyer. Indeed, the more I find out about my old friend the less I like it.'

'You can't desert her!' Hengan pleaded.

'For the sake of Stephen I won't! But I think we are finished here. Master Flaxwith will be waiting.'

'And afterwards?' Hengan asked.

'I'm hungry and thirsty. I'm going to visit the Lamb of God in Cheapside. You, master lawyer, Brother Athelstan, are welcome to join me. We'll take physical and spiritual comfort before we visit our friends in Newgate.'

Athelstan hurriedly took the manuscripts he had found and put them into his chancery bag, which now weighed heavy with the book the Venerable Veronica had given him. They went out on to the Tower green, thanked Colebrooke and walked down the narrow cobbled path which wound between the walls towards the Lion Gate.

The entrance to the Tower was busy with carts and sumpter ponies being taken in and out. Members of the garrison on patrol along the quayside were now returning. Chapmen, tinkers and traders had opened their booths to do a brisk trade. Cranston climbed on to a stone plinth and looked over the sea of heads and faces.

'Flaxwith!' he bellowed. 'Henry Flaxwith!'

Athelstan's attention was caught by a small crowd which had gathered round a Salamander King: one of those fire-eaters who went round the city performing their tricks. The man was assisted by a small boy who held the reins of a sumpter pony. A small booth had been set up for tankards of ale and the fire-eater was drawing onlookers to him. He was dressed in a mock scale armour with a red lion on the breast, brown leggings and thick leather boots. On his head he wore a tawdry coronet over a rather shabby wig with bright bracelets on each wrist. He'd lit a rush light and, as the crowd uttered gasps of wonder, lifted this and put it in his mouth chewing as one would a morsel of food. When he withdrew the rush light, the flame had gone. As the crowd clapped, he extended his clap-dish for contributions. Athelstan, intrigued, walked over. The Salamander King had suffered no ill-effect: his sunburned face broke into a smile as he glimpsed the friar.

'A miracle eh, Brother?'

'Everything's a miracle.' Athelstan grinned back. He offered the Salamander King a penny. 'I must hire you for St Erconwald's in Southwark, the children would love it.'

'I am always about the city, Brother. Just ask for the Salamander King.'

Athelstan thanked him. He was about to turn

away when he noticed something glinting against the pony's neck.

'Excuse me.'

He walked over and grasped the St Christopher medal hanging down from the saddle horn, which was almost identical to the one Bridget Sholter had shown him. It had the same thickness, but the chain was not so bright and the locket itself was dented and splattered with mud.

'What's the matter, Brother?' The Salamander King drew closer.

'I am intrigued, sir. This is a St Christopher medal. You don't wear it because it interferes with your tricks?'

'Of course not, Brother. This is a St Christopher locket, but you don't wear it round your neck. Here, I'll show you.'

He took the chain off the saddle horn and looped it over Athelstan's head. The locket itself lay against his stomach. The chain, being so thick, was rather heavy. He could certainly feel its weight.

The Salamander King took it off and put it back over his saddle. 'The locket is supposed to hang down so, as you get on and off your horse, you see it.' He picked up the medal and kissed it. 'That's what I do during my journey. I also touch it whenever I have to cross a rickety-looking bridge or ford a river.'

Athelstan closed his eyes. 'I should have known that,' he murmured. 'Oh friar, as Sir John would say, your wits are fuddled.'

'Are you all right, Brother?'

Athelstan opened his eyes and slipped another coin into the Salamander King's hands.

'God works in wondrous ways, sir,' he said. 'Angels do come in many forms.'

And, leaving the bemused fire-eater, Athelstan returned to where Sir John had at last traced his chief bailiff.

Chapter 9

Sir John wouldn't listen to what Flaxwith had to say but marched from the Tower as if he were leading a triumphant procession. He strode ahead up Eastchepe, Gracechurch Street, Lombard Street and into the Poultry. When they reached Cheapside it was thronged with crowds flocking round the stalls and markets. The pillories were full of miscreants trapped by their necks, fingers, arms or legs. Others had been herded into the great cage perched on top of the conduit which distributed water to the city. Sir John waved at all his 'lovelies' as he passed: night-walkers, rifflers, roaring-boys, pickpockets and drunks. He was met with sullen stares or abusive ribaldry.

The coroner was well known in the area, and his towering figure and luxuriant moustache and beard only highlighted his rubicund face. Ladies of the night, 'my little Magdalenas' as Sir John described them, disappeared at his approach up dark alleyways and runnels. He stopped to throw a penny at a whistling man who could imitate the call of the birds and roared at the cheap johns, their trays slung around their necks, to keep their distance. Flaxwith and two other bailiffs, plodding behind Athelstan, quietly laughed at some of the names Sir John was called. Abruptly the coroner stopped as if transfixed, blue eyes protuberant, mouth gaping.

'Oh Satan's tits!' he breathed.

Athelstan stood on tiptoe and saw heading for Sir John, Leif the one-legged beggarman.

'That bugger can move quicker than a grasshopper!'

Leif, together with his constant friend and companion, Raw Bum, always had an eye for Sir John. For some strange reason Lady Maude was much taken by this beggar who pleaded for alms and food outside kitchen doors and entertained the whole of Cheapside with his new found role as chanteur or carol-singer. Athelstan suspected that Lady Maude used Leif as a spy on Sir John's whereabouts, particularly his visits, fairly regular, to the Lamb of God.

'Ah, Sir John.'

Leif rested on the shoulder of Raw Bum, a rogue who'd suffered the misfortune of sitting down on a scalding pan of oil.

'Good morrow, Leif.' Sir John was already fishing into his purse for two pennies.

'The Lady Maude is well. She was much taken by my new carol: "I am a robin" . . .!'

'You will be a dead robin if you don't get out of my way!' Sir John growled.

'The Lady Maude is in good fettle,' Leif prattled on. 'But your two hounds Gog and Magog were in your carp pond and the two poppets . . .'

'What's wrong with the lovely lads?'

'Oh nothing, Sir John, they are just soaked and wet.'

'And?'

'The Lady Maude asked me to keep an eye open to see if you returned to Cheapside...' He took the pennies offered. 'But, of course, Sir John, I haven't seen you.'

And Leif, helped by Raw Bum, hobbled away.

Sir John, muttering curses under his breath, swept into the taproom of the Lamb of God. The taverner's wife bustled up. Sir John was taken to his favourite seat by the window where he ordered tankards for Athelstan, Hengan, Flaxwith and his two bailiffs. Once these had been served, the coroner leaned back in his seat.

'Well, Flaxwith?'

'I've been across to the Merry Pig, sir.'

'A well-known brothel house. Go on.'

'Alice Brokestreet entered the service of the Merry Pig weeks ago. Not as a whore, though she may have granted her favours, but more as a chamber girl and wine maid. She killed a clerk in a quarrel and escaped but the hue and cry were raised.'

'And?' Sir John asked testily. 'The vicar of hell?'

'The tavern-keeper said he had no knowledge of such a man.'

'I am sure he did.'

'But, he said that if he came across him, he would present the compliments of my lord coroner and Brother Athelstan.'

'Do you hear that, friar?'

Athelstan, lost in a reverie, started and looked at Sir John.

'A brothel-keeper knows you.'

'We are all God's children, Sir John.'

'What are you thinking about, Brother?'

Athelstan picked up his writing bag, took out a scrap of parchment, seal, inkpot and quill. He wrote a few lines.

'I'm thinking about St Christopher medals, Sir John.'

Athelstan shook the piece of parchment to ensure the ink was dry. He took a penny out of his purse and handed the coin and scrap of parchment to Flaxwith.

'When you've finished your ale, Henry, would you and your lads go back to Petty Wales. Seek out a young woman called Hilda Smallwode in Shoe Lane: she's maid to Bridget Sholter.'

'Oh, the widow of the murdered messenger?'

'Ask her the question I've written out. Did she see her master's medal hanging from his saddle horn or did she notice it in the house after he had left? You are to tell her you are from Sir John Cranston and she's to keep the matter secret.'

Flaxwith, eager to be away, drained his tankard and got to his feet, gesturing at his companions to follow.

'By the way,' Athelstan asked, 'where's Samson?'

'I've left him at a horse leech in Bodkin Lane.'

'Ah!' Sir John breathed. 'Don't say the darling boy's ill?'

'Something he ate, Sir John. He stole a string of sausages from a butcher's stall last night and the little fellow hasn't been the same since.'

Sir John raised his tankard and toasted him.

'Do give Samson my love.'

Flaxwith stamped out, complaining under his

breath about Sir John's attitude to his beloved dog.
The coroner ordered more tankards.

'I've got some bad news. While you were away looking at that fire-eater, Athelstan, I asked Henry about the accounts of the Paradise Tree but they've already been taken. Odo Whittock has, in the name of the chief justice, seized them already.' Sir John dug into the deep pocket in his cloak and drew out a tattered ledger. 'That's all he could find but it's five years old, the last year Stephen Vestler was alive. I was going to . . .'

'I'll have it, Sir John.'

Athelstan took the greasy-covered ledger, bound by pieces of red twine, and put it in his writing bag. Hengan was staring down at the table lost in his own thoughts.

'Master Ralph, you look sad.'

'Brother, I am more frightened.' Hengan sipped at the fresh tankard of ale. 'It does not augur well for Mistress Vestler. We know that the two corpses are those of Bartholomew the clerk and his sweetheart but there's also the question of the other skeletons.' He paused. 'Is it possible?'

'What?' Sir John demanded.

'Well, all the flesh and cloth had rotted away. Now around the city are numerous burial pits, relics of the great pestilence which swept through London thirty years ago. People were buried in gardens, any available piece of land.'

'And you think that's what happened in Black Meadow?' Athelstan asked.

'It's a possibility. I mean, if Mistress Vestler was a murderess, wouldn't we find or discover more corpses in the same state as Bartholomew?'

'There's one place I can look,' Athelstan added, 'my mother house in Blackfriars. When the pestilence swept through London the Dominican order did very good work. The brothers tended to the dead but they also made a careful list of burial grounds and, when the pestilence subsided, went out and blessed these.'

Sir John beamed from ear to ear.

'It's possible,' he whispered excitedly.

'But it makes little difference,' Hengan intervened. 'What does it matter if you hang for one or a dozen? Sir John, I think we should be going.'

They left the Lamb of God and made their way up through the milling crowds and into the open area before the grim doorway of Newgate. To one side ranged the fleshers' stalls and slaughterhouses. The cobbles ran with blood and ordure and the air was thick with the stench from the boiling cauldrons and vats.

Athelstan always hated the place. It stank of death, pain and punishment. The stocks in front of the prison were empty but a makeshift scaffold had been assembled. It was rarely used as an execution place but as a stark warning to the riff-raff who thronged about. In front of the massive gate swarmed beggars, grubby-faced clerks and scriveners eager to write messages for the unlettered. Turnkeys and gaolers moved about accepting bribes and gifts so people could be allowed through the metal-studded postern door into the yard beyond. Two prisoners had been released to beg for alms for those housed in the common cells. They wore nothing but loin cloths.

They were shackled together by long chains round their ankles and wrists, their emaciated, sore-covered bodies a pathetic reminder of the terrible conditions within. One of these pushed his clap-dish beneath Athelstan's chin.

'Some coins, Brother? Something for the poor within?'

Athelstan dropped a penny in but a sweaty-faced beadle was following the two prisoners so Athelstan wondered if the alms would go to those who needed them or the corrupt officials who regarded Newgate as their private fief. He followed Sir John up to the gate. The coroner had little time for the turnkeys. He simply showed his seal and thrust by them into the common yard. A gaoler took them across and up into the inner gatehouse.

Chambers stood on each floor. Athelstan glanced through an open door and recoiled in disgust: he was sure that a tray, lying within the doorway, held the severed ears of malefactors.

'Sir Jack,' he protested, 'I hate this place!'

They reached the fourth floor and the gaoler stopped before a heavy door set into the recess. When he unlocked the door Athelstan expected to see Mistress Brokestreet but it was flung open by a tall, black-haired man, thin-faced with a receding chin and a sharp-beaked nose which scythed the air. He was dressed from head to toe in a velvet gown of dark murrey trimmed with fur. The gaoler stepped hastily aside, almost knocking into Sir John in the narrow stairwell.

'Who are these people?' The man came out, closing the door behind him.

'Sir John Cranston, coroner of the city, and you, sir?'

'Master Odo Whittock, serjeant-at-law. Special emissary of Sir Henry Brabazon the chief justice.'

He looked over Sir John's shoulder, espied Hengan and his narrow eyes twinkled in amusement.

'I wager you've come to see Mistress Brokestreet. But the answer is no. Mistress Brokestreet is now a prisoner of the Crown and whatever you want to know can be learned in court.' He gestured with his finger. 'Above us lies Mistress Kathryn Vestler. I will not question her.' His lips parted in a smile. 'At least not now.'

And, without further ado, Whittock went back in, slamming the door behind him. The gaoler turned, his unshaven face creased into a smile.

'Sir John, I . . .'

'Oh bugger him!' Sir John growled. 'Let's see Mistress Vestler.'

The cell they were shown into was clean-swept, the shutters on the barred windows wide open; Mistress Vestler must have paid considerable amounts for a cell such as this. It contained a pallet bed, a bench, a table and two stools as well as a leather coffer with broken straps and buckles pushed against the wall. Clothes and blankets hung from pegs on the wall; on the table was an unfinished meal of bread, dried meat and some rather bruised apples. Mistress Vestler was staring out of the window and turned as they came in. If anything, Athelstan thought, she looked younger, more resolute than before. Her face was now hard set, no trace of any tears. She went and sat on the bed and watched as they came over. The gaoler locked the door behind them. She smiled up at Hengan.

'Have you come to take me home, Ralph?'

The lawyer coughed and shuffled his feet.

'Mistress, Sir John and I have questions for you.' She sighed, more concerned with straightening the dark-blue veil which covered her greying hair.

'I'm well looked after here,' she said. 'The place is clean. The gaoler says it's too high for the vermin.' She glanced at Athelstan who brought a stool across. 'It's good of you to come, Brother. I understand you have troubles of your own. A royal messenger killed in your parish?' She shook her head. 'It's so sad. I knew both Eccleshall and Sholter. Oh yes.' She saw the surprise in Athelstan's face. 'They often travelled from Westminster to the Tower and came striding into the Paradise Tree shouting for custom.'

'What were they like?' Athelstan asked as Sir John and Hengan brought across a bench.

'Oh, bully-boys both, especially Sholter; he would always swagger in roaring for a drink. Now he's gone! Life is truly a valley of shadows isn't it, Brother? But you have questions?' She didn't look at Sir John but at Athelstan. 'I also know your reputation: small and gentle with eyes which never miss anything.'

Athelstan smiled at the compliment. 'Mistress Kathryn, we are here to save you. I will be honest, that is going to be very hard.'

Mistress Vestler blinked, her lower lip quivered but she maintained her composure.

'Did you kill Bartholomew Menster and Margot Haden?'

'I did not.'

'Do you know how their corpses came to be buried in Black Meadow?'

'I do not.'

'Can you, Mistress Vestler,' Athelstan persisted, aware of how quiet this cell had fallen, 'remember the twenty-fifth June, the day after midsummer? That was the last day Bartholomew and Margot were seen alive.'

'I don't know, I can't remember.'

'What do you think happened?'

'Bartholomew must have come into the tavern to eat, drink and meet Margot.' She shook her head. 'But, apart from that . . .'

'Why did you burn Margot Haden's property?'

'I've told you that, it was tawdry, only cheap items. I thought she had eloped and wouldn't need them any more.'

Athelstan's heart sank: just a flicker of the eye but he was sure she was lying.

'Did Bartholomew Menster ever offer to marry you?'

'Of course not!'

'Were you jealous of his affection for Margot?'

She shook her head, and Athelstan sensed she was telling the truth.

'Did Bartholomew Menster ever discuss with you the legends of Bishop Gundulf's treasure, about it being like the sun?' He paused. 'And hidden beneath the sun.'

Athelstan abruptly recalled that no reference to the latter half of this cryptic riddle had been found in the manuscripts he had taken from the Tower.

Kathryn was now agitated, rubbing her hands together.

'The Tower is full of such legends,' she replied. 'Hidden gems, lost jewels, Gundulf's treasure hoard, Roman silver.'

'Did you and your late husband Stephen know about these lost treasures of the Tower?'

'Of course. We lived within bowshot of the Tower. Stephen was always buying artefacts from the garrison: shields, disused weapons and other curiosities. You've seen most of them yourself! True, Bartholomew discussed the legends with me but I just laughed.'

'Did he ever offer to buy the Paradise Tree?' Sir John broke in.

Kathryn was about to deny that.

'He did, didn't he?' Athelstan persisted.

'On two occasions,' she replied slowly, 'he made an offer but I refused.'

'And you never thought it strange,' Athelstan asked, 'that a clerk, a scribe from the Tower, was interested in the tavern? Didn't you think his interest in the treasure was, perhaps, more than a passing mood?'

'He made offers. I refused and that's the end of the matter.'

'Well, perhaps we have some good news,' Athelstan said. 'The other skeletons were probably victims of the plague: Black Meadow may have been a burial pit when the great pestilence raged.'

Kathryn smiled. 'It's possible. Perhaps that's why it was called Black Meadow.' She wiped her mouth on the back of her hand. 'Stephen always talked about ghosts being seen there.'

'More than ghosts, mistress. The Four Gospels,

that strange little company whom you so generously allowed to stay in Black Meadow, have reported barges coming in on the mud flats. Of dark shapes and shadows entering Black Meadow in the direction of the Paradise Tree.'

'I know nothing of that,' she retorted sharply. 'The Thames is like any highway, both good and bad travel there.'

'But where do they go to?' Athelstan asked.

'Petty Wales is a den of thieves.'

Athelstan fought to control his temper.

'Mistress Vestler, in this gatehouse is a serjeant-at-law, Master Odo Whittock. He and Sir Henry Brabazon are, to use Sir John's term, "two cheeks of the same face". They will dig and dig deeply. They will not be satisfied by your answers in court.'

'It's the only response they will get, Brother.'

'Mistress Vestler, I am trying to help. I have been to the Paradise Tree and it's a fine, prosperous tavern. Questions will be asked about your profits.'

'I am a good businesswoman,' she insisted. 'Brother, if I could have a cup of water?'

Athelstan rose, filled a cracked pewter cup and passed it over.

'My profits are what they are.' She sipped at the water. 'I can say no more.'

Athelstan saw his despair mirrored in Sir John's eyes.

'In which case, Mistress Vestler, I will pray for you and do what I can.'

'I will stay,' Hengan said. 'I need to talk about further matters.'

Sir John went across and hammered on the door.

The turnkey waiting on the other side opened it. They went down the steps and out into the cobbled yard. Athelstan plucked at the coroner's sleeve.

'It does not look well, Sir John.'

'No, Brother, it doesn't.' He paused at a scream which came from a darkened doorway. 'Hell's kitchen! That's what this place is: let's be gone!'

Outside the main gate, Henry Flaxwith stood holding a slavering, smiling Samson in his arms.

'You see, Sir Jack, he's well enough now.'

The dog lunged at Sir John, teeth bared.

'Samson is so pleased to see you, Sir John. You know he loves you.'

'Master Flaxwith, I'll take your word for it. Now, put the bloody thing down!'

Flaxwith lowered Samson gently down on to the cobbles and the ugly mastiff pounced on a scrap of meat from the fleshers' yard.

'And my errand?' Athelstan asked. 'To Hilda Smallwode?'

Flaxwith pulled a face. 'I am not too sure whether you will like this. The maid, who is honest enough, said she did not see Master Sholter actually leave, she was in the house. Her mistress stayed for a while but she did send Hilda upstairs to the bedchamber. The maid remembers seeing the St Christopher on a stool but didn't think anything of it. She certainly saw it again on Sunday morning when she called round to see if her mistress was well.'

Athelstan closed his eyes and quietly cursed.

'Well, well, Brother.' Sir John patted him on the shoulder. 'It would seem your theory will not hold up. Master Sholter did forget his St Christopher.'

Athelstan just rubbed the side of his face.

'Sir John, I must think while you must see your poppets.'

And, hitching his chancery bag over his shoulder, Athelstan despondently walked away, leaving a bemused coroner behind him.

Athelstan trudged on, oblivious to the crowds around him, to the constant shouts of the apprentices: 'What do you lack? What do you lack?' Tradesmen plucking at his sleeve, trying to attract his attention; whores flouncing out of doorways. All the little friar could think of was Mistress Vestler sitting there, telling lies while, across the city, two assassins hugged themselves in glee at the terrible crimes they had committed.

Athelstan paused, breathed in and coughed; the friar was suddenly aware that he had gone through the old city gates. He was now near the great Fleet Ditch which stank to high heaven of the saltpetre which covered the mounds of rubbish. Two urchins ran up, saying they would sing him a song for a penny. Athelstan tossed them a coin and sketched a blessing in the air.

'I'll give you that for silence,' he told them. 'Blackfriars!' he announced. 'I'll go to Blackfriars!'

'And then to heaven?' a chapman who had overheard him called out.

Athelstan smiled and walked on, lost in his thoughts and what he had learned.

At last he arrived at the mother house. A lay brother let him through the postern door. Athelstan seized him by the shoulders and stared into the man's vacant eyes, the saliva drooling from slack jaws.

'It's Brother Eustace, isn't it?'

'Abbot Eustace to you,' the lay brother replied.

Athelstan squeezed the old man's shoulder.

'And I am the Cardinal Bishop of Ostia,' he hissed.
'I've come to make a secret visitation, so don't tell
anyone I'm here.'

The lay brother chortled with glee. Athelstan
moved on across the cloister garth and into the
heavy oak scriptorium and library. The old librarian
was not there. Athelstan quietly thanked God, otherwise it would have been at least an hour of gossip
and chatter. The assistant, a young friar who introduced himself as Brother Sylvester, welcomed him
with the kiss of peace.

'I've heard of you, Brother Athelstan. They say
when you were a novice you ran away to war.' The
words came out in a rush. 'And your brother was
killed and you came back and so they made you
parish priest in Southwark.'

'Everyone knows my story.' Athelstan grinned.
'But, Brother, I am in a hurry. Is it possible to have a
history of the Tower and the Book of the Dead?'

'I know the former,' Brother Sylvester replied. 'But
the other?'

'It was written about twenty years ago,' Athelstan
explained. 'It lists all the burial pits left from the
pestilence.'

'I'll have a look.'

Athelstan sat down at one of the tables. The chair
was cushioned and comfortable. He noted the oaken
book shelves, the lectern with its precious calfskin
tomes chained to the stand; racks of parchments and
vellum. Books on scripture, theology, history and

science. Athelstan closed his eyes. It brought back memories of his novitiate, the smell of polish mingled with that of beeswax, dried leather and fresh parchment.

'Brother Athelstan?'

The assistant librarian had two tomes in his hand. He put these down in front then opened the window behind to provide more light. Athelstan begged a scrap of parchment and a quill before opening the tome with the title *Liber Mortuorum* engraved on the front. The pages were thin, yellowing with age, but the clerkly hand was still distinct. It listed the grave-yards of London, even at St Erconwald's. Athelstan scanned this entry quickly: two or three pages full of those buried there. He quietly promised himself that, one day, he would return and study it more closely. At the back the entries became more haphazard but, at last, he found the place: *Ager niger Prope Turrem*, Black Meadow near the Tower. '*In hoc loco*,' the entry began, 'In this place, many were buried in the autumn of the year of Our Lord 1349. The field was blessed and consecrated by Brother Reyward who tended to those,' here Athelstan had difficulty with the doggerel Latin, 'who had fallen sick and been placed in the tavern near the river, now used,' and Athelstan noticed the word '*hospicium*'.

'So, it was a hospital,' Athelstan murmured.

He took down the title of a book and the entry on a scrap of parchment.

'Have you found what you wanted, Brother?'

Athelstan smiled. 'Yes thank you.'

He should have felt elated but he was tired and hungry. Certainly the entry proved that at least

Mistress Vestler had not murdered indiscriminately. He sighed and opened the other book, *A History of the Tower and its Environs* by a chronicler who had lived fifty years earlier. It was not really a history but more a general description and chronicle of outstanding events, such as the legend that Julius Caesar built the Tower. Crudely drawn maps described the different buildings: the curtain wall, towers and chapel but nothing significant. Athelstan closed the book, thanked Brother Sylvester and left.

Once he was through the postern gate, Athelstan regretted not visiting the refectory or kitchen. Instead, he went into a tavern, the Mailed Gauntlet, a stone-built alehouse with a small rose garden beyond. The kindly tavern-keeper took him out to a turf seat and served him a pot of ale and a freshly baked meat pie. Athelstan sat and basked in the late afternoon sun. He would have liked to visit Sir John but what would he say? He should really be helping the coroner but, in truth, he felt a terrible anger against those two assassins playing 'lovers' cradle' in Mincham Lane.

'How did they do it?' he asked himself.

He thought of Sholter and Eccleshall riding across the bridge and, later that evening, a rider hurrying back.

'Of course!' Athelstan exclaimed. 'A horse is easy to get rid of but what about a saddle?'

Chapter 10

Athelstan left the alehouse determined to visit the Barque of St Peter, the rather eccentric name that eerie figure, the fisher of men, gave to his chapel or deathhouse. It was late afternoon and the crowds still thronged, particularly around the food stalls; they eagerly bought produce, reduced in price, before the market horn sounded for the end of the day's trading.

Athelstan, refreshed, made his way quickly along the streets. Above and around him three-storied houses, pinched and narrow, blocked out the sunlight, forcing people to knock and push each other in the busy lanes below. The friar threaded his way past the booths piled high with brightly coloured linen from Brussels, broad cloths from the West Country, drapes and wall sheets from Louvain and Dordrecht. Athelstan then entered Trinity where the traders sold more exotic goods, brought by the low-slung Venetian galleys now docked in the

Thames: chests of spices; bags of saffron; gingers and aniseed; casks full of dried figs; oranges and lemons from the islands of Spain; crates full of almonds and mace; sacks of ground sugar, pepper and salt.

At last Athelstan glimpsed the sails of ships and smelled the fresh tangy air of the river. He was now in La Reole where the quacks, fortune-sellers and relic-sellers swarmed like the plagues of Egypt. He noticed with amusement one bold fellow screaming above the rest that he had Herod's foreskin for sale, skinned by a demon and placed in the cave above the Dead Sea. There was a small stall, guarded by two burly assistants, selling books and manuscripts. Athelstan would have loved to stop there. Such merchandise was very rare and Athelstan, who was determined to study the night sky before winter set in, was always keen on discovering some book on astronomy or astrology. Such manuscripts were now flooding into the country, brought by travellers from the East and hastily copied by scribes and scriveners. Nevertheless, he had to press on. Once darkness fell, the fisher of men would set sail on his barge.

Athelstan heaved a sigh of relief when he rounded a corner and saw the fisher of men sitting on a bench outside his chapel. He was surrounded by his strange crew, outcasts and lepers, their faces and hands bound in dirty linen bandages. Only one was different, a young boy called Icthus. He had no hair, eyebrows or eyelids and, with his protuberant eyes, pouting lips and thin-ribbed body, he looked like a fish and, indeed, could swim like one.

Very few people approached these men who combed the waters of the Thames for corpses. Outside the chapel was a proclamation bearing the charges for bodies recovered:

**Accidents 3d. Suicides 4d.
Murders 6d. The mad and the insane 9d.**

The fisher of men rose as Athelstan approached.

'You have business with me, Brother?'

The fisher of men pulled back his cowl, his skull-like face bright with pleasure.

No one knew his origins. Some whispered that he was a sailor who had found his wife and children killed by marauders. He had lost his wits, wandered in the wastelands north of the city, before coming back to take up this most grisly position as an official of the City Corporation. He clapped his hands and a stool was produced from inside the chapel. The friar sat down.

'You wish to view a corpse?' the fisher of men asked. 'We have a fine array of goods today, Brother. A young man, deep in his cups, who tried to swim the Thames last night; a woman who threw herself off a bridge; a soldier from the Tower, as well as the usual collection of animals: five dogs, three cats, a sow and a pet weasel.' He grasped the skeletal arm of Icthus, his chief assistant. 'All plucked from the river by this child of God. And where is Sir John?' the fisher of men prattled on. 'The lord coroner does not visit me? I saw him today, coming out of Master Bapaume's, the goldsmith's.'

'It's good to see you sir,' Athelstan replied. 'And

may Christ smile on you and your endeavours. Sir John and I are involved in certain mysteries.'

'And you need my help?'

'Yes sir, we need your help.'

The thin, bony hands spread out. Athelstan noticed how long and clean the nails were, more like talons than human limbs.

'We have costs, Brother. I have a family to keep; pleasures to make.'

'What pleasures?' Athelstan asked curiously.

The fisher of men leaned forward. 'I visit Old Mother Harrowtooth on London Bridge. She offers me relief.'

'Yes, yes, quite.' Athelstan opened his purse and took out a silver coin, one of those Bladdersniff had handed over.

The fisher of men's eyes gleamed but Athelstan held on to the coin.

'I want to tell you a story,' the friar continued.

'When you are holding a piece of silver, Brother, I don't care how long it is.'

'I am an assassin,' Athelstan began.

The fisher of men started rocking backwards and forwards with laughter. The rest of his crew joined in.

'I am an assassin,' Athelstan repeated. 'I am riding back through the fields of Southwark. I do not cross the bridge. Instead, I dismount somewhere opposite Billingsgate or even the Wool Quay, a fairly deserted spot. I am disguised and intend to cross the river by barge.'

'So, it's useless making enquiries among the boatmen?' the fisher of men broke in.

'Precisely. I cross hidden by the cloak and cowl I have brought with me.'

'But you have to get rid of the horse?' The fisher of men's thin lips parted in a smile. 'In Southwark, that would be easy enough. A horse left wandering by itself is soon taken. What else, Brother?'

'I don't really care if the horse is taken or not,' Athelstan explained. 'But its harness and housings?'

'Ah, I see.' The fisher of men smiled. 'That must not be discovered. Very difficult to hide eh, Brother? So, if I were an assassin, I would go out somewhere along the mud flats and throw it into the river. If I understand you correctly, you wish us to search for it? A heavy saddle would sink and lie in the mud. However, it might take months before it was completely covered over.'

'Can you do it?'

'Before darkness falls: Brother, our barge awaits.'

'There is one other matter,' Athelstan persisted.

'The Paradise Tree?' The fisher of men spoke up. 'I know your business, Brother. The good tavern-owner, Kathryn Vestler, stands trial for her life. I cannot believe the stories. A kindly woman who has shown us and others great charity. She has given the Four Gospels the right to pitch camp and await the coming of St Michael and his angels.'

His words provoked laughter among his coven.

'They'll have to wait long,' he continued. 'We often see the beacon fire they light upon the bank. On dark nights when the moon is hidden, it gives us bearings.'

'I am not really interested in them,' Athelstan said.

'True, Brother, madcaps the lot of them. The

sounds we hear from their camp site are strange to say the least.'

'In your travels,' Athelstan chose his words carefully, 'especially at night, sir, you and your crew must see certain sights? Barges which have no lanterns, men masked, hooded and cowled?'

The fisher of men stared coldly back.

'Brother, I cannot tell you what happens along the Thames at night. We go unarmed. Oh, we carry an arbalest, a sword and a spear but we are left alone because we leave others alone.'

Athelstan sighed and got to his feet. He handed over the silver coin.

'But I can trust you on this matter?'

The fisher of men shook Athelstan's hand. The friar was surprised at the strength of his grip.

'You and Sir John are my friends. I have taken your silver. I have clasped your hand.'

Athelstan thanked them and went down towards the riverside where he hired a barge to take him across the now choppy Thames.

Athelstan dozed in the wherry then made his weary way along the valleys and runnels, passing the priory of St Mary Overy. All around him Southwark was coming to life at the approach of darkness. Taverns and ale-shops were opening; candles glowed in the windows. Dark shadows thronged at the mouths of alleyways or in doorways. Young bloods from the city, mice-eyed, heads held arrogantly, traipsed through their streets, thumbs stuck in their war belts: bully-boys looking for trouble, cheap ale and a fresh doxy.

Athelstan hated such men. They came from the

retinues of the nobles at Westminster to seek their pleasures. Fighting men, skilled with sword and dagger, they could challenge the like of Pike in his cups to a fight and, in the twinkling of an eye, stick him like a pig.

He passed the Piebald and sketched a blessing in the direction of Cecily the courtesan, dressed in a low, revealing smock, her hair freshly crimped, a blue ribbon tied round her throat.

'You'll get up to no mischief, Cecily?' Athelstan called out.

'Oh no, Brother,' she answered sweetly. 'I'll be good all evening.'

Athelstan smiled and made his way up the alley-way. The church forecourt was deserted and he sighed in relief. However, as he went down the side of the church towards his house, two figures came through the lych gate of the cemetery.

'Oswald Fitz-Joscelyn! Eleanor! What are you doing here?'

The young lovers looked rather dishevelled, bits of grass clung to Eleanor's dress and she had a daisy chain around her neck. The young man, sturdy and broad, with a good honest face, laughed and shook his head.

'Brother, we may have been lying down in the grass but we were talking to Godbless.'

Eleanor spoke up. 'Can we see you?'

Athelstan hid his disappointment at not being able to go in and relax.

'Of course! Of course!'

He took them into the kitchen. The fire was unlit but everything was scrubbed and cleaned: the pie on the table looked freshly baked. Beside it stood a small bowl of vegetables.

'Would you like to eat?' Athelstan offered.

'No, Brother.'

When the two young lovers sat down at the table Athelstan decided the pie could wait. The smiles had gone. Both looked troubled and Athelstan's heart went out to them. Oswald's hand covered Eleanor's; now and again he'd squeeze it.

'Brother, what are we going to do?'

'Trust in God, trust in me, say your prayers.'

'I can't wait.' Tears brimmed in Eleanor's eyes. 'Pike the ditcher's wife, her tongue clacks. All the parish know about your visit to the Venerable Veronica.'

'I'm sorry,' Oswald broke in. 'I know, Brother, you have troubles of your own: Mistress Vestler has been taken by the bailiffs.'

'Do you know her?'

'Oh yes. A generous woman, well-liked and respected among the victuallers. My father buys wine from her, the best claret of Bordeaux.'

'But what about your troubles?' Athelstan asked.

'What happens,' Eleanor enquired, 'if we do lie in the grass and become one? What happens if I become pregnant?'

'I cannot stop you doing that,' Athelstan replied coolly.

'They couldn't do anything about it then.'

'No, they couldn't.'

'Why do we have to be churched to be married?' she insisted.

'When a man and woman become one, they imitate the life of the Godhead. God is present. Such a sacred occasion must, in the eyes of the Church, be blessed, and witnessed, by Christ Himself.'

'But Christ will be with us?'

'Christ is always with you,' Athelstan assured her. 'But will you be with Him?'

'Brother!' Eleanor lowered her head.

'Listen.' Athelstan stretched across the table and touched both of them. 'Just trust me. Wait a while, don't do anything stupid, something you'll regret. Love is a marvellous thing, it will always find a way. You may not believe this but God smiles on you, help will come.'

Eleanor's face softened.

'Please!' Athelstan pleaded. 'For my sake!'

The two young lovers promised they would.

'Now, go straight home!' Athelstan warned as they opened the door. 'You will go straight home, won't you?'

'Brother, we have given our word.'

They closed the door behind them. Athelstan put his face in his hands.

'Oh friar,' he murmured. 'What happens if they can't trust you? What happens if they shouldn't?'

'Evening, Brother. Talking to yourself? You must want company?'

The friar took his hands away. 'Come in Godbless, there is enough pie for two.'

After the meal was finished, Athelstan left Godbless to clear up the kitchen. He took the keys and went across to the church intent on going up the tower, sitting there and studying stars. He'd revel in their glory, let their sheer vastness and majesty clear his mind. He had the key in the church door when he heard the scrape of steel and whirled round. There were five in all, masked and cowled, the leader standing slightly forward from the rest. He wore a red hood and a blue mask with slits for his eyes, nose and mouth.

'Well, good evening, Brother Athelstan.' The voice was taunting. He gave the most mocking bow. 'Off to study the stars, are we? Perhaps I should join you, it's the nearest I'll get to heaven.'

Athelstan felt behind him and turned the key in the lock. If necessary, he would flee into the church then lock and bar the door behind him.

'You know me?' Athelstan tried to control his fear.

'I understand your good friend the coroner, Sir John Cranston, wishes words with the vicar of hell?'

Athelstan relaxed. He had met this reprobate before and knew he posed no danger.

'Why do you come with swords and clubs?' Athelstan asked. 'I walk your streets daily.'

'So you do, Brother.' The vicar of hell resheathed his sword. 'Whether it be a visit to an alehouse or those strange creatures at the Barque of St Peter.'

He took off his mask and pushed back his hood, revealing a tanned, sardonic face and oiled black hair, tied in a queue behind. A pearl dangled from one ear lobe, his clean-shaven face had soft, even girlish features, except for the wry twist to the mouth and those ever-shifting eyes.

'We always have to be so careful with Sir Jack. I mean, here I am, Brother, a former priest, a sometime Jack-the-lad at whose feet all the crimes in London are laid.'

'Cranston's a man of honour,' Athelstan retorted. 'One day, sir, he'll catch you and you'll hang.'

'Oh no, I won't, Brother: that's why I brought my boys along, just in case old Jack stands hidden in the shadows with some archers from the Tower. I understand you've been there.' He turned and looked over his shoulder. 'Guard the alleyway,' he ordered softly. 'Let anyone come and go. But, if there's any sign of danger, give the usual signal. Brother Athelstan, shall we go into church?'

The shadowy figures behind the vicar melted into the darkness. Athelstan turned the key and went in. He led his unexpected visitor up the nave and into the sanctuary where he lit every available candle. The vicar of hell made him open the sacristy and the narrow coffin door which led into the cemetery.

'Just in case,' the rogue grinned, clapping Athelstan on the shoulder, 'I have to leave a little more speedily than I came.'

He sat down on the altar boys' bench but kept his head back, hidden in the dancing shadows.

'I was a priest once, Athelstan.' The vicar picked up the little hand bell. 'How does it go?' He rang the bell. 'Three times for the sanctus.' He rang it again. 'One to warn the faithful that the consecration is near.' Once more he shook the bell. 'Three times for the host; three times for the chalice and finally for communion: *Agnus Dei, Qui tollis peccata mundi . . .*'

'Don't blaspheme!' Athelstan protested.

'I am not blaspheming, Brother. Just remembering. I would have been a good priest. Like you. Ah, but the lure of the flesh, the world and the devil. Anyway, I like your church. You certainly have built a parish here, Brother. I remember the previous incumbent, William Fitzwolfe. Now, he was a wicked bastard!'

'Why have you come?' Athelstan sat on the altar steps facing him.

'Sir John wants to see me.'

'Then go and visit him yourself.'

The vicar of hell laughed. 'What is it you want, Brother? And I'll be gone.' He opened his purse and shook out some coins.

'I don't want your money.'

'Take it as an offering and tell me what you want.'

'Alice Brokestreet,' Athelstan began. 'She worked in a tavern, the Merry Pig, which is also a brothel.'

'I know it well. She stabbed a clerk with a firkin-opener, pierced him dead. A foul-tempered woman! Now I understand she'll see Mistress Vestler hang.'

'You know of the incident?'

'I was there when it happened, it was murder.'

'And Mistress Vestler?'

'A secretive one, our tavern-mistress: keeps herself to herself. I approached her on one occasion.'

'For what?'

'To see if we could do business together, moving goods around London. Perhaps hire one or two of my girls for her house but she refused.'

'And you know nothing of a barge which comes down the Thames at night and moors on the mud flats near the Paradise Tree?'

The vicar of hell laughed softly.

'The river is not my concern, Brother Athelstan: it belongs to people like the fisher of men. In my new vocation, friar, you have to be careful you do not tread on other people's toes. It's the only way you keep alive. However, I'll tell you one thing, I give it to you free: the corpses found in Black Meadow? Bartholomew Menster?' The vicar of hell clicked his tongue. 'Now, Bartholomew was a clerk, a royal official, yet he approached one of my associates. He asked what price would he pay if a large chunk of solid gold came into his possession!'

'What?' Athelstan leaned forward.

'Oh, it's common enough, Brother. Stealing a cup, a jewelled plate, a chalice or a pyx. You can't very well go down to a goldsmith and hand it over. The same goes for a slab of pure gold. Questions will be asked! It's treason to take treasure trove and not declare it to the Crown.'

'And Bartholomew Menster asked this? When?'

'Oh, at the beginning of June.'

'But the gold was never produced?'

'We were very interested but there's an eternity of difference between talk of gold and actually owning it.'

Suddenly, on the night air, came a sharp, piercing whistle. Athelstan jumped to his feet and went to the mouth of the rood screen.

'*Pax et bonum*, Brother,' came the whisper.

Athelstan turned but the vicar of hell had gone.

'*Pax et bonum*,' Athelstan replied. 'May Christ smile on you.'

He went and locked the coffin door and the sacristy and walked down the church. Godbless and Thaddeus were sitting on the steps. The beggarman stared up at him.

'I thought I heard a commotion, Brother, so I came out.'

'Nothing,' Athelstan replied. 'Nothing but shadows in the night, Godbless.'

'Are you well, Brother?'

Athelstan started. Benedicta came out of the alleyway, a lantern in one hand, in the other a linen parcel wrapped in twine.

'I've baked some bread,' she said.

'You shouldn't be out,' Athelstan replied.

'I was restless.' She pulled back her cloak. Athelstan glimpsed the Welsh stabbing dirk in her belt. 'I have friends in Southwark, no one would lift a hand against me.'

Athelstan went across to his house. He had given up any idea of studying the stars. Godbless had cleared the kitchen table and the lord of the alleyways was now stretched out before the fire-grate. Athelstan put the bread in the small buttery. He filled three cups of ale and shared them out.

'Why are you restless?' he asked.

'For poor Eleanor's sake.' Benedicta chewed her lip. 'It's so sad to see someone so young, so deeply in love.' She smiled. 'I understand you went to see Veronica the Venerable?'

'Ah yes.' Athelstan went to fetch the grimoire from his chancery bag. 'She had this, a relic from William Fitzwolfe, our former priest.'

Benedicta leafed through the pages.

'You can have it,' Athelstan told her. 'Take it over to the parchment sellers in St Paul's and you'll get a good price for the cover. In the meantime, Godbless, Benedicta, I want you to do a job for me.' He emptied the contents of the bag out on to the table, opened an inkpot and scratched a short message on a piece of parchment. 'Go down to London Bridge. If you can, collect Bladdersniff on the way, I want you to go to the gatekeeper.'

'The mannikin Robert Burdon?'

'Yes, that's the one. Give him this message. Ask him to think carefully then come back to me. He must tell the truth.'

Benedicta looked at the scrap of parchment, shrugged and, with Godbless and Thaddeus escorting her, left the house. Athelstan watched them go then closed and locked the door behind them. He went and sat back at the table.

'Right, friar.' He sighed. 'There's no rest for the wicked and that includes you.'

Bonaventure lifted his head then flopped down again. Athelstan wrote down his conclusions on the murder of Miles Sholter and the two other unfortunates.

'Very clever,' he said to himself. 'It's true that the sons and daughters of Cain are more cunning in their ways than the children of the light. But, saying it is one thing, proving it another.'

He wrote a title on a scrap of parchment: the Paradise Tree. Bonaventure jumped on to the table.

'You've come to listen, have you? We have a tavern-owner, Bonaventure.'

The cat nudged his hand and Athelstan stroked Bonaventure's good ear.

'We know she is a good victualler and what else? A widow. She allows those Four Gospels to camp on her land. She is undoubtedly innocent of the deaths of those other remains. They are simply the skeletons of poor people who died in the great pestilence.

But!' He spoke the word so loudly Bonaventure started. 'We have Bartholomew Menster and Margot Haden! They were undoubtedly killed on her land, either in the tavern itself or in Black Meadow. Their corpses were hurriedly buried. Why?' Athelstan closed his eyes. Gold! He thought: Bartholomew believed Gundulf's treasure was hidden in the church or chapel beside the Tower. It was a treasure which shone like gold. Bartholomew also made a reference, which I can't trace, something to do with the treasure shining like the sun buried beneath the sun. So, that means there's a scrap of parchment, some piece of evidence missing, probably destroyed.

Athelstan wrote down other conclusions.

Item – How could Bartholomew and Margot enter Black Meadow without Kathryn Vestler knowing?

Item – Was Kathryn Vestler jealous of Margot Haden?

Item – Bartholomew had offered to buy the Paradise Tree. Why? To search for gold? Or had Mistress Vestler already found it and decided to silence Bartholomew and his paramour? After all, if Bartholomew knew the gold had been found, he could blackmail Mistress Vestler over not revealing treasure trove to the Barons of the Exchequer.

Item – Why had she burned Margot Haden's possessions?

Athelstan lifted his head. 'We know nothing about the dead girl,' he said. 'But I wager Master Whittock does.'

Athelstan returned to his writing. What were those black shapes and shadows glimpsed by the Four Gospels? What had they to do with Mistress Vestler? Athelstan paused.

'I am missing something,' he whispered. 'Master Cat, I am missing something but I can't remember what.'

Bonaventure yawned and stretched. Athelstan went into the buttery and brought back a small dish of milk and the remains of the pie. He put these down near the hearth and watched as Bonaventure delicately sipped and ate. The friar sat in the chair and closed his eyes. What was missing? Something he had learned? Athelstan rubbed his arms. If matters don't improve, he thought, Mistress Vestler will hang and that will be the end of the matter.

'It's this gold!' Athelstan declared loudly. 'These legends about Gundulf's treasure!'

He remembered the accounts book Flaxwith had taken from the Paradise Tree. He took a candle from the table and sat, going through the dirty, well-thumbed ledger. The accounts were a few years old. He could tell from the different entries that they marked the year Kathryn Vestler became a widow. There were Mass offerings made to a local church for her husband's requiem as well as regular payments to a chantry priest to say Mass for the repose of the soul of Stephen Vestler. Items bought and sold. Athelstan turned to the front of the ledger and noted the date 1374 to 1375. He studied the last page and whistled softly at the profits the Paradise Tree made, hundreds of pounds sterling.

'I am sure Master Whittock's found the same,'

Athelstan mused. 'And how can Kathryn explain such profits?'

He went through the items bought. A number of entries chilled his blood. Margot Haden was apparently a favourite of Mistress Kathryn. A list of expenses showed cloaks, caps, gowns and petticoats, shoes, belts and embroidered purses bought for the young chambermaid. At one item Athelstan closed his eyes.

'*O Jesu miserere!*' he prayed.

He picked up the ledger, holding it close to the candlelight, and read the item aloud.

'For a Book of Hours, bought for the said Margot Haden, so she could recite her prayers and make her own entries.'

Athelstan threw the ledger down on the floor. He was sure the documents Whittock had seized would show similar entries. How could Kathryn Vestler explain why she had burned what she described as 'paltry items'? A Book of Hours? Hadn't Kathryn Vestler really destroyed important evidence which, in any court, would surely send her to the scaffold?

Chapter 11

'*Ecce Agnus Dei. Ecce qui tollis peccata mundi*:
Behold the Lamb of God, behold Him who takes
away the sins of the world!'

Athelstan stood with his back to the altar and
lifted the host above the chalice. He was celebrating
a late Mass and most of his parishioners were
present, huddled in the entrance to the rood screen.
Athelstan turned back to the altar. He ate the host
and drank from the chalice.

'May the body and blood of Christ,' he whispered,
'be not to my damnation but a source of eternal life.'
He closed his eyes. 'Help me Lord,' he prayed. 'Make
me as innocent as a dove and as cunning as a serpent.
Send Your spirit to guide me. I thank You for the
great favour You have shown.'

Athelstan could have hugged himself. He'd fallen
asleep in the chair and woken in the early hours of
the morning to see the scrap of parchment Benedicta
had kindly pushed under the door. Master Burdon

had told the truth. Athelstan, for the first time, could see a path through the tangle of troubles besetting him.

He heard a commotion at the back of the church and looked round. The fisher of men had entered with his strange coven around him. This caused consternation among the parishioners. The fisher of men was much feared, regarded as an outcast, and the members of St Erconwald's hastened to move away. Athelstan, however, continued with the Mass. He brought the ciborium down and distributed the hosts. He then went out into the nave and held a host up before the fisher of men.

'*Ecce Corpus Christi!* Behold the Body of Christ!'

The fisher of men's eyes filled with tears.

'We are not worthy, Brother.'

'No man is,' Athelstan said. '*Ecce Corpus Christi!*'

'Amen!'

The fisher of men closed his eyes and opened his mouth. Athelstan put the host on his tongue. He then moved round the other members of the coven. Some objected. Athelstan felt a deep compassion for these most wretched of people, their eyes and mouths ringed with sores. He walked back to the altar and finished the Mass. However, he did not return to the sacristy but stood on the top of the altar steps.

'The fisher of men,' he told his congregation, 'is my guest.'

'Brother.' Watkin spoke up. 'They search for the dead and . . .'

'Do their job well, Watkin, just like you sweep the streets of Southwark.'

'They are ugly,' Pernell the Fleming woman objected.

Athelstan, looking at her garish hair, thought he had never seen such a clear case of the pot calling the pan black.

'God does not think they are ugly,' Athelstan replied. 'All He sees are His children.'

A murmur of dissent greeted his words.

'They are our guests,' Athelstan urged. 'Now go, the Mass is ended!'

He went into the nave of the church where the fisher of men sat with his back to one of the pillars, his motley crew around him.

'Would you like something to eat or drink?' Athelstan asked.

'No, Brother, what you did and what you said is good enough.' The fisher of men's skull-like face broke into a grin; he grasped the shoulder of young Icthus who stared, fish-like, his cod mouth protuberant. 'Go on boy,' the fisher of men said. 'Show what we found.'

The parishioners on the other side of the church watched anxiously. Icthus skipped down the nave and Athelstan saw a bundle just inside the doorway covered with a canvas sheet. It was still dripping wet. Icthus picked it up and placed it at Athelstan's feet. When the fisher of men triumphantly plucked the sheet away Athelstan gazed down at a dirty, mud-slimed saddle, beneath whose heavy leather horn was the royal escutcheon. He turned the saddle over, and saw burned on the leather beneath, the letters M. S.

'Miles Sholter!' he breathed. 'This is a royal messenger's saddle!'

'And, Brother, look in the pouch.'

The friar turned the saddle back over, his hands and cuffs now soaked with the dirty river water. The fisher of men tapped the small leather pouch tucked into the saddle.

'Go on, Brother!'

Athelstan dug his fingers in. He could have cried 'Alleluia! Alleluia!' at what he felt. He took out the large St Christopher medal and couldn't resist doing a small dance of joy. His parishioners flocked closer, now seriously concerned about their little priest's wits.

'Is everything all right, Brother?' Pike glared at the fisher of men.

'Pike!' Athelstan exclaimed. 'God forgive you, but sometimes you are a great fool! And the same goes for all of you!' He grasped the fisher of men's shoulder. 'I prayed for deliverance. Oh, it's true what scripture says: "Angels come in many forms. This man has delivered us. Yea!".' Athelstan quoted from the psalms. ' "From the pit others had dug for us!" We will not have to pay a fine!'

That was it for the parishioners. Led by Benedicta, they streamed across the nave, thronging around the fisher of men, clapping him on the shoulder. Merry Legs, the pie shop owner, loudly proclaimed that each of them should receive the freshest and sweetest of pastries. Joscelyn the taverner, not wishing to be outdone, said he'd broach a fresh cask of ale. Athelstan had never seen a church empty so quickly. The fisher of men and his coven were bundled through the door, the parishioners loudly singing their praises, though they were still in doubt as to what miracle these strange creatures had wrought. Crim came speeding out across the sanctuary but Athelstan caught him by the shoulder.

'Crim!' He fished under his robes and took a penny from his purse. 'Merry Legs will keep a pie for you. Benedicta, bring the fisher of men back here.'

The widow woman hurried out and returned with their unexpected visitor.

'Where did you find it?' Athelstan asked.

'There's nothing the river can hide from us, Brother. In the reeds opposite Botolph's Wharf. I would wager someone went into the mud and threw it as far as they could. However, the silt and the weeds at the bottom caught and held it fast. Whoever did it must have been in a hurry.'

'Oh yes they were,' Athelstan agreed. 'And now they can hurry to the scaffold and answer to God. Benedicta, see to our guests. Crim, go to Sir John Cranston. He is to bring his bailiffs and meet me outside Mistress Sholter's house in Mincham Lane. Now go, boy! Benedicta will see that your portion of pie is kept.'

Athelstan disrobed, piling his vestments on a stool just inside the sanctuary. He gave Benedicta the keys of the church and asked her to clear up the sacred vessels, thanked the fisher of men again and hastened across to his house. Pike followed him over.

'Brother?'

'Yes, Pike?'

'The Community of the Realm.' The ditcher shuffled his feet. 'They had nothing to do with these murders.'

Athelstan smiled. 'Yes, Pike, I can see that now.'

An hour later, a slightly breathless, sweat-soaked Athelstan walked into Mincham Lane. The day was a fine one, the autumn sun strong and warm. Athelstan, however, had barely noticed the weather as he hurried out of Southwark and across London Bridge. He realised he hadn't broken his fast and stopped for a quick stoup of ale and some fresh bread in a cookshop. Now he looked down the lane, quietly groaned then jumped as Sir John Cranston appeared like the Angel Gabriel out of the mouth of an alleyway, his bailiffs behind him.

'You look in good fettle, Sir John.'

Cranston wore a flat grey cap over his tousled white hair, a white linen shirt beneath a burgundy-coloured doublet. His broad war belt was strapped around his ponderous girth, fingers tapping the hilt.

'And you, Brother, look as if you've been dragged through a hedge backwards. What's all this excitement?'

Athelstan took him aside and whispered his news.

'Oh by Queen Mab's tits!' Sir John exclaimed. 'Oh, Satan's futtocks! What a little terrier you are, Athelstan.' He brought two hands down on the friar's shoulders. 'Just look at you. The face of a maid and the heart of a lawyer. Oh, come, come! Mistress Sholter awaits us!'

Cranston didn't stand on ceremony but brushed by the apprentices and into the suspect's house. Mistress Sholter was in the parlour, sitting at a counting table, a row of coins stacked before her. On the window seat behind, Hilda the maid was examining a broken strap one of the apprentices had brought in.

'Is Master Eccleshall here?' Sir John boomed.

'Of course not.'

Mistress Sholter rose in alarm. She was still dressed in widow's weeds, her face pale. Athelstan abruptly realised how deep her voice could be.

'Well, you can get out for a start!' Sir John pointed to the maid.

Athelstan heard a dog yapping; Flaxwith and Samson had joined them. Sir John went to the door.

'Henry, keep everybody out of here! Brother Athelstan and I wish words with Mistress Sholter.'

The coroner slammed the door behind him and drew the bolts. Mistress Sholter had retaken her seat.

'What is this?' Her eyes had a guarded look. 'Why do you come here like this? I am a widow, my husband is not yet buried.'

'You are a murderess.' Cranston eased himself down into a chair and leaned against the wooden panelling.

Athelstan sat on a high stool before the counting desk. He felt like a bird perched on a branch. The widow kept her poise but her nervousness was apparent. She kept shifting the stacks of coins.

'Tell her, Brother.'

'Last Saturday,' Athelstan began. 'You do remember last Saturday, Mistress Sholter?'

'Of course!'

'Your lover and accomplice Eccleshall brought horses from the royal stables.'

'My lover!'

'Yes, yes, quite. I'll come to that later. Anyway, your husband left, spurred, sword belt about him. He kissed you goodbye and mounted his horse. As he was riding down the street, or even before, he took out the St Christopher medal he always kept with him and hung it, like many travellers do, over the horn of his saddle.'

'Impossible!' Mistress Sholter spat out. 'He left it here. It's still upstairs.'

'No, mistress, your husband had two medals. A common enough habit with something precious. I shall tell you what happened. He and Eccleshall left Mincham Lane and rode down towards London Bridge. As is customary, because they are royal messengers, they had officially to notify the gatekeeper, Robert Burdon. He remembers your husband, and I have a testified statement that Burdon distinctly remembers the St Christopher medal hanging from your husband's saddle horn.'

'It may have been something else,' she intervened.

'I don't think so. The riders continued through Southwark and then, for God knows what reason, Eccleshall managed to persuade your husband to leave the road and climb a hill to a derelict house once owned by an old miser. The house is a gaunt, sprawling affair, allegedly haunted, so a rather lonely place. If Eccleshall noticed anyone he would probably have chosen a different location. As I said, God knows what excuse was used. Perhaps Eccleshall feigned illness, something wrong with his horse? Or just a curiosity to visit the old ruin? Once inside the house, however, Eccleshall continued with the plan he'd hatched with you. He killed your husband. The poor man would never dream that such an attack would be launched.' Athelstan paused. 'You know what happened then, mistress. They had taken their time crossing the bridge which would provide enough time for you to clear away the stall, dispense with your maid and hurry down through Petty Wales. You'd go disguised, cowled and hooded: one among many on a busy Saturday evening. Once on Southwark side you hastened along the lanes. I wonder if you arrived before they did?'

Mistress Sholter was now breathing quickly, leaning back in her chair.

'You took your husband's corpse and hid it in the cellar of that house. Your husband was clean-shaven, with long black hair. You would be the same height, mistress. You dressed in his clothes, boots, cloak, and wore his insignia. You and Eccleshall then travelled on to the Silken Thomas.'

'Someone would have noticed,' she interrupted.

'Oh, but they didn't. Eccleshall did all the talking. A room was quickly hired and up to the chamber you go. I am sure, mistress, where necessary, you could lower your voice, make it sound like a man's. Why should anyone think differently? Why should they suspect you weren't a man? You were a stranger at the Silken Thomas, cowled and cloaked. Most people are wary of royal messengers. Not like the Paradise Tree, eh?'

'The Paradise Tree!' she exclaimed.

'Yes, the tavern in Petty Wales where Miles and his so-called friend Eccleshall often went to drink. Strange, isn't it? The taverner there said your husband was known for his bully-boy ways, shouting his orders. At the Silken Thomas he was, apparently, quiet as a mouse.'

'And then there's the medal,' Sir John put in.

203

'Yes, I always had grave doubts about that,' Athelstan continued. 'Here is a man who leaves his house. He has a devotion to St Christopher. He didn't wear the medal round his neck but kept it in a pouch on his saddle and hung it over the saddle horn. Are you saying he forgot to do that for a long journey to Canterbury? That nothing jolted his memory, even when he stopped at St Thomas à Becket's chapel on London Bridge to pray for safe passage?' Athelstan noticed the beads of sweat running down the woman's face. 'It was a clumsy ploy,' he went on. 'But you had to explain how your husband was killed well away from Eccleshall's company.'

'I . . . I . . .'

'Hush now, mistress. Let me finish.' Athelstan cleared his throat. 'You left the Silken Thomas pretending to be your husband riding back to collect his medal. But we know the truth, don't we? Your husband had two medals. You reached a lonely spot on the riverside opposite Botolph's Wharf when darkness was falling. You put on the great cloak you probably carried in a bag. You unstrap the saddle and harness, wade into the weeds and throw it into the river. The mud is deep, the water fast flowing. In days it might be swept away or begin to rot. You then clamber back on the bank. The horse you leave grazing; it won't stay free for long, someone will take it. In the gathering dusk you hire a barge across to Petty Wales and return by stealth to your house where, once again, you assume your proper attire. You dispose of any incriminating evidence and prepare to act the role of the grieving widow.' Athelstan paused. 'You made one real mistake: in your haste you forgot to remove that St Christopher medal. If you had, any talk of your husband having two could be easily dismissed.'

'Meanwhile,' Sir John took up the story, 'your accomplice sleeps on at the Silken Thomas. He has proven witnesses who will swear he never left the tavern. On Sunday he acts the distraught friend, riding hither and thither. Of course, he was waiting for nightfall.' Sir John took a swig of wine. 'Only the good Lord knows what you truly intended. Set fire to the old ruin where your husband's corpse was hidden? Or take it out, under the cover of darkness, and bury it in some desolate spot never to be discovered?' He pulled a face. 'What do you care? No one will ever know the truth and the blame will be laid at the door of robbers or rebels.'

Cranston took another swig and offered Athelstan the wineskin but the friar shook his head. He did not like the look on Mistress Sholter's face: arrogant, slightly mocking.

'You didn't really care, did you,' the friar demanded, 'who took the blame? My innocent parishioners would have to pay. You and your friend would play the roles you assumed. Time would pass, memory would dim. Tell me, when did you first plot it? Days, weeks, months ago? For what? So you could lie in adulterous passion and play the two-backed beast?'

Mistress Sholter moved some of the stacks of coins.

'What a farrago of nonsense!' she snapped. 'How can you prove that I left Petty Wales and journeyed to the Silken Thomas disguised as my husband?

True, he had two medals. Maybe he had forgotten that? Perhaps he was riding back for something else? Did he have a mistress in the city? Anyway, he's ambushed on a lonely road. The saddle bears the royal insignia so it's thrown in the river and the horse is taken and sold elsewhere.' She paused. 'I really don't know what you are talking about!' She preened herself.

'You know full well!' Athelstan insisted. 'You were party to your husband's murder; Eccleshall killed those other two because their arrival hindered his plans. One corpse is easy to hide or burn. But three? Did he panic? Did he flee? I am sure Mistress Sholter that, if you had been present, those corpses would never have been discovered.'

'I don't know what you are talking about,' she repeated.

Sir John sprang to his feet as he heard raised voices outside and, before Athelstan could stop him, he grabbed the St Christopher medal from his hands and walked out of the door. Eccleshall was standing by the stall held back by Flaxwith. Sir John strode up to him, slamming the front door shut. He held up the St Christopher medal.

'Pinion his arms!' he ordered.

The bailiffs grabbed the royal messenger and, before he could protest, took cords from their belts and bound his wrists.

'What is this?' Eccleshall spluttered.

Cranston pushed him along past the stalls and down a narrow alleyway. The coroner quietly prayed that Athelstan would keep Mistress Sholter busy. He grasped Eccleshall by the chin and held up the medal.

'She's confessed all, you know. How she met you at the old miser's house, stripped Miles' body and then journeyed in disguise with you to the Silken Thomas.'

Eccleshall blinked and wetted his lips.

'Our little songbird wishes to save her neck, doesn't she, lads?'

The bemused bailiffs nodded.

'She's told us how she rode down to the Thames and threw the saddle into the river then cast the horse loose. How she used Miles' second medal to distract the maid: a pretext for his supposed journey from the Silken Thomas. How you waited until Sunday evening to dispose of the corpse but then had to kill those two others who surprised you. She has turned King's evidence in return for a pardon.'

'The bitch!' Spit bubbled on Eccleshall's lips. He lunged to the mouth of the alleyway but the bailiffs held him fast. 'She's as guilty as me! She may be cold as ice now but she's a whore in bed!'

'Are you saying that she's your accomplice?'

'More than that! She plotted it from the start.'

'And those two other corpses?'

Eccleshall sagged against his captors. 'I had no choice,' he mumbled. 'I heard them coming. I loaded the arbalest I carried. The man died immediately. The young whore was going to scream.'

'Thank you very much.' Sir John gestured with his head. 'Take him to Newgate! Keep him well away from his accomplice!'

Mistress Sholter's face, when Sir John confronted her, twisted into a grimace of hatred. She cast the coins about and would have run to the door but he seized her by the wrist, twisting her round and throwing her against the wall.

'You'll both hang,' he said quietly, 'for the deaths of three innocents.' He opened the door and gestured Athelstan out. 'Take one last look around your house, Mistress Sholter: it's Newgate for you.'

After Sir John left instructions with the bailiffs, he and Athelstan walked up Mincham Lane.

'You did very well, Brother. Very well indeed.'

'And that was quick of you, Sir John. If they had met, Mistress Sholter's guilt would have been hard to prove.' The friar nudged the coroner playfully in the ribs. 'So it's true what they say about you, Jack? Swift as a greyhound, more tenacious than a swooping hawk!'

Sir John stood in the middle of the street and took a quick gulp from his wineskin.

'You think I'm swift now, Brother. Let me tell you about the time before Poitiers. We were going along a country lane . . .'

Athelstan closed his eyes. He'd heard this story at least six times and jumped when he heard his name being shrieked.

'Brother Athelstan! Brother Athelstan!'

Crim the altar boy came speeding from an alleyway, his face covered in the remains of a meat pie, black hair sticking up. He stopped before the friar, grasping his robe.

'Brother!' he gasped. 'Brother, I've . . .!'

Athelstan patted him gently on the shoulder.

'Come over here.'

He led the little altar boy between two stalls and

made him sit on a makeshift bench outside an alehouse.

'Has the church burned down?' Athelstan asked.

Crim shook his head.

'Are Watkin and Pike at daggers drawn?'

Again the shake of the head.

'It's Mistress Benedicta,' Crim gasped.

Athelstan went cold. 'What's happened to her?'

'Come on, lad!' Sir John sat beside the boy. He opened his wallet and took out a piece of marchpane. 'One of my poppets put that in my purse this morning. They don't like to think of Daddy being hungry. I only found it after I had left. Now, tell us what's happened.'

Athelstan found it difficult to breathe.

'Benedicta,' Crim gasped. 'Benedicta, grim . . .'

'I beg your pardon?'

'Benedicta, grim . . . No, grimoire!'

Athelstan recalled the book he had given to Benedicta.

'She's in our house, Brother. She's all excited. She says you've got to come now.'

'Well, in which case, we'll go.'

Together they strode down Eastchepe, fought their way through the fish stalls at Billingsgate and hired a barge, Sir John offering the rowers an extra penny. The wherrymen needed no further bidding but pulled at their oars. Crim, his mouth now full of marchpane, sat wedged between the coroner and Athelstan, who had to give up in despair at questioning him further.

The wherry turned midstream, gathering speed as it headed towards the arches under London Bridge.

Crim sat wide-eyed, looking up at the poles jutting out, bearing the severed heads of traitors and river pirates. They entered the shadows of the bridge, the wherrymen pulling their oars in as the river gathered speed, carrying them by its own force under the arch and out to the other side.

A short while later they reached the Southwark quayside and clambered out. Sir John strode along the lanes, shoving people aside, Athelstan and Crim bustling behind him. Athelstan expected to find the yard in front of St Erconwald's busy and thronging but it was deserted. Only Bonaventure slept like some lazy sentry on the top step of the church.

'She's in the house,' Crim explained. 'She said she hadn't told anyone. She wanted to show you first.'

'Jack, you needn't have come!' Athelstan said.

'Brother, if you find it exciting, so do I. Anyway, I like to see Benedicta.'

The widow woman opened the door and gave a gasp of surprise as Sir John embraced her, kissing her loudly on the cheeks.

'You are a lovely woman, Benedicta, and what's all this clamour about?'

Benedicta was certainly excited. She had taken her veil off, her raven-black hair tumbling down to her shoulders. She skipped away from Sir John, clapped her hands and pointed to the parchment littering Athelstan's table.

'It's the grimoire,' she explained, taking a seat at the top. 'Now, when William Fitzwolfe, the former priest, had this bound he used parts of the old blood book and different parish records to stiffen the binding.'

Athelstan sat down at the table. Benedicta had

undone the red binding which held the grimoire together, loosened the pages and pulled these apart.

'It was when I looked at the cover I noticed how thick it was.'

Athelstan picked it up. It was nothing more than a strip of leather laid out flat and strongly reinforced with a thick wadge of parchment glued together at the edges and then placed against the leather to strengthen it. He leafed through the pages. He saw entries: 'Fulke, son of Thurston the labourer and Hawisia his wife . . .' Athelstan smiled: that was Watkin's father. Page after page was filled with these faded, scrawled ink entries made by successive priests over the years.

'Now, look at this!' Benedicta took the pages from him and pointed to one entry already marked with a piece of ash from the fireplace. 'If you check again, Brother, you will find that these two women are the great-grandmothers, respectively, of Joscelyn the tavern-keeper and Basil the blacksmith. They were apparently married on the same day.'

Athelstan read the entry on Agnes Fitz-Joscelyn and Ann, daughter of William the warrener.

'They definitely had different fathers,' Athelstan said. 'But they are described as "*sorores*", sisters, in the marriage entry.'

'Ah yes.'

Benedicta took the parchment from him. She leafed through and showed another entry. This time the page had a title, written neatly by a learned clerk: 'The Confraternity of St Erconwald'. The first column listed 'brothers of the Confraternity', the second a similar list of 'sisters'. Agnes Fitz-Joscelyn and Ann, daughter of William the warrener, were grouped together as 'sisters'.

Sir John, who had been looking over his shoulder, chuckled.

'You've told me about this problem, Brother.' He tapped the parchment. 'And there's your answer. In my treatise "On the Governance of this City", I have come across many such confraternities. At one time they were very strong in different parishes. The Confraternity of the Blessed Sacrament, the Confraternity of the Angels, the Confraternity of St Luke.'

Athelstan gazed wistfully at the piece of parchment.

'It's a very good idea,' he said. 'And there must have been one here: the Confraternity of St Erconwald's. What I suspect happened is this. Agnes and Ann were bosom friends: that's apparent from the fact that they married on the same day. They were also members, perhaps leading ones, of the parish confraternity. They called each other sister. When the blood book disappeared there was no explanation for why they did this. The Venerable Veronica was speaking the truth. These two women lived and died many years ago. All Veronica could remember is that they called each other sister, hence the mistake.'

'Benedicta!'

The widow woman backed away from Sir John who came, arms stretched out, towards her.

'You should have been a coroner. I mean, after all, you can't be a friar.'

'Benedicta,' Athelstan echoed. 'Your sharp eyes and keen wit have made two young lovers very, very happy.'

'Will that mean there's going to be more feasting?' Crim spoke up from where he stood just within the doorway.

'Oh, yes,' Athelstan replied. 'Feasting and dancing, Crim. Now, haste away. Don't tell them what we've found but bring Eleanor and Oswald here!'

Chapter 12

Alice Brokestreet was unaware that she was only minutes away from the death she thought she had so cleverly cheated. She sat in her cell of the gatehouse at Newgate and contemplated the table bearing a pewter jug, cup and a trauncher covered with a linen cloth: gifts, the gaoler had said, from a benefactor. Deciding these could wait, she got up and went to the window to look down into the yard. Fowls and pigs roamed freely about; fierce-looking dogs preyed on the garbage heaps, competing with marauding crows. These scattered as huge vats of water, used for washing, were emptied out to cleanse the yard.

Alice was about to turn away when she noticed two bailiffs drag a cunning man out from the dungeons on the far side. The man was to be branded as a forger, the letter 'F' burned into his cheek. The executioners trailed out after him, their branding-irons already red-hot. One of the bailiffs hastily read out how 'Richard Bracklett, forger, perjurer, had sold false relics, including a piece of Elijah's mantle, two legs of one of the Holy Innocents, a skull of one of the Eleven Thousand Virgins from Cologne.'

'Yet,' the bailiff bawled across the yard, 'the said Richard knew that these were nothing but items of rubbish and the certificates he bore were forged.'

Alice turned away as the executioner advanced on the pinioned man, closing her ears to the terrible screams which rang up from the yard. She sat down on the bed. She was nervous. Tomorrow morning she would be taken into court and the case against Kathryn Vestler would be presented.

'All I have to do,' she murmured, 'is tell the truth.' She smiled to herself. 'Well, as I see it!'

She would repeat her story. How Kathryn Vestler, full of frustrated passion, poisoned the clerk Bartholomew Menster and the tavern wench, Margot Haden, and forced her, Alice, to help her bury them out in Black Meadow.

She breathed in. She felt safe with Master Whittock, that hawk-eyed man with his searching eyes and harsh, guttural voice. He had learned a surprising amount about the Paradise Tree and its owner: stories of hidden treasure, of visitors at night. Time and again he'd refer to other evidence. Time and again he would make her repeat her story. Alice chewed her lip. She had been promised a pardon but was there something else? Whittock had been deeply interested in the stories about the hidden treasure of Gundulf. She had seen Whittock wet his lips and noticed the gleam in his eyes. If Mistress Vestler hanged, she wondered, would the serjeant-at-law buy the tavern and continue the search?

Alice felt her stomach rumble. She went and took the linen cloth from the trauncher revealing a pastry. Then she removed the piece of parchment over the jug and filled the tin cup. Taking that and the pastry, she sat on a stool and began to eat. She also drank rather quickly so the poison in the wine soon made its presence felt with searing pains in her belly which ran up into her chest, sealing off her throat. Alice dropped the cup, spilling the dregs out on to her gown. She staggered towards the door but the pain was dagger-sharp, she couldn't breathe and collapsed on the floor. She stretched out her hand, opened her mouth to scream but no sound came. All she could think of, strangely enough, was Black Meadow, that great oak tree and those graves beneath it.

In St Erconwald's the celebrations were well under way. Athelstan had informed the happy couple that he could now see no impediment to their marriage: at Mass, the following Sunday, he would proclaim their forthcoming nuptials for all to hear. Eleanor and Oswald fairly danced with joy and the news had quickly spread. The Piebald tavern was closed. Basil the blacksmith did the same with his forge. Watkin and Pike, only too eager to hurry from their work, also spread the good news and the parishioners thronged in front of the church steps. Athelstan, Sir John smiling beatifically beside him, announced that they would not pay the fine. The assassins responsible for the murder of Miles Sholter had been unmasked and were now already lodged in the King's prison of Newgate.

'We'll have a celebration!' Pike shouted.

'The parish council will have a celebration!' Watkin declared, eager to exercise his authority. He glared spitefully at Pike's sour-faced wife who kept in the shadows, muttering that she was glad 'the difficulty had been resolved'.

Tables were set up, benches brought out from the church; Watkin brought his bagpipes; Ranulf the rat-catcher his lute; Manger the hangman his tambours. Merry Legs provided pies and pastries which, he proclaimed, were only two days old. Other offerings were made and Joscelyn was cheered to the heavens when he rolled barrels of ale and beer along from the Piebald. Athelstan promised that some of the expense would be met from the parish coffers.

Sir John, of course, was determined to stay. He drank two blackjacks of ale and, when challenged by Watkin and Pike, drank another faster than they. Afterwards he danced a jig with Ursula the pig woman and Pernell the Fleming: even Crim declared him light on his feet and nimble as a juggler.

Athelstan sat on the steps and watched it all. He drank his stoup of ale a little too fast and felt rather tired. Eventually he and Sir Jack left the parishioners and retired to the priest's house where the coroner threw his beaver hat and cloak into a corner, took off his doublet and sat on a bench opposite Athelstan, mopping his face.

'I sometimes curse your parishioners, Athelstan, yet they are a merry lot: it's so good to dance! Did I tell you I was at Windsor when the Countess of Salisbury lost her garter?'

'Tomorrow, Sir John, another lady will lose more than her garter!'

Sir John sobered up. 'Aye, Athelstan. What we've learned is bad enough but only the good Lord knows how much Master Whittock has unearthed. I hope Hengan's wits are sharp and keen for he is going to need all his power to defend Mistress Vestler.'

'Let us say,' Athelstan ventured, 'for sake of argument, that Mistress Brokestreet is a liar.'

'Which she is.'

'Then how, my dear coroner, did she know about those two corpses? That's the nub of the case. The murder of two innocents is not something you proclaim for all the world to hear.'

'So?'

'There are a number of possibilities, Sir Jack. Firstly, Kathryn Vestler told her about the corpses, but that's hardly likely. Secondly, somehow or other, Alice Brokestreet found out about the murders and kept the secret to herself.'

'In which case,' Sir John mused, 'we must ask why the assassin should tell her?'

'And that's my third point, Sir Jack. If Alice Brokestreet is lying and Mistress Vestler is innocent, someone else murdered Bartholomew and Margot. He, or she, then gave the secret to Brokestreet so she could escape execution by approving Mistress Vestler.'

'So Brokestreet will know the identity of the assassin?'

'Not necessarily, Sir John. She could have been informed by letter, or by a mysterious visitor to Newgate or even before she committed her own murder. Brokestreet is not the problem. She is only the cat's-paw. She was informed by the assassin who,

I suspect, will take care of Mistress Brokestreet in his own way and at his own time. Now Vestler is a widow. If she's found guilty of a felony and hanged, the Crown will seize the Paradise Tree and sell it to the highest bidder.'

'So?'

'The real assassin could be the one who buys it in order to search for Gundulf's treasure.'

Sir John whistled under his breath.

'That's going to be hard to prove, little friar. The Paradise Tree is a profitable, spacious tavern; there will be many bids for it.'

'Yes, I know,' Athelstan sighed. 'So I suppose my conclusion is weak. However, it will not go well for us tomorrow. The profits of the Paradise Tree will have to be explained; as will those mysterious visitors at night and, above all, two corpses in Black Meadow. You went to Bapaume the goldsmith?'

Sir John nodded. 'He told me that Bartholomew Menster had intimated he was drawing all his gold and silver out to buy something but he didn't say what!' He tapped Athelstan on the back of the hand. 'But you did well, Brother. At least Mistress Vestler is cleared of the deaths of those other skeletons. I just hope Chief Justice Brabazon accepts your plea that Black Meadow was a cemetery during the great pestilence.'

He started at a knock on the door.

'Come in!' Athelstan shouted.

Joscelyn, the one-armed tavern-keeper, staggered in, his face wreathed in smiles. Under his arm he carried a small tun of wine which he lowered on to the table.

'Sir Jack,' he slurred. 'This is the best cask of Bordeaux claret, held in the cellars of the Piebald for such an occasion. It's only right that you and Brother Athelstan are the first to broach it.'

Cranston scooped it up like a mother would a favourite child. He examined the markings on the side, drew his dagger and began to cut at the twine which held the lid securely on. Then he paused, put the dagger down and held the cask up, inspecting it carefully.

Joscelyn's smile faded. 'What's the matter, Sir John?'

'You know full well, sir. I am the King's officer.'

Joscelyn licked his lips nervously and lowered himself on to a stool at the far end of the table.

'Sir Jack?' Athelstan asked. 'Is there a problem?'

'Yes there is, Brother.' Sir John tapped the top of the cask. 'This is rich claret brought from Bordeaux.' He pointed out the markings on the side. 'This tells you the year and the vineyard. But, Joscelyn,' he added sweetly, 'would you like to tell your priest what is wrong?'

'Why should I, my lord coroner? You are the King's officer.'

'The good tavern-master here,' Sir John said, 'has very generously brought a cask of wine to broach but one thing's missing: all wine from Bordeaux brought into this realm must pay duty. Each cask is marked with a brand saying it has come through customs. It is then sealed showing the port of entry. Such marks are very hard to forge.'

'Oh, Joscelyn, no!' Athelstan groaned. 'You haven't been involved in smuggling along the river?'

'Sir John, Brother, I brought it as a gift. Such casks are common among the victuallers and tavern-masters of London.'

'True.' Sir John smacked his lips. 'I am only here to celebrate and I am not a customs official.'

'Joscelyn, you should be careful,' Athelstan warned. A memory stirred. 'Where did you buy it from? Come on, Joscelyn. If you were involved in smuggling, my precious parish council would be involved up to their necks: Moleskin, Watkin and Pike. Are they? I don't want to see them dance on the end of a rope.'

Joscelyn swallowed hard.

'You bought this from someone else, didn't you? Your son talked about the Paradise Tree and Mistress Vestler.'

Sir John opened the cask with his dagger and groaned with pleasure.

'Don't lie to your priest!' Athelstan stood over the tavern-keeper.

'Yes, Brother, I bought it from Mistress Vestler. There are a number of tavern-keepers in South-wark . . .'

'Enough said.' Athelstan patted him on the shoulder. 'Go on, Joscelyn, thank you for the wine. Join the revellers, your secret's safe with us.'

Joscelyn, all sobered up, sped out the door.

Sir John had broached the cask and was now filling two cups.

'Is it a sin to drink it, monk?'

'Friar, Sir John. No, I don't think it is. The Lord giveth and the Lord taketh away. Moreover, the mood I am in, I recall St Paul's words: "Use a little wine for thy stomach's sake", even if the customs duty has not been paid!' Athelstan sat opposite his friend and sipped the wine.

Sir John closed his eyes, smacked his lips and sighed. 'Oh this is truly a gift from heaven.'

'Well, we've solved one mystery,' Athelstan said. 'We now know who Mistress Vestler's midnight visitors are: river smugglers. They take their barges out to the wine ships before their cargo is unloaded, pay the captain a good price, then it's along to the Paradise Tree and other riverside taverns. Mistress Vestler must have done a roaring trade.' He thought of that lonely stretch along the mud flats and laughed. 'It also explains her charity, Sir John.'

The coroner, more interested in the wine, looked puzzled.

'The Four Gospels,' Athelstan explained. 'That's why she let them camp there. Do you remember what they told us? How they lit a fire on the mud flats in case St Michael came by night? The fisher of men referred to it as a beacon.'

'Of course! And, on a moonless night with a river mist swirling in, there's nothing like a fire to draw a smuggler in. I wager a cup of wine to a cup of wine that Master Whittock knows something of this. No wonder Kathryn wouldn't tell us.'

Athelstan turned as the door opened.

'Yes, Benedicta?'

'Brother, you have a visitor.'

She stood aside and Hengan, cloak about him, swept into the house.

'I will leave you,' Benedicta called out and closed the door.

The lawyer sat down, unhitched his cloak and tossed it on the floor. He put his face in his hands.

'Master Ralph, what's the matter?'

'Alice Brokestreet's been murdered!'

'What!' Sir John exclaimed.

'Someone took a flask of poisoned wine and a pastry to the gatehouse. Now, because Brokestreet was a prisoner of the Crown, her gaolers treat her tenderly. All they remember is a man cowled like a monk.' He smiled thinly. 'He actually had the impudence to say it was a gift from Master Odo Whittock. Of course, our good serjeant-of-law knows nothing of this. Now, in other circumstances the gaolers would have drunk or eaten it themselves but the jug or flask was sealed. Both Brabazon and Whittock are well known for their long arms and vindictive tempers so the wine was safely delivered. Mistress Brokestreet must have died immediately; there was more arsenic in it than grape.'

'Does that mean her testimony will collapse?' Athelstan asked.

'No,' Sir John said. 'She made a solemn declaration before the chief justice and, if Master Whittock has a brain in his head, he will have taken a sworn affidavit.'

'It's more dangerous than that,' Hengan continued. 'Brabazon will ask who wanted Mistress Brokestreet dead? And they'll lay the blame at Kathryn's door.'

'But that's not right!' Athelstan expostulated. 'Mistress Vestler herself is a prisoner. How could she be held responsible?'

'Oh, Whittock will weave his webs. He'll say that Kathryn has an accomplice outside.'

'Aye, and it will get worse,' the coroner growled.

He succinctly informed Hengan what they had discovered regarding Mistress Vestler's smuggling activities. The lawyer groaned.

'You know nothing of this, sir?'

'Of course not!' Hengan snapped. 'Yet, be honest, Sir John, there's not a tavern in London which does not receive smuggled wine. Even the royal household is involved in it. It's almost a national pastime, yet I understand what you say. If Whittock discovers it, and I am sure he will, he'll allege that Mistress Vestler consorts with well-known outlaws and smugglers.'

'And she arranged for one of these to carry out Brokestreet's murder?'

'Precisely, Brother.'

Athelstan went to the door and opened it. The night air cooled his face as he looked out at where the parishioners were still dancing and singing.

'Why the interest?' he asked, turning round. 'I mean, Alice Brokestreet has made a declaration; the case against Kathryn is overwhelming. So why is Whittock involved? She can only hang once.'

'What I suspect,' Hengan replied, 'is the Crown now knows about Gundulf's treasure. Maybe the Regent himself is involved? There are thousands upon thousands of pounds at stake. They may even think Mistress Vestler has discovered its whereabouts.' Hengan pulled a face. 'That's serious enough. However, you must also remember Bartholomew Menster was a royal clerk. The Crown does not take lightly to its minions being ruthlessly murdered.'

'It will come down to this.' Sir John, despite the ale and wine he had drunk, remained calm and level-headed. 'It will come down to,' he repeated, 'the twenty-fifth of June this year, when Bartholomew was last seen.'

'He definitely worked in the Tower on the twenty-fifth, the morrow of the birth of John the Baptist,' Hengan said. 'He left his chamber late in the day and, as we know, said he was going to the Paradise Tree. He was never seen again. I've also established that Margot Haden was last seen in the tavern on that day. According to witnesses she went out and never came back.'

'What!' Athelstan exclaimed.

'Well.' Hengan raised his hand. 'We know Bartholomew visited the tavern and they both left.'

'And Mistress Vestler?'

'Oh, she was definitely there.'

'How do we know that?'

'From the servants . . .' Hengan rubbed his chin. 'I wish I had been there.'

'Where were you, Master Ralph?'

'Well, the Feast of St John the Baptist is a holy day. The day before, the twenty-fourth, I went on a pilgrimage to Canterbury, the regular pilgrimage by the Inns of Court.' He shrugged. 'I stayed at the Chequer Board tavern. I even had the pleasure of meeting Master Whittock there as well. We both prayed at the tomb of St Thomas à Becket. I came home on the feast of St Peter and St Paul, the twenty-ninth of June. Kathryn mentioned that Margot and Bartholomew had eloped, but I thought nothing of it.'

Athelstan took a stool to the top of the table and sat down, cupping his face in his hand.

'So, we have Bartholomew and Margot leaving the

tavern late on the twenty-fifth of June. No one knew where they were going. Some months later their corpses are discovered in Black Meadow. I can see the line Master Whittock will follow. Bartholomew and the tavern wench went down to Black Meadow. Somebody met them there, gave them poisoned wine and buried their corpses.' Athelstan shook his head.

'Even the dimmest member of the jury will draw one conclusion: Kathryn Vestler killed them!'

'Hear ye! Hear ye! All ye who have business before the King's justices of Oyer and Terminer seated in the Guildhall of the King's own city of London, draw close and witness the King's justice being done!'

The herald standing before the bar of the court proclaimed the message twice again. In a blare of trumpets, the justices sat down on their cushioned seats beneath the great scarlet canopy. Athelstan, next to Sir John on the witness benches, closed his eyes, bowed his head and prayed. Brabazon looked in fine fettle, florid face beaming round the court. He was the King's justice and the other judges, who flanked him on either side, mere appendages to his own majesty. On the red and gold steps below, Master Whittock, dressed in a russet robe lined with lambswool, sat like the chief justice's hunting dog. The serjeant-at-law leaned slightly forward, keen eyes studying members of the jury as they took their seats and swore the oath. At the far end of the hall, men-at-arms in the royal livery held back the crowds. The news had spread throughout the city and many had flocked to the Guildhall to witness the unfolding drama.

The witnesses' and spectators' benches were full, so that Sir John had had to use all his authority to gain admission. Now he sat in his blue and gold doublet, cloak thrown across his green hose, legs slightly parted, tapping his high-heeled boots on the wooden platform. He kept glaring at the chief justice. Athelstan, who felt slightly tired after the previous day's revelry, looked down at Mistress Vestler. She had been brought up in chains and now stood at the bar flanked by two tipstaffs carrying their white wands of office. Behind her stood a line of archers, arbalests hooked to their war belts.

'May the good Lord and St Antony help her!' Athelstan prayed.

Mistress Vestler looked pale in mourning weeds, black gown and a veil of the same colour.

'You'd think she was dead already,' Sir John whispered. 'But she holds herself well. Pleas for mercy will find no echo here.'

Beside Mistress Vestler, Ralph Hengan sat and shuffled among certain papers. The small gate to the bar was open; two clerks carried forward a lectern which bore a book of the gospels. This was where the witnesses would stand, take the oath and give their testimony. Chief Justice Brabazon made a cutting movement with his hand. The two heralds stepped forward and gave a shrill blast on their silver-plated trumpets. The clerks seated at the foot of the steps rose, turned and bowed to Sir Henry. He nodded.

'The court is in session!' the chief clerk proclaimed. 'Let the charges be read!'

Confusion immediately followed. Whittock sprang to his feet and walked down to stand at the other side of the bar from Mistress Vestler.

'You are?' Sir Henry Brabazon asked.

'Odo Whittock, serjeant-at-law. My lord, before the charges are read, I must inform the court that its principal witnesses Alice Brokestreet has been found poisoned.'

'In which case,' Hengan interrupted, 'the case should be dismissed.'

'Not so! Not so!' Whittock retorted. He held up a sheaf of parchments. 'Mistress Brokestreet had made a statement under oath; her testimony has been accepted by the court.'

'Are you implying,' Master Hengan snapped, 'that Mistress Brokestreet's murder must be laid at the door of Kathryn Vestler?'

'What does it matter?' Whittock replied languidly. 'Hang for one, hang for ten, you are still hanged!'

Sir Henry smiled.

'In which case,' Hengan said, leaning against the bar, 'I would also like the other matters to be discussed.'

'What other matters?' Sir Henry asked.

'My lord, the corpses of Bartholomew Menster and Margot Haden were discovered in Black Meadow, which belongs to my client. However, my lord,' Hengan pointed to Athelstan, 'I can produce good witnesses and sound testimony that Black Meadow was used as a burial ground for victims of the pestilence. These human remains, pathetic though they may be, are not a matter for this court to consider.'

Sir Henry played with his scarlet skullcap and conferred quickly with colleagues on either side.

'All this,' he replied, 'is wasting the court's time. Hanged for one is the same as being hanged for ten.

The murder of Alice Brokestreet is beyond the power of this court. As regards the other matter, there is no need to call Brother Athelstan.' The chief justice beamed in Sir John's direction. 'I will accept what you say, Master Hengan. Clerk, read out the indictment!'

Athelstan relaxed. He was glad he wasn't called as a witness. He listened to the charge, grim and stark that, 'Kathryn Vestler did, on or around the twenty-fifth of June thirteen-eighty, feloniously slay by poison Bartholomew Menster and Margot Haden.'

'My lord.' Hengan rose, grasping the bar. 'My client goes on oath and pleads not guilty to this and all other specified charges which may be levelled against her.'

'Of course. Of course.' Sir Henry smiled. 'Master clerk, read out the sworn statement of Alice Brokestreet.'

The statement produced nothing new. Master Whittock had been very careful not to introduce any other charge which could be challenged. It stated that Mistress Vestler had slain Bartholomew and Margot by an infusion of poison, that Brokestreet had helped take the corpses out in a handcart and bury them under the great oak tree in Black Meadow. How the felonious deed was Mistress Vestler's doing and she, Brokestreet, had no choice but to co-operate. The clerk sat down.

'My lord,' Hengan began. 'Mistress Vestler is a good woman, a respected member of the parish. She keeps a dole cupboard for the poor, gives alms gener-ously and observes the King's peace.'

'Does she now? Does she now?' Whittock came down the steps. 'Mistress Vestler, you put yourself on oath in Newgate, when you denied these charges?'

'I did.'

'And you say you are a woman of good reputation?'

'I am,' came the calm reply.

'Even though you smuggle?'

Mistress Vestler, warned by Hengan about what Sir John had discovered, remained silent.

'We have found in the cellars of the Paradise Tree,' Whittock continued, 'small casks of Bordeaux, and even some from Alsace, which bear no customs mark.'

'My lord,' Hengan interrupted. 'My client has been charged with murder, not with smuggling. She need not incriminate herself on charges she has had little time to reflect on.'

'True, true,' Whittock replied in a mock whisper. 'I concede that, but you started this hare, Master Hengan, so I think my observation is relevant.'

'My lord.' Hengan desperately tried to move away from the matter. 'The indictment claims that Mistress Brokestreet knew that Kathryn Vestler poisoned her two alleged victims. However, we have it on good report that Margot Haden and Bartholomew Menster left the Paradise Tree on the evening of the twenty-fifth of June."

Yes, yes,' Whittock interrupted. 'But, my lord, Mistress Brokestreet has sworn that the crime was committed that night. In other words, Bartholomew and Margot may well have returned to the Paradise Tree and the crime been committed when the tavern was empty, no witnesses being around. I will also demonstrate that Mistress Vestler had a great deal to hide on that evening. It's best, my lord, if we listen to all the witnesses before we start proclaiming the truth.'

Sir Henry agreed.

'In which case,' Whittock went on, 'I call Master Tapler, ale-taster at the Paradise Tree.'

The clerks of the court shouted the witness's name. From a small chamber at the other side of the hall, hidden in one of the transepts, Mistress Vestler's ale-taster shuffled out. The man was nervous and, as he took the oath, hand on the book of the gospels, the judge bellowed at him to speak up.

'Well, well, sir.' Whittock smiled across at him. 'We know who you are. We know where you work.'

Master Tapler looked decidedly agitated.

'I want you, sir,' Whittock's voice was almost a purr, 'to recall what happened on the twenty-fifth of June of this year. You had all returned to work after the Holy Day, hadn't you?'

'Yes, sir, we had.'

'And the tavern was busy?'

'No, sir.'

'Oh, so what time did you close?'

'Well, sir, because it was summer, the curfew didn't toll till about an hour before midnight.'

'What happened that evening? Anything extraordinary? Come, come, sir,' Whittock continued sharply. 'You know why you are here. Did Master Bartholomew come to the tavern?'

'Yes, sir, between the hours of nine and ten. It was a beautiful summer's day, the sun hadn't set.'

'And what happened?'

'He stayed for a stoup of ale; rather excited he was. Then he and Margot left.'

'Do you know where to?'

'No, sir.'

'And was Mistress Vestler around?'

'She always is, sir.'

'That particular night, what did Mistress Vestler do?'

'Sir, she was most insistent that the cooks and scullions, tapboys and slatterns, myself included, all had to leave early.'

'She was decidedly nervous, Master Tapler?'

'Yes, sir, she was.'

Athelstan glanced at Sir John.

'Oh, forgive me,' the friar whispered. 'Lost in my own troubles I should have questioned those people myself.'

Whittock, apparently distracted by the whisper, glanced across and smiled.

'And what happened then, Master Tapler?'

'Mistress Vestler urged us to leave, customers included.'

'Why?'

'I had the distinct impression,' Tapler's voice fell to a mumble, 'that she was expecting someone.'

Whittock smiled from ear to ear.

'Master Tapler, I thank you.'

Chapter 13

Hengan did his best with the ale-taster but it was a losing battle. In fact, the more he questioned the more damaging it became.

'It was very rare for Mistress Vestler to urge us to leave the tavern early, so why that night?'

Hengan realised the harm he was doing, stopped his questioning and Tapler was dismissed.

'She'll hang,' Sir John murmured. 'God save us, Athelstan, but I think she's guilty myself.'

'The court calls Isobel Haden!' the clerk shouted.

Athelstan's head came up. A young woman came out of the adjoining chamber into the well of the court. The clerk escorted her to the witness stand and again the oath was taken. Whittock was now thoroughly enjoying himself.

'We have your name and occupation,' he began. 'You are a seamstress in the parish of St Mary Bethlehem near Holywell. And your sister Margot was a tavern wench at the Paradise Tree?'

'Yes, sir.'

Sir Henry was now leaning forward.

'Did your sister enjoy her work?'

'Yes, sir, she did.'

'How do you know that? Come on, girl, tell the court.'

'My sister wrote me letters.'

'My lord.' Whittock glanced at Sir Henry. 'If necessary, I can produce these letters.'

The chief justice looked at Hengan who shook his head despairingly.

'So, your sister, even though only a tavern wench, was lettered?' Whittock asked.

'Oh yes, sir, our father was a wool merchant. We attended the parish school and learned our horn books. He was very proud of Margot.' Her voice trembled. 'She could read and write.'

'So she was more than just a tavern wench?' Whittock insisted. 'A young woman who might well attract the likes of Bartholomew Menster?'

'Yes, sir. Margot only entered service because she wanted to leave the parish. A good lass, Margot,' Isobel continued defiantly, looking balefully down at Mistress Vestler. 'She would have made a fine marriage.'

'And your sister wrote to you about her work?'

'To be honest, sir, she liked the Paradise Tree. Miss Vestler was kind: she gave her money, clothes, as well as a Book of Hours.'

'Did she now?' Whittock purred. 'My lord, a matter we will return to in the very near future. Mistress Isobel, in those letters, your sister told you how she had met Bartholomew Menster, a clerk of the Tower, that he was sweet on her but Mistress Vestler did not like it?'

'Indeed, on one occasion, Master Bartholomew had sharp words with her.'

'Over what?' Whittock persisted.

'According to the letter, Mistress Vestler had snapped: "I wish you'd leave the matter alone. You have my thoughts on it." '

'And you think Mistress Vestler was talking about your sister?'

'Yes, sir, and Margot did as well.'

'Did Bartholomew propose to your sister?'

'Yes, sir, he did. Margot had high hopes that they would exchange vows at the church door.'

'Did your sister talk about anything else?'

'Oh yes, sir.' Isobel paused and dabbed at her eyes with the cuff of her brown smock.

Athelstan could see Isobel had been well prepared for this. She was undoubtedly telling the truth but Whittock's questions were extracting this piece by piece so the jury could follow and understand the way he was leading.

'Tell us,' Whittock said softly.

'My sister wrote that Master Bartholomew had high hopes of tracing certain lost treasures.'

Her words created murmurs in the court. Sir Henry tapped his knee excitedly.

'My lord.' Whittock walked back to the foot of the steps and glanced up at the justices. 'There seems to be good evidence that Gundulf, Bishop of Rochester, who built the Tower, may have buried his treasure somewhere in the grounds of the Paradise Tree.'

'And have you looked for this treasure?' Sir Henry asked.

'My lord, I have conducted a careful search of the gardens and cellars.' Whittock smiled. 'That's how we found the casks of wine which had not passed through customs.'

'My lord.' Hengan sprang to his feet. 'Is this relevant? Is Mistress Vestler being accused of seizing treasure trove and hiding it from the Crown? She is on trial for murder, not for petty treason!'

Sir Henry pursed his lips. 'True, true, Master Hengan. Master Whittock, this questioning?'

'My lord, my lord.' Whittock spread his hands. 'I simply wish to demonstrate to the court that Mistress Vestler may have had a number of grudges against Master Bartholomew. Not only young Margot but the possible whereabouts of this treasure.' He bowed. 'However, if it's your wish, I shall let the matter rest.' Whittock turned back to the witness. 'Your sister, how long did she serve at the Paradise Tree?'

'About three years.'

'And she spent her money well on clothes, gowns, robes?'

'Yes, she told me she kept careful accounts at the back of her Book of Hours.'

'Ah yes, yes.' Whittock rubbed his chin and tapped the end of his pointed nose. 'Would you say that your sister was a sober young woman, industrious, of sharp wit?'

'Of course!'

'She was not the sort,' Whittock said, then paused, 'to elope in the dead of night, leaving all her possessions behind her?'

'No, sir, she would not.'

'But, that is the story Mistress Vestler gave you when you made enquiries at the Paradise Tree?'

'It was.'

'And then you went there yourself?'

'At the end of July, I stayed three days.'

'And you were shown Margot's chamber?'

'A garret, sir, at the top of the house. It was stripped bare.'

'And your sister's possessions?'

'Mistress Vestler said that's how it had been left. Nothing of what remained could be sold or kept so she had burned it.'

'And what did you think of that?'

'At the time I thought it strange but, perhaps, Margot had taken her possessions with her. Now . . .' Her voice faltered. 'I cannot understand why Mistress Vestler burned everything.'

'No, no,' Whittock replied, 'and, to tell you the truth, mistress, neither can I.'

Whittock finished with a flourish and Hengan went to the bar where he stared across at Isobel Haden.

'You are on oath, madam.'

'I know I am.'

'And have you told the truth?'

'As God is my witness.'

'But, at the time, you really did think your sister had eloped with Master Menster?'

'Yes, sir, I did.'

'And, when you went to the Paradise Tree, you believed Mistress Vestler?'

'Of course. She seemed a kindly woman. Margot had talked highly of her.'

'And now?'

The young woman became confused. 'She said my sister had eloped but she hadn't. All the time, her corpse lay beneath that oak tree.' Her voice trembled.

'Do you find it hard to accept that Mistress Vestler would do your sister such mortal injury?'

'Yes . . .'

'Remember, you are on oath!'

'Yes, yes, sir, I do. But why should she burn my poor sister's possessions?'

Hengan thanked the young woman. Her departure was followed by hushed conversation, both among the jury and the spectators.

'I can't understand this,' Athelstan whispered. 'Whittock's had only a few days yet he's ferreted out one thing after another.'

'He is good,' Sir John replied. 'They intend Kathryn to hang and the Crown will put the Paradise Tree under the most careful scrutiny.'

Athelstan glanced up as the clerk called the next witness, a thin, spindle-shanked fellow, his greasy hair tied at the back by a red ribbon. He wore a soiled leather jacket, darned hose and scuffed boots. A chapman or tinker, Athelstan thought: he was proved correct when Matthew Biddlecombe, chapman and trader, took the oath.

'Now, sir,' Whittock began. 'On the twenty-fifth of June last I was travelling to Canterbury to pray before the shrine of blessed Thomas à Becket.' He pointed to Hengan. 'My learned colleague over there was also on pilgrimage. Sir Henry Brabazon, our noble judge, was holding Commissions of the Peace in Middlesex. Mistress Vestler was in the Paradise Tree. So, sir, where were you?'

The chapman shuffled his feet.

'She's very kind,' he muttered.

'Where were you?' Whittock almost shouted.

'I travel the city, sir.' Biddlecombe looked up at the chief justice. 'From Clerkenwell down to Westminster. I sell ribbons and laces, needles, gew-gaws . . .'

'And very good ones too, I'm sure,' Sir Henry broke in sardonically. 'Pray, Master Matthew, do continue.'

'I do not earn enough to hire a chamber,' the fellow declared. 'But Mistress Vestler lets me sleep in one of her outhouses. She gives me ale and cold pie . . .'

'Yes, yes, quite,' Whittock intervened. 'Your belly, sir, does not concern us: your words do.' He sniffed noisily. 'I was talking about Midsummer's Day earlier this year. You are on oath, sir; for perjury you can be pressed.'

'I, I know,' Biddlecombe stammered, refusing to glance at Mistress Vestler. 'I arrived at the Paradise Tree on Midsummer's Eve. I intended to stay three days. On the Holy Day itself I went to the fair held outside the Tower.'

'And the day after?'

'I went to London Bridge and returned late. I fell asleep in the outhouse. It was a beautiful night. I woke because I felt strange. The tavern was quiet, then I heard a sound in the yard. When I opened the door and peered out, Mistress Vestler was there.'

'And what was she doing?' Whittock asked quietly.

'She had a mattock, hoe and spade in a small barrow. I remember seeing her clearly; she had taken her shoes off and was wearing a pair of boots.'

'And what time was that, sir?'

'I don't know. Darkness had fallen though the night sky was clear.'

'So,' Whittock insisted. 'Was she going somewhere or coming back?'

'Oh, coming back. She put the mattock and the other implements up against one of the doors, wheeled the barrow away and went into the scullery.'

'You must have thought it was strange? I mean, why should a tavern-keeper, so prosperous and with so many servants, be gardening or digging at such a late hour? That's what you thought, wasn't it, Master Biddlecombe?'

'Yes, sir.'

'And what else?' Whittock leaned back like a reproving schoolmaster.

'Well, sir, she was quiet, as if she didn't want anyone to see or hear what she was doing.'

'I am sure she did not.' Master Whittock spread his hands and looked at Hengan.

Hengan didn't bother to rise from his stool.

'Master Biddlecombe, how did you know it was Mistress Vestler?'

'She held a lantern horn.'

'Thank you.' Hengan rubbed his face in his hands, a despairing gesture.

Whittock, however, had not finished. A tree-feller was called; he took the oath glibly and loudly proclaimed that, on the morning of the 27th of June, Mistress Vestler had hired him to go out and lop the branches on the oak tree in Black Meadow.

'That was early, wasn't it?' Whittock asked.

'Yes, sir. Pruning of trees is not usually done till

autumn and, to be honest, I really couldn't see why she wanted to cut such a great tree. I mean, it stands by itself in Black Meadow.'

'What's the relevance of this?' Hengan rose, his face suffused with anger.

Sir Henry chose to overlook his discourtesy.

'Master Whittock?' he asked.

'Why, my lord, the relevance is quite clear. The corpses of the two victims were found beneath the oak tree. If you have a labourer moving around cutting branches, the grass and soil are disturbed, branches and twigs fall down.'

'In other words,' Sir Henry observed, 'Mistress Vestler didn't want the oak tree pruned but rather the ground which covered the graves to be disguised.'

Whittock bowed. 'My lord, you are, as ever, most perceptive.'

Whittock's last witness caused a stir. Athelstan didn't recognise the name, Walter Trumpington, until First Gospel came striding out of the chamber and across to take the oath. He had the sense not to play his games here, but took the oath, gave his name and claimed he belonged to an order called the Four Gospels who had the use of a small plot of land in Black Meadow.

'You recall the morning of the twenty-sixth of June last?' Whittock demanded.

'Yes.'

'Why?'

'Mistress Vestler came down to see us. She asked if, the previous day, we had seen anyone we knew in Black Meadow.'

'And had you?'

'No, sir, we had not.'

'Did Mistress Vestler often make such a request of you?'

First Gospel, careful not to look at Mistress Vestler, shook his head.

'She was good and kind to us but I thought it was strange at the time.'

Hengan rose to question but First Gospel would not be shaken: he and his community remembered the incident quite clearly.

Brabazon then called Kathryn Vestler to the stand.

Hengan made careful play of her pious works, her good reputation and character but he could elicit nothing to shake the testimony of so many witnesses. Whittock closed like a weasel would on a rabbit, biting and tearing. Once again Mistress Vestler refused to discuss Gundulf's treasure or the allegation of smuggling. She confessed to burning Margot Haden's clothing and property. She admitted to hiring the woodcutter and, when confronted with the chapman's testimony, did not even bother to make an excuse.

'What I do on my own property and when I do it,' she declared defiantly, 'is my own concern!'

Nor did she deny approaching First Gospel and asking the question.

Athelstan didn't really listen to the interrogation. He studied Mistress Vestler closely. She stood resolute and pale-faced, drained of all bonhomie. Athelstan recognised that logic, every item of evidence, spoke against her yet there was something dreadfully wrong. He sensed she was lying, but why?

The clerks gathered to ask Chief Justice Brabazon whether there would be a recess but he waved his sprig of rosemary: he had scented blood, the hunt would continue until the quarry was brought down. Whittock summarised the evidence. Hengan followed with an impassioned and eloquent plea on behalf of his client but his desperation was apparent. At one time he even hinted that, if Mistress Vestler produced Gundulf's treasure, the Crown might consider a pardon for all past offences. Sir Henry chose to ignore this. He conferred with his fellow justices then gave a pithy but damning summation of the case against Mistress Vestler. An hour candle was lit. The jury withdrew but the candle was scarcely burning before the foreman came back and announced that they had reached their verdict. The jury filed back into their pews. The clerk reread the indictment and tolled a hand bell.

'Members of the jury!' he intoned. 'Look upon the prisoner. Do you find her guilty or not guilty as charged?'

'Guilty with no recommendation for mercy!' came the foreman's stark reply.

Kathryn Vestler swayed a little. Hengan hid his face in his hands. Sir John was wiping at his eyes but Athelstan, hands clasped, watched the piece of black silk being placed over Chief Justice Brabazon's skullcap.

'Kathryn Vestler,' he began. 'You have been found guilty of the hideous crime alleged against you. A jury of your peers has decided that you, maliciously and heinously, murdered Bartholomew Menster and Margot Haden. You claim you are a woman of good repute. The court does not believe this. We know of no reason why you should not suffer the full rigours of the law.' He paused. 'Kathryn Vestler, it is the sentence of this court that you be taken to the place from whence you came and confined in chains. On Monday next, at the hour before noon, you shall be taken to the lawful place of execution at Smithfield and hanged by your neck until dead, your corpse interred in the common grave. May the Lord,' Sir Henry concluded, 'have mercy on your soul! Bailiffs, take her down! Members of the jury, you are thanked and discharged!'

Kathryn Vestler was immediately hustled away. Athelstan heard the cat-calls and cries from outside as she was led to the execution cart. Sir Henry and all the retinue of the court formally processed out. Sir John sat, legs apart, hands on his knees, staring down at the floor.

'I am sorry, Stephen,' he muttered as if his dead friend could hear him. 'I am sorry but I could do no more.'

Hengan still sat on the lawyer's stool, pale-faced and sweating.

'Come on man!' Sir John called over. 'This is no time and place for tears!'

They left the Guildhall by a side entrance. A quack doctor came running up, offering a sure remedy for rotting of the gums.

'It's a distillation of sage water.'

But he saw the look on the coroner's face and, grasping his tray, scuttled away.

Sir John marched up Cheapside, Athelstan walking beside Hengan. Now and again he glanced sideways;

the lawyer looked truly stricken, lips moving wordlessly, dabbing at his sweaty face with a rag. He seemed unaware of the crowds, of the gentlemen and their ladies, the apprentices screaming for custom, the criers shouting for every household to keep a vat of water near the doorway in case of fire.

Sir John, also, was in no mood for distractions. Leif the beggarman came hopping over but Sir John raised a clenched fist and the beggarman hobbled away as if he, too, knew this was not the time for his importunate pleas.

Once inside the Holy Lamb of God Sir John sat down on the window seat and crossly demanded a meat pie and three blackjacks of ale. Athelstan found his throat and mouth dry. He could not believe what had happened. He leaned over and grasped Hengan's hand, which was cold as ice.

'You did your best, Master Ralph.'

'I wish I could do more,' the lawyer grated. 'I tell you this, Brother, I am Mistress Vestler's executor. Once I have refreshed myself, I am going to the Paradise Tree to search it from top to bottom. I'll find Gundulf's gold for you, Sir Jack, for old friendship's sake.'

'If you find it,' Sir John replied, lowering the blackjack, 'I'll seek an immediate audience with my Lord of Gaunt. I'll do that anyway. A stay of execution, a pardon? Who knows, they may even agree to Kathryn being hanged by the purse and leave it at that.'

'But you don't think so, do you?' Athelstan asked.

Sir John shook his head. 'The murder was malice aforethought. Mistress Vestler refused to plead guilty, while Bartholomew was a royal clerk. The Crown will not listen to pleas of mitigation.'

'How did Whittock know all that?' Athelstan asked.

Hengan was staring into his tankard.

'Ralph?'

'I'm sorry. I was thinking how the Crown must be pleased that Brokestreet is dead. After all, she was a condemned felon who killed a man with a firkin opener. Rumour will now place her death at Mistress Vestler's door. The gossips will argue that it was in her interests for Mistress Brokestreet to be killed; Kathryn had relationships with outlaws or smugglers and they did the bloody deed. I am sorry, Brother, I am confused. What I am really saying is any real plea for pardon will be turned down; Mistress Vestler will be regarded as a murderess on many counts. I must find that treasure.' He paused. '*Thesaurus in ecclesia prope turrem*: I wonder what that means?' He smiled at Athelstan. 'I'm sorry, Brother, you asked a question?'

'How did Master Whittock know to call all those witnesses?'

'Oh, quite easy,' Sir John said. 'I've been thinking of that myself. The accounts books, eh Master Ralph?'

The lawyer nodded. 'The accounts books, Sir Jack, have a great deal to answer for. They'll show all the monies spent by Kathryn Vestler on Margot Haden, including pennies given to chapmen to deliver messages to her sister. The same will be true of the tree pruner and Master Biddlecombe. Whittock's clerks searched all these out.' He finished his tankard and got to his feet. 'Sir Jack, Brother Athelstan, today is Thursday: in three days' time Mistress Vestler hangs. I will see what I can do.'

Athelstan watched him go then became distracted by a beggarman who brought in a weasel for sale. Sir John threw the fellow a coin and told him to go away.

'There's little we can do, is there, Brother?'

'Sir Jack.' Athelstan got to his feet. 'You can pray and we can think.'

And, giving the most absentminded of farewells, Athelstan left. Sir John was so bemused, he had to call for a further blackjack of ale to clear his wits.

Meanwhile the little friar trudged down Cheapside. As he went he pulled his cowl over his head, pushing his hands up his sleeves.

'Isn't it strange?' he asked himself. 'Sir Jack and I.' He paused. Yes, that's why he was confused! He and the coroner hunted murderers down, sent assassins to their just deserts. Now he was desperately trying to free one.

Athelstan crossed London Bridge. He stopped half-way and went into the chapel of St Thomas à Becket where he sat in the cool darkness staring up at the sanctuary lamp. He found it hard to pray. His mind was all a-jumble: scenes from the court, the witnesses being called, raising their hands; Whittock's persistent questions; Brabazon's smile; the lowering looks of the jury men; Mistress Vestler standing poised but defiant. Athelstan crossed himself and left.

When he reached St Erconwald's the churchyard was empty but the door was open so Athelstan slipped inside. Huddle the painter was sitting dreamily on a stool. This self-appointed artist of the parish was determined, given Brother Athelstan's patronage, to cover every bare expanse of wall in the church.

'What's on your mind, Huddle?'

'The marriage feast at Cana. I have Eleanor and Oswald. Joscelyn can be the wine-taster. Benedicta can be Our Lady, Sir Jack would be one of the guests. Just think of it, Brother.'

'And what will Pike the ditcher's wife be?'

'Why, she will be Herod's wife.'

'Herod's wife didn't attend the marriage feast at Cana.'

'How do we know, Brother?'

Athelstan patted him on the shoulder.

'You have the key to the church?'

'Benedicta left it with me. She gave me a pot of the rabbit stew she made for you. It's in the kitchen. I also took some of the ale.'

'We are a truly sharing community,' Athelstan remarked.

He went and checked on Philomel. The horse lay so silently Athelstan wondered if it had died but it was only sleeping. In the cemetery Godbless was lying on one of the tombstones sunning himself, Thaddeus quietly cropping the grass beside him.

Athelstan tiptoed back. He found the house in order. Bonaventure was out and Athelstan sat in his chair next to the empty grate. Something troubled him. Something he had seen and heard this morning, but he kept it to one side. He recalled Master Whittock's questions, the line of witnesses he had summoned. Athelstan searched out the old accounts book. He sat at the table and leafed through the pages. Yes, it all made sense. Mistress Vestler was a good householder. She and her husband had kept meticulous accounts. Items purchased; guests who had called; alms given to beggars. He noticed the name of Biddlecombe the chapman, a regular visitor, often given a fresh bed of straw in the outhouse. Athelstan's eyes grew heavy and he was about to turn the page when one entry, a purchase by Kathryn's husband, caught his eye.

Chapter 14

Athelstan went through the ledger very carefully, noting that there were other entries beside the two he had already discovered. He secretly admired their detail. No wonder the serjeant-at-law had been able to present such a compelling case. The suspicions which had nagged his mind now grew and took shape. Athelstan sadly reflected on the power of love: the damage, as well as the good, it could do. Time and again he went through the journal, only wishing he had the others to inspect. As the evening drew on Bonaventure came back and pestered him for food and milk.

'You are a riffler. Do you know that?' Athelstan lectured him. 'You prowl the alleyways and you come back in a bad temper.' He got to his feet. 'Bad-tempered cats, Bonaventure, will never enter the kingdom of heaven. If you are not a Jesus cat what hope is there for you?'

Bonaventure just rubbed himself against the friar's

legs, arching his back, persisting in his demands until Athelstan fetched him a dish of milk. Huddle brought the key across and Athelstan went out to check that all was well. He was too tired to study the stars but retired early and fell asleep thinking about Kathryn Vestler manacled in the condemned cell and said a quick prayer for her.

The next morning Athelstan surprised Crim by taking out the special red vestments reserved for the feast of Pentecost: a beautiful chasuble with gold and silver crosses sewn on the back and front.

'We need God's help,' he told the heavy-eyed altar boy. 'I doubt if many of my parishioners are here this morning. It will take some time for the effects of all that revelry to wear off.'

Athelstan celebrated his Mass, praying that God would make him as innocent as a dove and as cunning as a serpent.

'Because, Lord,' he concluded, 'today justice must be done.'

Athelstan finished his Mass, hastily broke his fast then locked up the house and church. He hurried through the streets down to the riverside. Although he passed the occasional parishioner he kept his eyes lowered, unwilling to be distracted or drawn into conversation. The river mist still hung heavy but a taciturn Moleskin soon rowed him across the other side. The fish market was preparing to open as Athelstan landed on the quayside and hastened up through Petty Wales to the Paradise Tree.

The ale-master came out to meet him; he looked rather sheepish and rubbed his hands.

'I am sorry, Brother,' he mumbled as he led the

friar into the taproom still not yet cleaned from the previous evening. 'But I had no choice. Master Whittock was most insistent.'

Athelstan took a seat near the window and looked out across the garden, savouring the early morning freshness. Sparrows squabbled in the trees; house martins dived and swooped over the flower beds, still covered with a crystal-white morning frost. Then he turned to the ale-master.

'Please bring me a cup of watered wine and some bread and cheese.'

The man hurried away. Now and again servants popped their heads round the door of the kitchen to study this little friar who had become so immersed in their mistress's affairs. Athelstan hoped Sir John would not be late. Before he had celebrated Mass, he'd despatched Godbless with an urgent message for the coroner to meet him here.

'The tavern will be closed on Monday,' the ale-master mournfully informed him. 'And what will happen then, eh, Brother?'

'I don't know. Was Master Hengan here yesterday?'

'Oh yes, sir, conducting the most scrupulous of searches.'

Athelstan thanked him and turned away. He heard a dog bark and Sir John's bell-like voice.

'For the love of God, Henry, keep that bloody dog away from me!'

Sir John, followed by Flaxwith and the ever-slavering Samson, walked into the taproom. The coroner clapped his hands and beamed around, but Athelstan could see he was pretending: he looked heavy-eyed, haggard-faced. He had not even bothered to change his shirt or doublet. He slumped down on the stool opposite Athelstan and threw his beaver hat on to the table.

'I don't know about you, Brother, but I will not be in London on Monday. Flaxwith!' He turned to his ever-patient chief bailiff. 'Join the rest and take Samson with you!'

'No, Henry.' Athelstan beckoned him over. 'I want you to do more than that. Take your lovely dog for a walk through Black Meadow. Tell the Four Gospels, those strange creatures who dwell in the cottage down near the river, that the lord coroner and Brother Athelstan wish words with them beneath the oak tree.'

Flaxwith went out. Sir John looked narrow-eyed at his companion.

'What's this, Brother?'

'Just drink your ale,' Athelstan replied.

The coroner obeyed but his impatience was apparent.

'Right!' Athelstan got to his feet. 'Come on, Sir John! I've got a few surprises for you.'

The garden was beautiful. Athelstan passed the sundial and noticed how its bronze face glittered in the early morning sunlight.

'First things first,' he whispered.

Cranston stopped at the lych gate leading to Black Meadow.

'What's this all about, Brother?'

'Walter Trumpington.'

Cranston furrowed his brow.

'Walter Trumpington,' Athelstan repeated. 'Doesn't the name ring a bell?'

'Well, yes, it does, that rogue, the First Gospel.'

'And Kathryn Vestler?'

'What about her, Brother?'

'What's her maiden name?'

'Oh, I don't know. She came from a village outside Cambridge. She and Stephen were married years . . .' Sir John's jaw sagged. 'It's not Trumpington, is it?'

'Yes, Sir John, it is. Our First Gospel, I suspect, is Kathryn's younger brother.'

'But she never said!'

'No one ever asked her. He's no more waiting the return of St Michael and his angels than Flaxwith's dog. Come on, Sir John, let me prove it!'

The Four Gospels were gathered beneath the outstretched branches of the oak tree. There were the usual greetings and mumblings of apology.

'We had no choice,' First Gospel wailed. 'Master Whittock was most insistent.'

'Let me see one of those medals,' Athelstan demanded. 'You offered me one when I first met you.'

The fellow took one from his wallet.

'It's specially blessed . . .'

'Oh, shut up!' Athelstan went up and stared into the man's face. 'Do you know something, Walter Trumpington? I've yet to meet one of your kind who's got a spark of religion in him.'

First Gospel looked both hurt and puzzled.

'Are you going to act for me now? Why didn't you tell the court? Why didn't you tell me or Master Whittock that you are Kathryn Vestler's younger brother? I found an entry in the accounts book from years ago. You've tried everything, haven't you,

Walter? Chapman, tinker, mountebank, soldier? But, when times are hard, it's always back to sister Kathryn for help. She's soft-hearted, isn't she? Now, you can stand here with your three sisters and act the innocent. So I'll tell you the truth. You are a pimp, Walter, and these three ladies are whores.'

'How dare you!' one of them screeched.

'Shut up!' Sir John growled. He was as surprised as any of them but was enjoying Athelstan's fiery temper. 'If any of you make another sound,' the coroner continued, pointing across to where Flaxwith was walking up and down, Samson trotting behind him, 'I'll order my bailiff across here: he'll put you across his knee and whip your buttocks! Now, sir.' He poked First Gospel in the chest. 'Either you answer my secretarius' questions or I'll have you driven from the city!'

'Now, I don't know how you did it, how you persuaded her,' Athelstan continued, 'but Walter Trumpington decided to return to the Paradise Tree when he learned that Stephen Vestler was dead. When he was alive, the taverner kept some control over his wife's generosity to her wayward brother but, once he was gone, back you came. She's a lovely woman, isn't she, Walter?'

Athelstan paused and looked up at the tree where a blackbird had begun to sing.

'She loves you completely, doesn't she? You are the family rascal. I wager you could act the prodigal son or, in this case, the prodigal brother. In truth you are a cunning man. Anyway, Kathryn gives you a cottage on the edge of Black Meadow. You pretend to be one of our latter-day prophets. However, you are involved in quite a lucrative business: buying smuggled wine from ships, then selling it on to the likes of Kathryn, who can refuse you nothing. I wonder how much gold and silver you have hidden beneath the floor of that cottage?'

'May I sit down?' Walter's face became pleading. 'I don't feel very well, Brother.'

'Of course!'

First Gospel and his three sisters slumped to their knees. Athelstan crouched down to face them.

'In fact it was a subtle, clever ploy,' he went on. 'On one side of your cottage snakes a river where roguery thrives like weeds in rich soil. On the other side stands a deserted meadow and a prosperous tavern owned by a loving sister. No wonder you lit a fire every night – smugglers must have a beacon light to draw them in.'

'I told you about those,' First Gospel mumbled.

'Rubbish! There were no barges full of shadowy, cowled men, that was to distract us. When I and Sir Jack, coroner of the city, arrived in Black Meadow surrounded by bailiffs, you must have had the fright of your life. But that's not all you are involved in, is it, sir? The King's warships, the wool cogs and wine barges throng the Thames. Sailors are sometimes not given shore leave: so, what better for sailors, starved of female kind, than to drop the ship's bum-boat and sail up river for a tryst with one of our ladies here? And what a place to make love, particularly in summertime, along the hedges of Black Meadow? No wonder the fisher of men heard strange sounds and cries at night.'

'Do you know the sentence?' Sir John asked. 'For

keeping a brothel? You can be whipped at the tail of a cart from one end of the city to the other.'

'And the gold?' Athelstan asked. 'Gundulf's treasure?'

'Oh no.' First Gospel waved his hand. 'Mistress Vestler was very firm on that: I was not to enter the tavern. Kathryn can be a strict woman. She gave me the cottage and the use of the land provided I left her and her tavern alone.'

'Is that why you did business with Master Whittock?' Athelstan asked. 'Do you have a soul? Do you have a heart? Do you realise your sister could hang? Is that why you decided to flatter the King's lawyer? To keep your place here?'

'I'm a villain!' First Gospel's face turned ugly. 'And true, Brother, I have wandered the face of the earth.' He paused. 'How did you know about the ladies?'

'Oh, something the fisher of men said. You've seen him combing the river for corpses, as well as someone else.' Athelstan smiled. 'Dead men do tell tales. Do you remember a strange character called the preacher? Tall, black hair, face burned by the sun?'

'He may have come here.'

'He took one of your cheap little medals depicting St Michael. He hired some poor whore in Southwark and got both himself and her killed. The medal was found on his corpse. However, we were talking about your sister: you gave that information to Whittock?'

First Gospel ran his tongue round his sharp, white teeth, reminding Athelstan of a hungry dog.

'He came down here.' One of the women spoke up. 'He asked if we had seen anything untoward.'

'But what you told him,' Sir John persisted, 'was not the truth.'

'No, my lord coroner, it wasn't,' First Gospel snarled, getting to his feet, standing legs apart.

He paused and looked across the field. Flaxwith had now sat down near the hedge, one arm round his beloved mastiff.

'The lawyer came down here. He asked questions. I could see he would stay until he got an answer. I told him the truth, or at least half of it. Kathryn did come down here on the morning of the twenty-sixth. She asked if I had seen anyone I knew in Black Meadow. I replied I hadn't.'

'You said it was half the truth?'

'Well, the night before, my girls were busy down behind the hedgerow. It was a balmy, soft night. I thought I would walk.' He shot a glance at Athelstan. 'I didn't tell Whittock this. I saw lantern-light, just a pinprick, so I crept up the hill.'

'And what did you see?'

'My beloved sister Kathryn. She was digging. Or rather she was finishing what she had dug. She was piling in the earth.'

'And weren't you curious?'

'Brother, I survive by keeping my nose out of other people's business. Yes, I wondered what she could be burying at the dead of night. I was tempted to search there myself.'

'You did, didn't you?' Athelstan asked. 'Don't tell lies!'

'Yes, Brother, I did, a few days later. I came across a stinking corpse so I pushed the earth back and left it alone.'

Athelstan looked at the horror-stricken coroner.

'So you see, if I wished to do my sister real damage, I could have taken the oath and told them that.'

'And you never approached your sister?'

'I've already answered that, Brother. Kathryn is kind. She showed me great charity. If I had my way I'd have dug the corpses up and slung them in the river. Anyway, I've smuggled a little wine and allowed my girls to pleasure some sailors. What are you going to do, my lord coroner, arrest me?'

'No, sir, I'm not.' Sir John turned away. 'Today is Friday. I shall return on Tuesday. And you must be gone.'

'There will be no trouble,' Athelstan added, as he undid his pouch and pulled out a piece of parchment. 'Provided you answer one question.' The friar felt a tingle of excitement as he approached the main reason for this meeting. 'When you were on oath, Master Whittock asked you about your sister's question on the morning of the twenty-sixth of June last?'

'Did I see anyone I knew here in Black Meadow?'

'Look at that list,' Athelstan said. 'You are lettered?'

'Of course, Brother.' The First Gospel grinned. 'Father always said schooling was the beginning of my downfall.'

'This is a list of names of all those who use the Paradise Tree. Which of them do you recognise?'

First Gospel studied the list carefully. Athelstan winked at Sir John. He had drawn up the names this morning in bald, round letters.

'This one,' First Gospel said, jabbing his finger.

'And, of course, this one and this one, but those two are dead.'

'Anyone else?' Athelstan asked. 'Anyone I have missed out?'

First Gospel shook his head and handed the piece of parchment back.

'Is there anything else, Brother?'

'No, sir, there isn't.' The friar turned. 'Angels might not come on time,' he declared, 'but, sometimes, God does work in wondrous ways. Master Trumpington, ladies, I will not trouble you again.'

Athelstan, followed by a bemused Sir John, walked back to the Paradise Tree.

They sat in the garden and were joined by Flaxwith. Cranston hurriedly brought the mastiff a large, cooked sausage from the kitchen. The dog seized it, grinning evilly at his benefactor.

'Just keep him away, Henry!'

A sullen tapster brought tankards of ale.

'Master Flaxwith,' Athelstan said. 'When you have finished your ale, I would be grateful if you would go for Master Ralph Hengan. You know where he lives?'

Flaxwith nodded.

'Bring him here. Tell him we'll meet him under the great oak tree in Black Meadow.'

'And if he's busy?'

'Oh, he'll come. Tell him we have found Gundulf's treasure.'

Flaxwith choked on his ale. Cranston nearly dropped his blackjack; even Samson stopped chewing the sausage.

'Brother, are you witless?'

'No, Sir John, I am not. The treasure is not very far

from us. Master Flaxwith, I beg you to go.'

Flaxwith finished his ale and hurried off, Samson loping behind him.

'Where's the treasure, Brother?' Sir John whispered.

'Here in the garden.'

'Friar, don't play games. If we find the treasure, God knows we could turn Gaunt's mind to mercy.'

'Oh, I'll do more than that, Sir John. Now, do you remember when we went to the Tower?' Athelstan asked. 'We do know Bartholomew read manuscripts we never saw. However, there was an entry in that chronicle about the treasure glowing like the sun. What was it now? *"In ecclesia prope turrem"?'*

'That's right. Which we translated as "in the chapel or church near the tower": the site of the Paradise Tree.'

'I don't think so.' Athelstan smiled. 'You see, Sir John, Gundulf was a bishop. He held the See of Rochester. I read a book at Blackfriars. His real interest wasn't theology but mathematics: he loved buildings and measurements. He was fascinated by anything which could calculate, weight or measure. Because he was William the Conqueror's favourite stone mason, Gundulf also amassed a treasure. Before his death he had it all smelted down, fashioned into one great block.'

'Yes, yes, we all know that,' Sir John interrupted.

'He was a churchman,' Athelstan continued. 'And, before he died, he used his status to hide the treasure away.'

'Where?' Sir John almost bawled.

'Why, Sir John, he had it smelted down and then covered with a brass face.'

'What?'

Athelstan pointed to the sundial. 'I think it's in there.'

Sir John stared open-mouthed at the sundial. The stone pillar which held it was covered in lichen and chipped. It reminded him of a long-stemmed chalice with the cup holding the sundial at the top. The coroner went across and tapped it with his finger.

'But it's only a sundial, Brother. Look, it has an arm.' He peered down. 'And it's divided into Roman numerals.'

Athelstan joined the coroner.

'When Gundulf talked of his treasure being in *"ecclesia prope turrem"* we thought he was referring to the Paradise Tree but he wasn't, Sir John. You see, since his day, the Tower has been extended and strengthened. However, when Gundulf built the great keep, that was his *"turris"*. The church he was referring to . . .'

'Of course!' Sir John exclaimed. 'St Peter ad Vincula! The little chapel in the Tower grounds which stands next to the keep.'

'That,' Athelstan agreed, 'is what Gundulf was referring to. He had his treasure melted down, covered with a brass sundial and placed in the stone pillar outside the chapel of St Peter ad Vincula. The years passed. People found references to the treasure being hidden but they forgot that, in Gundulf's day, the word "tower" referred to the keep, not to the walls and fortifications we know now.'

'So how did you know it was here?'

He placed his hands around the edge of the sundial and tried to move it but couldn't.

'It was in that accounts book. Do you remember, Sir John, when we first came here? Someone told us how Stephen Vestler loved curiosities? How he'd brought shields and swords from the Tower to hang on the wall.'

'Yes!' Sir John breathed. 'And Stephen had a love of ancient things.'

'Apparently, Sir John, Stephen Vestler bought the sundial from the new Constable of the Tower. There's a reference to a cart being hired, labourers being paid for this sundial to be brought here.'

'Satan's tits!'

'And when I was in the Tower last week,' Athelstan continued, 'I could see that the small churchyard outside the Tower had been refurbished. Some of the old tombstones had disappeared. When I read that entry, I began to think.' Athelstan sighed. 'Ah well, Sir John, you are coroner, an official of the city. This tavern will soon be in the hands of the Crown.'

Sir John took his dagger out and tried to slide it between the rim dividing the sundial from the greystone which held it.

'I doubt if you can move it,' Athelstan said.

The coroner went back to the Paradise Tree and returned carrying a heavy hammer. The ale-master came out protesting.

'Oh, shut up!' Sir John bellowed. 'And stand well back!'

He threw his cloak over his shoulder and began to smash the stone cup which held the sundial. At first all he raised were small chips of flying stone. Time and again he brought the hammer down. The stone split, crashed and rolled on to the grass. Even before the dust cleared Athelstan knew he was correct. The stone cup had broken; on the grass, covered in a grey film of dirt, was a circle of glowing yellow about a foot across and at least nine inches thick. It lay like the cup of a chalice without the stem, beside the thin bronze face of the old sundial. Sir John and Athelstan crouched down, the rest of the servants clustered round. Athelstan took the hem of his robe and rubbed the yellow metal until it glowed, catching the rays of the sun.

'*Fulgens sicut sol!*' Athelstan said. 'Glowing like the sun and hidden under the sun!'

The gold, because of the way it tapered at the end, tipped and turned. Everyone's face, including Sir John's, had a strange look, eyes fixed, mouths open.

'I've never seen so much!' the coroner said wistfully. 'Not even the booty of war piled high on a cart.'

'As the preacher says,' Athelstan remarked, 'the love of wealth is the root of all evil. This was Gundulf's secret as well as his little joke. He was dying, probably a sickly man, and he thought he'd used his treasure for something useful. So he left the riddle for those who wished to search for it. Time passed and people made mistakes.' Athelstan tapped the gold with his finger. 'This has been the cause of all our troubles. Sir John, you'd best tell people here to keep a still tongue.'

Sir John got to his feet and drew his sword.

'This is the King's treasure!' he bellowed. 'To take it, to even think of stealing it, is high treason!' He pointed to the ale-master. 'You, sir, bring a barrow!'

The man didn't move, his eyes still on the gold. Sir

John lifted his sword and pricked him under the chin.

'Bring a barrow and a piece of cloth. Brother, we are going to need a company of archers to take this to the Tower.'

'We are not taking it there, Sir John, but into Black Meadow,' Athelstan said quietly. 'Go on, man!' he ordered the ale-master. 'Do what the coroner says!'

The fellow hurried away. A short while later he returned trundling a wheelbarrow, a dirty canvas sheet folded inside it. They tried to lift the gold in but it was too difficult and slippery so the handcart was laid on its side, the gold was eased in and covered with the sheet. With the help of the ale-master Sir John trundled it out of the garden and down under the shade of the great oak tree.

'Good man.' Athelstan smiled. 'Now, fetch Sir John and me two blackjacks of ale. When Master Hengan arrives bring him here!'

The fellow obeyed. Athelstan sat with his back to the oak tree. He sipped at the ale which was brought, cool and tangy; through the trees he could make out the turrets and crenellations of the Tower.

'Where is all this leading to?'

The friar turned and glimpsed Hengan coming through the lych gate.

'To the truth, Sir John, but here is Master Ralph.'

The lawyer came over, cloak flapping, his face flushed with excitement.

'You've found the treasure!' he exclaimed.

Athelstan pulled the sheet back. Hengan slumped to his knees, like a knight before the Holy Grail. His sallow, sharp face softened, all severity gone. He stretched out his hand and touched it, caressing it like a mother would a favourite child.

'It's so beautiful,' he whispered. 'Gundulf's gold!'

He eased his leather chancery bag off his shoulder, Athelstan noticing how heavy it was, and put it on the ground. Hengan pressed his face against the gold.

'Where did you find it?'

In sharp, pithy phrases Athelstan explained how he had unlocked the secret cipher. All the time he watched the lawyer's eyes and saw the resentment flare.

'So easy,' Hengan said. 'So very, very easy.'

Athelstan made to cover the gold up.

'No! No!'

Sir John was staring at him curiously.

'Master Ralph, this should be taken to the Tower. Couriers should be sent to my Lord of Gaunt at the Savoy.'

'Yes, yes, quite.' Hengan was still stroking the gold.

'Was it worth it?' Athelstan asked sharply.

'Oh, yes.'

'For that,' Athelstan snapped, 'you are quite prepared to see Mistress Vestler hang!'

The lawyer lifted his face. 'What do you mean?'

'You know full well,' Athelstan replied. 'Here we are, Master Hengan, under the oak tree in Black Meadow. A place you know well. After all, wasn't it here that you killed Bartholomew Menster and Margot Haden?'

Hengan sat back on his heels. 'Me? I was . . .'

'You are an assassin,' Athelstan said quietly. 'You killed Bartholomew, Margot and that miserable unfortunate Alice Brokestreet, and you were quite prepared to see Mistress Vestler hang!'

Chapter 15

Hengan reminded Athelstan of a cat about to spring. He sat back on his heels but his body was quivering, lean face slightly turned.

'This is preposterous!' he stammered. 'A mistake!'

'Nothing of the sort,' Athelstan replied. 'Here under this oak tree I'll present the case against you. It's only fitting. After all, this is where you killed Bartholomew and Margot on a beautiful summer's evening.'

'I was in Canterbury.'

'You were no more in Canterbury than I was!'

Athelstan glanced at Sir John, who was nodding as if he understood the full case against Hengan but, later on, Athelstan would have to explain and apologise. He also quietly cursed his own arrogance. He'd thought it was appropriate to confront Hengan here but, now they were moving towards the truth, Hengan had changed. It was as if seeing and touching the gold had brought about a subtle shift. He seemed stronger, more resolute.

'You dreamed of this, didn't you?' Athelstan began. 'I wonder where the root of your greed lies? A lawyer who had everything. Were you born in Petty Wales, Master Ralph?'

Hengan waved a finger. 'Very good, Brother. Yes I was, in the shadow of the Tower. I know every part of that fortress, its story, its legends! As far back as I can remember, I knew about Gundulf's treasure. But it was only when I entered the Inns of Court that the dream became a reality. I began to collect manuscripts, documents, old chronicles and histories. I came across references to gold shining like the sun, being hidden in a chapel near the Tower. I also discovered the history of the Paradise Tree.' He paused. 'All the stories about it once being the site of an old chapel or church.'

'Did you know Black Meadow had been used as the burial ground for the pestilence?' Athelstan asked.

'Oh yes, but that didn't concern me.'

'Stephen and Kathryn Vestler did, didn't they?' Athelstan asked. 'You became their friend and eventually, as you intended, their family lawyer. You could visit the Paradise Tree whenever you wished. Months passed into years; you still held fast to your greed. You wouldn't discuss it with the Vestlers but used every opportunity to look around, to search, to make careful enquiries. It was very clever because now you were party to all documents, household accounts and memoranda. You could watch for anything untoward. Poor Stephen died and you became counsellor to his widow. It was only a matter of time, wasn't it?'

'You are sharp of eye, friar,' Hengan answered. 'Sharper than I thought.'

'I don't think so. I pray a lot, Master Hengan. Prayer sharpens the mind and hones the wit. Perhaps God wanted justice done and an innocent woman saved from hanging?'

Hengan pulled his chancery bag towards him.

'It's a beautiful day,' he observed, staring up at the branches. 'I always thought it would be like this, with the gold before me.'

'It's not yours,' Athelstan told him. 'Never has been and never will. You are going to hang.'

'On what evidence?' the lawyer retorted sharply. 'You attended Mistress Vestler's trial.'

'It's true what they say.' Sir John spoke up. ' "Cacullus non facit monachum: the cowl doesn't make the monk." You are two men aren't you, Master Ralph? The kindly lawyer, but that's only a shroud for the rottenness beneath.'

'Now, now, Sir John, are you envious of me? Do you secretly lust after Mistress Vestler's sweetness?'

Sir John would have lunged at him but Athelstan held his hand out.

'Let me speak,' he ordered. 'Everything in your garden, master lawyer, was grass and roses until Master Bartholomew Menster appeared: a studious clerk from the Tower who becomes sweet on a tavern wench at the Paradise Tree. To your horror you realise that he is a learned man with access to manuscripts and who has the same determination to discover Gundulf's treasure as yourself. Nevertheless, you kept up the pretence. I wager you never talked with Bartholomew in the presence of Mistress Vestler but away, in some other place. It wouldn't have taken you long to realise how close this interfering clerk was to the truth, so you decided to kill him.'

'And Margot?' Sir John asked.

'Margot was just as dangerous,' Athelstan said. 'You heard the evidence in court. Margot was schooled and sharp-witted, determined to make a good marriage. She was prepared to hitch her fortunes to a well-paid clerk who, one day, might discover secret treasure. What did you do, Hengan? Offer to share information? Act the kindly lawyer, willing to help?'

Hengan seemed more intent on the gold than Athelstan's words.

'You pretended to go to Canterbury,' Athelstan continued. 'You left the city but made a hasty journey back up the Thames to where you could hide away in many a tavern or alehouse suitably disguised. What you did do, however, was lure Bartholomew and Margot to a meeting. You'd send no letter, nothing which could be traced; perhaps just a hushed, excited whisper that you had discovered where the gold was, how you would meet Bartholomew and Margot at a certain time here, beneath the oak tree in Black Meadow.'

'Are you sure your evidence is sound?' Hengan taunted. 'Wouldn't Bartholomew or Margot chatter?'

'Why should they?' Athelstan retorted. 'Mention gold, mention treasure and people lick their lips and narrow their eyes, their fingers itch as yours did. And why should Bartholomew and Margot distrust a respected man such as yourself? On the evening of the twenty-fifth they left the Paradise Tree and came here. You, like Satan, slid out of the shadows. In this deserted place, hooded and cowled, who'd notice you? I doubt if you stayed long. You gave them a present of wine, a token of your friendship. Perhaps you claimed you'd left a manuscript or document somewhere and away you'd go. Bartholomew and Margot are happy, joyous, in love with each other. They would be only too eager to share your flask of wine, something which could not later be traced. Cups are filled, thirsts slaked: death would have followed soon after.' Athelstan pointed across the meadow. 'Were you hiding somewhere over there? Did you come back just for a short while, as the shadows lengthened, to ensure they were truly dead? Pick up the flask of wine and any documents Bartholomew may have been carrying? You are in the countryside near the Thames. The deed done, you hurry back towards the river, hire a wherry and then continue your journey to Canterbury.'

'But I was there, friar.'

'Oh, I am sure you were. You'd travel fast and, in the confusion, who'd remember you coming and going?'

'And Mistress Vestler?' Hengan asked.

'I don't know what you planned for the future. Who would be blamed? Certainly Mistress Vestler would not escape scrutiny but then she implicated herself, didn't she? Darkness falls and Margot doesn't return. Did Bartholomew and Margot often come here? Anyway, when Mistress Vestler came looking she discovered two corpses lying beneath an oak tree in her own meadow. Did she suspect? Did she wonder? She could not hide the corpses away so she hurried back for mattock and hoe and hastily buried them here.

'The next day, to cover the disturbance, she hired a tree-cutter to come and cut the branches, cover the ground in leaves and twigs so no one would notice.'

Athelstan watched Hengan. The lawyer was leaning forward, clutching the chancery bag tightly. Sir John, too, was nervous, hand on the hilt of his dagger.

'Mistress Vestler's thoughts are her own,' Athelstan continued. 'But she was in a fair panic. She searched the Paradise Tree and did something rather stupid. She collected Margot's possessions and promptly burned them. Why, I don't yet know. Later, when Bartholomew's absence becomes noted, a search is made but nothing can be found. Other enquirers are turned away, forced to accept the unlikely story that Bartholomew and the tavern wench had eloped.'

'And Alice Brokestreet?' Hengan asked. 'She was the one who laid allegations against Mistress Vestler, not myself.'

'Brokestreet was a harlot at heart, with no real love for Mistress Vestler. You knew that. Anyway, master lawyer, you were committed. You'd killed two people for Gundulf's treasure. But, what if someone else took Bartholomew's place? There was only one thing to do. Mistress Vestler also had to be removed, as quickly as possible.'

'Why should I do that?' Hengan asked abruptly. 'Mistress Vestler was sweet and kind to me.'

'For two reasons,' Athelstan snapped. 'First, like all gold hunters, Hengan, you couldn't share with anyone.'

'And secondly?' Hengan asked quietly. 'There is a further reason, friar?'

'Yes there is, lawyer. On your return from Canterbury you must have been surprised to see nothing had changed. Mistress Vestler still managed the Paradise Tree. Bartholomew and Margot had disappeared into thin air; I wager you suspected what had happened. Of course, you must have reflected on the possibility that Mistress Vestler may have entertained suspicions about you. In other words, Hengan, she had to be silenced. You couldn't poison her like you had Bartholomew and Margot. After all, you were one of the closest persons to her. So you'd sit and wait. News arrives that Alice Brokestreet was taken for killing a man in the Merry Pig. Did she know you, Master Hengan?'

'Mistress Brokestreet never had the pleasure of meeting me,' came the sardonic reply.

'No, I'm sure she didn't. The great lawyer would make sure of that. I suppose in the condemned cell at Newgate, dressed like a friar with the cowl pulled over, you could have been anyone.'

'You went there dressed like that?' Sir John asked abruptly.

'Sir Jack, do you really expect me to answer that?'

'Yes, he did,' Athelstan said. 'You've seen the condemned cell at Newgate, my lord coroner, black as pitch. Our good lawyer would be disguised, the same is true of his voice. Not that Alice Brokestreet would care. All she could see was the hangman's noose waiting for her and, abruptly, salvation is at hand. Our good lawyer tells her what to do: she will accuse Mistress Vestler, say no more than that and she will be a free woman. I doubt if Brokestreet cared if her visitor was Satan from hell.' Athelstan sighed.

'So the game began. Mistress Vestler was accused and sentenced to the gallows.'

'But the Crown would then seize the Paradise Tree?' Hengan spoke softly like a schoolmaster correcting a pupil.

'Oh come, Master Hengan: you are Mistress Vestler's executor with the right to poke and pry into her affairs; in reality, search around, looking for the treasure. Heaven knows even, when the time was right, buy the Paradise Tree, like Bartholomew Menster wanted to. He probably raised the matter with you, didn't he? You must have learned about that and become very alarmed.'

'As a lawyer,' Hengan protested, 'I maintain the evidence still points to Mistress Vestler.'

'All the evidence,' Athelstan pointed out, 'came from her own household books, and that made me curious. As Mistress Vestler's lawyer and good friend, why didn't you seize them, hide or burn them? It might be illegal, but something you'd expect a good friend to do in such circumstances. As it was, Master Whittock seized them and was able to track down the tree-cutter and the chapman, not to mention Margot Haden's sister.'

Hengan's gaze had shifted back to the cart. He was watching it carefully, like a cat would a mousehole.

'Brokestreet was another victim.' Sir John spoke up. 'You sent the poisoned wine to her so she'd cause no further problems. In that tangled brain of yours you probably saw it as some reparation for Mistress Vestler's pains.'

'This is all well and good.' Hengan placed his chancery bag beside him, dabbing his face with the long cuff of his gown. 'But you are missing one important factor: Mistress Vestler buried the corpses.'

'You guessed that,' Athelstan interrupted. 'It's a question of logic as well as self-defence. I am sure you later walked out into Black Meadow to carefully study the ground. Who knows, one dark night you may even have taken mattock and hoe and dug it yourself, just to make sure?'

'Yes, yes,' Hengan replied. 'But why didn't she accuse me? Why didn't she just tell the truth on oath?'

Athelstan shook his head. 'Ever the lawyer, Master Hengan! What proof did she have? That she went out and found two corpses on a summer evening, so she buried them then hurried back to her tavern to burn Margot Haden's possessions? Oh, I am sure she can explain it, but now is neither the time nor the place. As for further proof . . .'

Athelstan glanced back towards the lych gate where he thought he saw a flash of colour, but all was quiet.

'You told me that Brokestreet killed a man with a firkin opener? The only other person who knew that was the vicar of hell. How did you know? Unless you made a very careful scrutiny of Mistress Brokestreet before you approached her? Secondly, after the trial, you quoted accurately, word for word, the quotation from the chronicle we found in the Tower. Yet you only saw it for a few seconds. Finally, I was fascinated by Mistress Vestler's actions on the morning following Bartholomew's and Margot's disappearance. She came down to Black Meadow and asked the Four Gospels a very specific question. Had they, the previous day, seen anyone they knew in the meadow? Now, those rogues.' He saw the change of expression on Hengan's face. 'Yes, they are rogues, were kept well away from the Paradise Tree. The only people they knew were Bartholomew, Margot, you and herself. We know where Kathryn Vestler was. We also know the fate of Bartholomew and Margot. In an oblique way Mistress Vestler was asking about you.'

'God knows,' Sir John said as he moved his war belt to sit more comfortably, 'why Mistress Vestler didn't really speak the truth but I have my own suspicions.' He thrust his face closer. 'I believe she loved you, lawyer, but you wouldn't understand that, would you? "What does it profit a man if," ' he quoted from the gospels, ' "he gains the whole world but loses his soul?" You lost your soul for that gold, you were quite prepared to kill because of it.'

Hengan pulled a wry face. 'I have heard the evidence. It's not as conclusive as a court would want.'

'Oh, we haven't begun yet,' Athelstan remarked. 'Not really. Sir John here will take his bailiffs and search your house. We'll find manuscripts showing your extraordinary interest in Gundulf's treasure. We may find other documents. Then we can despatch royal couriers to Canterbury. Just where were you on each particular evening and day? Did you leave for the shrine on the twenty-third? If so, at which tavern did you stop? We will reach the conclusion that people saw you there but they can't remember you arriving in Canterbury for one or two days after you claim. Moreover, does your house contain poisons? Alice Brokestreet was poisoned. Perhaps the memory of the gaolers at Newgate can be pricked? Whatever.' Athelstan emphasised the points on his fingers. 'Mistress Vestler will not hang. You will never have the gold and you must face the most cruel interrogation.'

Hengan looked towards the lych gate where Master Flaxwith stood gesturing with his hand; around the bushes came other figures including Whittock, behind him a group of royal archers wearing the blue, red and gold livery. Hengan opened his chancery bag and took out a small arbalest. Sir John started forward but Hengan sprang to his feet.

'Brother Athelstan! Sir John!' the serjeant-at-law called out. 'Is all well? I understand you have the treasure?'

'What are you going to do?' Athelstan asked quietly.

'Oh, I had a madcap idea,' Hengan said smiling, 'that I would force Sir Jack to take the barrow down to the Thames and I'd escape with the gold. But this is life, not some troubadour song.'

'What are you going to do?' Athelstan repeated.

Hengan took a bolt from the large wallet he carried on his belt and slipped it into the groove on the arbalest.

'I confess all, Brother. To a certain extent I am sorry. Sorry for myself, for Kathryn, for all this sordid mess. I don't want to hang. I don't want to dance in the air. This is much quicker.'

And, before Athelstan could stop him, Hengan ran towards Whittock. Confusion and chaos broke out. At first Whittock didn't understand what was happening until Hengan stopped and loosed the quarrel.

The crossbow bolt went awry, lost in the long grass. Hengan fumbled for another. Whittock shouted an order. Two of the bowmen hurried through the lych gate, bows bent, arrows pulled back. Hengan began to run, lifting the arbalest, a stupid, futile gesture. The two longbows twanged. One arrow caught Hengan full in the neck, the other in the chest. He flung his arms up against the sky and crashed to the ground where he rolled on his side, legs moving, then lay still. The two archers ran across and turned the corpse over.

'Dead, sir!' one of them called out.

Whittock hardly spared the fallen man a glance. He strode across the meadow and, without a by-your-leave, pulled back the canvas sheet and stared open-mouthed at the gold.

'Gundulf's treasure at last!' he breathed. 'Did you find it, Sir John?'

'I would like to say I did, Master Whittock, but the truth is that Brother Athelstan found it.'

'How did you know?' the friar asked.

The serjeant-at-law's harsh features broke into a smile.

'I am the Crown's officer. I have a right to know. I also paid the servants and scullions at the Paradise Tree good silver to keep me informed of everything that happened there. I was at the Guildhall when the news arrived so I went to the Tower, collected these merry lads and came here.'

'You do not seem concerned about Master Hengan?' Athelstan asked.

'I stood and watched for a while. It was apparent, how can I put it, that events had rapidly changed.'

'Did you have any suspicions?'

Whittock clicked his tongue. 'I would like to say yes.' He grinned. 'No lawyer wants to be wrong. How can I put it, Brother? I did sense something amiss and wondered if Mistress Vestler had an accomplice. The only thing I found truly strange was that Hengan never hid those household accounts which told me so much. He was responsible, wasn't he?'

Sir John nodded.

'The Crown will need a full report, Sir Jack.'

Whittock snapped his fingers and called the archers over.

'Have the corpse taken to the death house in the Tower! This,' he pointed to the barrow, 'will also be taken there and guarded until His Grace the Regent inspects it.'

'It's treasure trove,' Sir John said quietly. 'And, according to the law, a portion of it should be given to the person on whose land it was found and to the finder.'

Whittock scratched a cheek and, bending down, picked up Hengan's chancery bag.

'Oh, don't worry, Sir John, in the end justice will be done. I will take care of our dead lawyer and the Crown's gold. And you, sir, have my permission to go to Newgate. Within the hour a letter of release will be despatched. All charges against Mistress Vestler, including that of smuggling, will be withdrawn. A good day's work, Sir John.' He bowed. 'Brother Athelstan, I bid you adieu.'

Later that day, just as the bells of St Mary-le-Bow began to toll over the great marketplaces of London,

Sir John and Athelstan escorted a weeping, pale-faced Kathryn Vestler into the dark coolness of the Lamb of God tavern. Sir John had taken her out of the condemned cell, not even waiting for Whittock's letter of release. Now he sat holding her hand, talking to her quietly, telling her everything that had happened.

Kathryn had lost her calm poise, her air of resignation had crumbled into bitter sobs. She sipped at a cup of wine, refusing a portion of the beef pie Cranston had also ordered from the kitchens.

'Mistress Vestler.' Athelstan put his blackjack down. 'Do you still think you are for a hanging? This is a time for celebration!'

'No, Brother.' Kathryn wiped her eyes. 'This is the time for questions, isn't it? I am sorry, Sir Jack, and you, Brother, for all your trouble.'

'Why?' Sir John asked. 'Just tell us that, Kathryn, why?'

'I loved him,' she began. 'God forgive me, Jack, I loved Ralph Hengan more than life itself, even more than Stephen. I met him before my husband died. He wasn't as fine a man as Stephen, Ralph was secretive, withdrawn, but, Brother, it's as if your heart isn't whole, then you meet someone and it becomes so.'

'You knew he was interested in the treasure?' Athelstan asked.

'Yes and no. Oh, he asked questions, but nothing out of the ordinary. He often came to the Paradise Tree when it was fairly deserted and, on reflection, he was always wandering around. Occasionally, I'd see him talking to Bartholomew but, again, nothing out of the ordinary.' She paused. 'After Stephen's death I actually thought of asking Ralph to marry me, yet he anticipated that. Well.' She raised her head. 'He told me he had no love or liking for womankind. Perhaps he was trying to save me the humiliation of a refusal! I was happy with his friendship. I could see that something about Bartholomew agitated him. I didn't inform Ralph that the clerk was trying to buy the Paradise Tree. So,' she shrugged. 'Life went on.'

'And at midsummer?' Athelstan asked.

'Well, on the evening of the twenty-fifth of June, Bartholomew came to the tavern. He was truly sweet on Margot. I didn't really care. Bartholomew was pleasant enough though I always thought Margot was ruled by her pocket rather than her heart. Anyway, Bartholomew was very excited. He and Margot sat in a corner whispering. They said they had to go out.' She shrugged. 'I let them go. It was only afterwards that I realised they had not left by the front or side entrance but through the garden.' She smiled through her tears. 'You've also learned the truth about First Gospel? I wondered if he was up to any villainy.'

She glanced across the taproom. Athelstan could see she was no longer there but retracing her steps on that fateful summer evening.

'Yes, that's right. They had gone out of the back gate through the back garden into Black Meadow. So I went out myself. It was a beautiful evening; the sun was like a fiery red ball and the garden was full of perfume. Strange, isn't it? I stopped to look at the sundial: Stephen was very proud of that. He loved such curiosities.' Kathryn wiped her eyes. 'I went into Black Meadow. The shadows were growing longer. I couldn't believe my eyes. At first I thought two dark pieces of wood were lying beneath the oak tree. I ran across to find Bartholomew and Margot sprawled there. They were dead, terrible expressions on their faces. It was apparent that they had died in agony. One thing I must say to you, little Margot's Book of Hours? She always took it with her. I noticed it was gone while someone had also been through Bartholomew's chancery bag. I did not know what to do. Two corpses, murder victims in my meadow! I was the last to see them alive. I'd discovered their corpses. It was obvious to a simpleton that they had been poisoned and that I would be accused.'

'So you returned to the tavern?' Athelstan asked. 'And told everyone to leave?'

'Yes, of course I did. Later, in the dead of night, I went out. I dug shallow graves and heaved the bodies in. Then I started to think. Black Meadow is not used by customers, it's private land.'

'Did you wonder about your brother the First Gospel?'

Kathryn smiled. 'He's a rogue born and bred, but murder? I did wonder if it was Ralph. The next morning I went down to see the Four Gospels but they could tell me nothing.'

'Of course,' Sir John put in. 'And you found it difficult to suspect our lawyer friend because Master Hengan was supposed to be in Canterbury?'

Kathryn tightened her lips, fought back the tears and nodded.

'I had the oak tree pruned,' she continued, 'to hide any signs. When Ralph returned I watched him closely but I didn't notice anything untoward. I loved him then and I love him now, perhaps that made me blind.'

'But why didn't you say anything?' Athelstan insisted. 'Why not just tell the truth?'

'You are a good friar.' Kathryn took Athelstan's hand and squeezed it. 'But you've also got the mind of a lawyer. You know the reason why. Who would believe me? What real proof did I have? How could I approve someone else like Alice Brokestreet did, lay false allegations? I wasn't sure myself. Was it Ralph? Would my brother be blamed?' She shrugged. 'I left it in God's hands and God replied.' She glanced at Sir John. 'Sir Jack, if you would take me back to the Paradise Tree. I would love to bathe, change and sleep in my own bed. Brother, when I am more fit and merry company, you must be my guest.'

'Will you come?' Sir John asked.

Athelstan shook his head. 'For once, Sir John, let me be the last to leave the tavern, not you!'

The friar watched them go. He sat in the deserted taproom then raised his tankard in a silent salute.

'Whom are you toasting, Brother?'

Athelstan glanced round to see the merry-faced taverner's wife standing in the doorway wiping her hands.

'Why, mistress, I'm toasting love: in all its beauty and all its terror!'

Headline hopes you have enjoyed THE FIELD OF BLOOD, and invites you to sample THE ANUBIS SLAYINGS, Paul Doherty's new ancient Egyptian crime thriller now available from Headline . . .

Prologue

Silence shattered the Temple of Anubis which lay to the north of Thebes within bowshot of the shimmering, snaking Nile. The evening sacrifice was finished. The god had been put to bed, the naos doors closed. The flagstaffs which surmounted the soaring pylons on each side of the principal gateways were stripped of their coloured pennants. The conch horn wailed: night was fast approaching. The great sanctuary with its black and gold statue of the jackal-headed god was now empty except for a young novice priest. He sat cross-legged, half asleep, savouring the fragrant incense which curled like a forgotten prayer through the temple.

He started and stared fearfully across at the throne of Anubis. Wasn't that the howling of dogs? He relaxed with a sigh. He was new to the temple. He had forgotten about the great pit where the pack of wild dogs sacred to Anubis were kept. A fanciful notion of the high priests: the dogs were savage, a gift sent by a tribe south of Nubia. The young priest had visited the pit once: a great rocky cavern where the dogs prowled in the caves and were fed morning and night by the Dog Master. The novice priest remembered himself. He dipped his hand into a nearby stoup of holy water and rubbed his lips with the tips of his fingers, as an act of purification before bowing his head in silent prayer. It was his task to keep vigil. He must pray for the temple, its high priest and hierarchy of scholars, librarians and priests. Nor must he forget the Lord Senenmut, vizier, some people even whispered lover, of the Pharaoh-Queen Hatusu. The Temple of Anubis had been chosen as a meeting ground where Senenmut could negotiate with the envoys of the Mitanni king Tushratta. A great peace treaty was planned. Tushratta would give his daughter to one of Hatusu's kinsmen in marriage. The Mitanni king's armies had been decisively defeated by Hatusu and, despite his arrogance, Tushratta desperately needed the peace. Egyptian armies now controlled the Horus road across the Sinai desert. Chariot squadrons, Egypt's best, massed along Mitanni's borders. Tushratta could fight but common sense dictated peace.

The novice priest had listened very carefully to the temple gossip. The Pharaoh-Queen was now accepted at home. She had usurped the throne after her half-brother and husband's mysterious death. Once Tushratta signed the treaty, Egypt's most powerful enemy was publicly accepting her, so in time the Nubians, the Hittites, the Libyans and the rest would bow the knee and kiss her sandalled foot. The novice priest dreamed on.

The Anubis temple settled for the night. The great hypostyle hall with its blue ceiling and gold star-bursts was clear of pilgrims: its sacred walls, covered with inscriptions to Anubis, were no longer studied. The repellent, evil animals and reptiles, hacked by daggers to keep them immobile, stood in silent watch. The columns, decorated at base and top in green and red and garlanded with banners, stood in shadowy rows. Elsewhere in the temple, all was locked and bolted with clasps made from the finest Asiatic copper. Only soldiers, wearing the insignia of Anubis, stood on guard, spears and shields in hand. The scholars of the House of Life had doused the lights. The works they were copying or reading, the books and great parchments sheathed in pure leather listing spells for the overthrow of the Evil One or the repelling of crocodiles, had been stowed away: they would not be reopened until the following morning. Tetiky, the captain of the guard, in bare feet because he was on sacred ground, patrolled the mysterious portals, the small side chapels, the House of Delectation where banquets were held; the House of the Heart's Desire where, during the day, the handmaids of the gods waited; the raiment room where the sacred cloths were held. Satisfied, the captain passed on. The sanctuary and libraries were secure, as were the granaries stocked with barley and oil, wine, incense and precious cedar wood from Lebanon.

Tetiky went into the heart of the temple, the warren of corridors around the Holy Chapel where the sacred amethyst, the Glory of Anubis, was held. He passed a priestess, a handmaid of the god, and turned to admire her sinuous walk, hips swaying, long hair swinging. The priestess carried a jug. Tetiky frowned, angry at not being able to recall her name. Ah yes! Ita, she was responsible for bringing refreshments to Khety, the priest who guarded the door to the Sacred Chapel. Tetiky walked to the end of the gallery. Khety squatted there, leaning against the cedarwood door. Inside, the vigil priest, Nemrath, guarded the sacred amethyst. Nemrath kept the key; he would allow no one in until he was relieved just before the dawn sacrifice. A long night, Tetiky reflected, without food and drink. The captain shivered. His men talked of the god Anubis, jackal-masked, being seen walking his temple. Did he visit the Sacred Chapel and gaze on that gorgeous sacred amethyst winking from its statue? A sombre place the Sacred Chapel, with its pool guarding the door, its recessed walls and soaring roof. Tetiky remembered himself and coughed. Khety heard this, turned and raised his hand as a sign that all was well.

Satisfied, Tetiky went out into the gardens. He paused to savour the scent of resin and sandalwood. The temple grounds were a veritable paradise with their shimmering lakes, well-watered lawns, flower-beds and shady trees dark against the night sky. Tetiky heard the sound of singing and grinned. A dancing girl, a heset, was probably entertaining a client. He walked on past the cattle-byres, the beasts within lowing vainly against the morning and the waiting slaughterer's knife. He paused and bowed as a group of priests, in their linen kilts and panther shawls, passed by on their way into the city.

Tetiky returned to his post. He did not know it but heinous murder was to visit the Temple of Anubis that evening. Seth, the red-haired slayer, would make his presence felt yet the victim, the dancing girl in one of the small garden pavilions, was full of life. She was naked except for a loincloth. Her hair, drenched in oil and fringed with beads, moved like a black veil from side to side as she swayed, shaking the sacred sistra. She glanced quickly at her customer. Was he one of the Mitanni? Male or female? All she could glimpse were arms; the rest of her customer's body was hidden in a white gauffered lined robe, head and face hidden by that terrifying black jackal mask.

The heset had been approached earlier in the day whilst walking along one of the temple's dark-shaded porticoes. She would have refused except for the silver bracelet the masked customer had offered. He, or she, now sat in the shadows but the bracelet lay shimmering in the pool of light from an oil lamp the girl had brought. The heset was a professional dancer, a singer in one of the temple choirs. She was also a courtesan, skilled in the art of love with both male and female, of enticing the most jaded customer to excitement. She danced and swayed, moving her oil-drenched body alluringly, turning her back, glancing coquettishly over her shoulder. She would earn the silver bracelet, boast about it then sell it in the marketplace. All she had to do was please this customer. She moved closer and began to sing a love song, one of the hymns the priests chanted to Anubis.

'Thou art crowned with the majesty of thy beauty.
The light of your eye warms my face.
I will come to you and be one with you.'

The dancer paused

'Are you happy?' she whispered into the darkness 'Am I not comely? Do I not please you?'

She felt a trickle of sweat run down from her neck as well as a pang of annoyance. She had danced and sung for some time. All she had heard was a grunt of approval but no clapping, no invitation for her to go out and lie in the darkness.

'I am tired.' She tried to keep the petulance out of her voice. 'The day is finished. Shall we stay here? Or go out beneath a sycamore tree? The evening is cool.'

'Then you should sleep,' the voice whispered.

The dancing girl stepped back. There was something in the tone she did not like. She heard a long sigh and felt the quick prick of pain. What was that? She stood shocked; her hand went to her belly. Had she been poisoned? She turned towards the door but she was already dying. Her chest felt so heavy, a strange froth soured the back of her throat. She could hear a voice counting and then she collapsed. For a short while her body shuddered. Only when she lay quiet did her killer stop counting, get up and walk towards the corpse.